PROBABLE CAUSE

Theresa Schwegel

Quercus

First published in Great Britain in 2007 by Quercus
This paperback edition published in 2008 by

Quercus
21 Bloomsbury Square
London
WC1A 2NS

The moral right of Theresa Schwegel to be
identified as the author of this work has been
asserted in accordance with the Copyright,
Designs and Patents Act, 1988.

A CIP catalogue
fr

978 1 84724 299 0

This book is a work of fiction. Names, characters,
businesses, organizations, places and events are
either the product of the author's imagination
or are used fictitiously. Any resemblance to
actual persons, living or dead, events or
locales is entirely coincidental.

10 9 8 7 6 5 4 3 2 1

Typeset by E-Type, Aintree, Liverpool
Printed and bound in Great Britain by Clays Ltd, St Ives plc.

for Rodney

CHAPTER ONE

The store's alarm doesn't startle anyone. Two blocks away, in a rehabbed three-flat on Washtenaw Avenue, an underwhelmed DePaul professor hears it. He momentarily loses his place in a *Tribune* article, skims through something about the mayor's unfair hiring practices, yawns, and skips to the METRO section, assuming the alarm is part of whatever movie-of-the-week his wife is watching downstairs on TV. Downstairs, it doesn't matter what's on TV, because his wife is already well into a bottle of average cabernet and the first stages of sleep, dreaming of being appreciated.

A block away, at the intersection of Lincoln and Foster, a taxi driver hears the alarm while he waits at the light. Sirens all sound the same after ten years driving this route: bau, bau, bau, bau; whup-whup-whup-whup-whup-whup – *whatever*, the driver thinks. The sound is mildly irritating, like any red light. He steps on the gas and makes a right for Lake Shore Drive.

On the sidewalk in front of the store, a homeless woman wanders and, believing the alarm is a signal from her God, is confused as to why there is no church. No church, just Lucky Mike's Electronics: neon-yellow signage over a locked-up storefront, its windows and door fortified top to bottom by steel curtains. The woman moves on, ready to tell any other living soul her predicament.

A decal on Lucky Mike's blacked-out door declares security courtesy of WESTEC: area office located exactly 9.2 miles from the store. There, a little red light blinks on a console, summoning some dispatcher to get off his ass for the third time this shift and send a car. He finishes his pastrami on rye. The dispatcher is used to false alarms.

Seven and a half miles from the store at Spiaggia restaurant, Officer Ray Weiss probably wishes he could hear the alarm. It'd be a nice way to ditch the horrendous dinner date his mother guilted him into making. Monica has already ordered an appetizer and a twenty-dollar glass of some kind of wine she couldn't pronounce, and now she won't shut up about the shopping on Oak Street. She says 'eww' in a baby voice when he cracks his knuckles. Weiss tries to act interested in her and decipher the menu at the same time, but he's never heard of half the items, and every one costs more than both his shirt and tie. He orders something with sweetbreads, expecting, well, sweet bread. He's twenty-three. He wants a burger. He wants to get out of there and catch bad guys.

No, the store's alarm doesn't startle anyone, but Jed Pagorski thinks he can feel the adrenaline coming out of his ears. In the alley behind the store, his hands are slippery in his gloves as he jimmies the loading dock's heavy garage door. 'Noise' Dubois is over his shoulder, watching, making sure Jed doesn't slip up. *It's the heat of the night*, Jed thinks; that's why he's sweating. Can Noise tell?

'Rent-a-cops will be here in ten minutes, tops,' Jed says.

Noise's look says: No shit.

Too late to back out now, Jed thinks. Not that he would. He slides one leg underneath the door, then the other, then his torso, the weight of the door held by his twitching arms like a stacked bench press.

Ten minutes. Less.

'Hold this fucking door up for me.' *Be in control,* Jed thinks. *It's all under control.* Noise's fingers appear in front of Jed's nose, healthy pink nails against black skin. Underhanded, Noise holds the door.

As soon as Jed slides through, the garage door hits the pavement like a guillotine.

Nine minutes, no counting.

Jed pulls a flashlight from his belt, turns it on, and sweeps the space with light. Layout looks like the map Noise penciled on a napkin at Hamilton's earlier tonight: a doorway behind opens to outside and runs ahead to the showroom; inventory is there to the right; alarm keypad is mounted on the wall, over there.

Nine-one-zero-one-six, Jed repeats in his head, the code memorized easily, after so much practice. The gloves prove difficult as he disables the alarm. The siren stops; his ears ring in the silence. He thinks he hears his own heartbeat. He remembers to breathe.

Jed hears the car pull up out back, just like they

planned. One of the tires crunches broken glass in the alley. Car door slams. *Seven minutes*, Jed thinks, *to be on the safe side*. To be out of there with no trouble. He approaches the door to the right of the loading dock and presses his ear against it, waiting for the signal. He turns off his flashlight like a conscience. He waits, counting backward from ten three times over, and again, the numbers steadying his concentration.

Jed smiles. He's in it: he's in the game. And he won't get caught – can't, really. He smiles, notices his jaw is clenched. He's so god damn tense he wishes he'd taken Noise up on that drink back at Hamilton's. Sweat trickles through his brow and into his eyes and he wonders, *where the hell is Noise?*

Be in control. It's all under control. He grips his flashlight like a weapon in his right hand and reaches for the door with his weak left. He turns the lock, it clicks; he pulls the handle down and inches the door open to get a look outside.

Before he can make sense of it the barrel of a gun slips through the crack. The muzzle stops an inch from his face. He drops the flashlight and turns to take cover, but the door is pushed open quickly and with so much force that Jed can't get his feet set. He tumbles to the floor and covers his face with his forearms like a little girl would.

Noise doesn't say anything. Just holsters his gun and stands there, shaking his head.

'God damn, Noise, what the fuck?'

'Is that a question?' Noise swipes Jed's flashlight, then helps Jed to his feet. Through the open door Jed sees the car, trunk open.

Five minutes left, no time for Jed's answer.

He follows Noise into the showroom. The only light comes from a flickering EXIT sign just above them; the front windows are blacked and reinforced, shielding the merchandise from bad reflection during the day and undue interest at night – a security measure, backfired. Noise shines the flashlight over surround sound stereos, home theater systems, digital projection packages. He stops, focuses the beam of light on a 48-inch Sony plasma television.

Jed can't see Noise in the dark so he asks, 'That's it?'

'It's a nice TV.'

'I know, but that's all we're taking?'

'You think we should load up the backseat? Strap a big screen to the hood?'

Jed knows better than to ask stupid questions. He knows that. He also knows he has to be the one to lift the TV. Sometimes he thinks they only want him for his muscle. *Suck it up*, he thinks. *One TV, maybe three minutes and one fucking nice TV*, and he's in no matter why they want him.

Noise disappears as Jed disconnects the control box from the screen. He can't carry both at once, so he takes the box first, out the back, down the steps. He sets it in the trunk like it's his mother's favorite porcelain figurine. Noise sticks his head out the back door, uses Jed's flashlight to inspect the job.

Jed hustles back up the stairs past Noise, says, 'I know,' assuming Noise's pursed lips were about to squeeze out a customary *Be careful*.

Jed goes inside, and he can see the finish line now,

his vision narrowed in the showroom. He hoists the 48-inch screen under his right arm and negotiates his way through the dark, out the back. Noise isn't there, but there's no time to wonder where he went.

Jed hopes Noise won't harp on him about the screen's scraped edge. Forty-eight inches happen to be a perfect fit for the trunk, except he didn't know that when he gave the screen a little too much elbow grease on the way in.

Jed shuts the trunk and closes his eyes, sealing his fate in the trunk: he is one of them. Finally. And with at least a minute to spare.

'Jed.' Noise's tone is far from congratulatory.

Jed looks up: Noise is standing at the top of the steps, holding a VHS tape. *Be careful.* Jed had mocked him, instead of checking for cameras.

'Surveillance. Man, Noise, I thought—'

'Don't tell me what you thought. Tell me what you know.'

Jed's answer comes out like a reflex: 'Cover your ass.'

Noise stops short of a nod. His body seems to tense from the inside out. Jed watches him, waiting to maybe get yelled at.

A car turns into the alley, shining its high beams on the men. Noise tucks the tape in his jacket and remains on the steps.

'Shit,' says Jed, thinking he fucked this up somehow, took too long, and now they'll have his ass. He leans over the trunk, his arms spread, head hanging, like he's ready to get frisked.

The driver pulls up, gets out, says, 'What is going on?'

'Mr Lukas?' Noise comes down the steps cautiously, gun drawn, held close to his leg. Jed is afraid to turn around.

'Yes,' the driver says. 'What in the hell happened?'

Jed can feel the rush in his veins. He stands up, reaches into his jacket, waits for his cue.

'Well?' the driver asks.

Of course Noise doesn't say anything.

Be in control, Jed tells himself. *It's all under control*. Then he turns slowly, arrogantly, and produces his badge. 'I'm sorry, sir, it seems there's been a burglary.'

CHAPTER TWO

A serious-looking white woman grips a knife, her eyes glaring at the camera, her skin tinged orange by the TV's poor color calibration. 'To a police officer,' she says, 'this dagger is a potential weapon.' She palms the handle, presents it for a close-up. 'But to a Sikh man, this is a *kirpan*, a sacred symbol carried as a sign of spiritual devotion.' The camera zooms out to reveal she's standing in Lincoln Park, next to a Sikh. She smiles at him like he's retarded, then hands him the knife. He bows slightly and steps out of the frame. She notices his turban is casting a distracting shadow, so she moves to the left. 'How can we ever understand one another?' she asks the camera. Then she pauses, takes a step forward, and says, 'If strength comes from knowledge, cultural sensitivity is muscle.'

Ray Weiss cracks his knuckles, looks around the briefing room cautiously, like he's cheating on a test. He's trying to get a read on the other beat cops, to see if anyone else thinks this is complete bullshit.

As the woman starts in about how Saudi Arabians mean yes when they shake their heads from left to right, Field Training Officer Jack Fiore whispers an indecipherable though predictably vulgar comment to his colleague, Noise Dubois. Next to Weiss, Officer Gary Anzalone rocks on the back legs of his metal chair, his iffy balance providing self-entertainment. Across the room, Jed Pagorski is sound asleep. All the guys in between pretend to watch the monitor, their eyes glazed over by real life.

Weiss looks at the District 20 beat map on the wall to his left, though he's studied it so often he sees it when he closes his eyes. To his right, he glances at another ineffective use of space: a corkboard tacked with familiar and otherwise useless information: Beat events, CAPS information, memos about crystal meth pushers in the LGBT community. Sex offenders, Most Wanteds. Weiss wishes the room had a window. Anzalone beats him to a sigh.

On the TV, some guy in a pinstripe suit says, 'With security concerns paramount in current times of turmoil, it is critical to have strong elements of trust and understanding between our law enforcement agencies and the communities they serve.' He's probably from the State's Attorney's Office, Weiss figures, since his statement sounds rehearsed and the camera caught him on his way out of the courthouse on La Salle.

When the orange woman returns, pamphlet in hand, Weiss is reminded of the information the stewardess gives you before you fly: great in theory, but when your plane is falling out of the sky, you're going to be shitting your pants, not locating your flotation device. Just like if some Latin King puts a gun in your face – you aren't going to be concerned with his personal space or his religious rights. Weiss looks at his watch. Twenty minutes 'til his four o'clock shift.

'In a city as diverse as Chicago,' the orange woman says, 'we have many different cultures that view the police from varying perspectives.' The Sikh steps up behind her, followed by a black woman, and an Asian couple. A Hispanic woman joins them, holding a vacant-eyed baby; a Hasidic Jew brings up the rear. *It's a regular rainbow coalition*, Weiss thinks.

'As police officers,' the woman says, 'you have the responsibility to understand those perspectives to better serve and protect our communities. You earned your badge; now earn their respect.' Cue the feel-good music.

Sergeant Flagherty turns on the overhead lights; Weiss' eyes adjust. Flagherty looks like he used to be fat and he walks like he still carries the weight. He goes to the VCR and shuts off the tape, triggering static noise that jerks Jed from sleep. He wipes drool from the corner of his mouth, runs his hand over his buzz cut, tries to focus. *Fucking guy*, Weiss thinks.

Flagherty picks up a Magic Marker and scrawls on the Dry Erase board: SENSITIVITY. From the back corner of the room, Johnny Giantolli groans like he does when he's imitating his wife.

'We have to do this, guys,' Flagherty says, his pronunciation heavy on the *a*.

'We do this,' Walter Guzman says, two seats over from Weiss, 'and I still got to spend all day in court with some spic who says I arrested him because he's Mexican.' Everyone laughs – even Jed, who just yesterday spent the better part of their workout insisting that Guzman was Japanese. Sure, he has Asian features, Weiss agreed. But what about his name? And the time that guy from the twenty-fourth called him 'Galtero'? What about the picture of the Virgin Mary in his locker? Nope, Jed insisted: Guzman's Japanese. Look at his hair. The shape of his eyes.

And now Jed sits there, his big mouth fixed in a contagious, stupid grin, like he knew all along. Weiss wishes he could let himself off as easily.

On the board under SENSITIVITY, Flagherty writes the word SPIC.

'Guzman's only sensitive about his sexual preference,' Giantolli says.

'You'd know, you faggot,' Mark Sikula says. Weiss thinks he sounds angry, but Giantolli's his partner, so who knows. In the front row, Sikula doesn't turn around.

Flagherty writes FAGGOT on the board.

'Sarge, what's the point here, huh?' Guzman asks. 'We don't need a seminar on how to piss each other off.'

'It's city-mandated. The department has suffered some serious blows lately. With all the trouble in the twenty-third, cops getting killed—'

'The twenty-third: your old stomping ground,' Fiore says.

'Did you know that woman cop?' Giantolli asks Flagherty. 'Was it her fault?'

'It's complicated.'

'Leave it to a woman,' Fiore says.

Flagherty ignores him. 'We've got problems on the southside, too: racial profiling, police brutality. The press is up the mayor's ass about all this, and he's got enough on his plate. He wants this nipped in the bud, ground level. So the superintendent is cracking down on corruption.'

'With a videotape?' Guzman asks.

'They should be showing us *National Geographic*, the fucking animals we deal with,' from under Sikula's breath.

'I'm just following orders,' Flaherty says. 'You should all give it a try.' Flaherty turns back to the board and adds ANIMAL to his list.

'This is ridiculous,' Giantolli says. 'I need a cup of coffee. Or something I can hang myself with.'

'Hey, Flaherty,' Fiore says casually. 'Why don't you write *nigger* up there.'

There are other black cops in the room, but this was clearly intended for Noise, who is sitting right behind Weiss. Noise Dubois, given name Innis, is a quiet, observant cop – his nickname a testament to his aural acuity, not his mouth – but when he speaks, he always has something to say.

So far, he hasn't. Nobody has said anything. The air in the room is as still as a dead man.

Finally, Flaherty says, 'Look, guys. I think the point is made.' He puts down the marker, addresses Noise: 'None of us is immune to insult.'

Weiss hears Noise's chair slide across the linoleum. Uh-oh.

Flaherty swallows hard. He's fairly new to the district, and he isn't quite standing up straight yet. Weiss is pretty sure Noise isn't about to help him feel welcome.

'This whole exercise has been an insult to my intelligence,' Noise says, each word like it's capitalized. 'Some woman talk-show host, telling me to be nice. A group of model citizens pleading for my understanding. I'm not in the job to make friends and didn't come to work today to sit here and talk about racial epithets. Because you know what? When I get out on the street, I'd rather be called a nigger than a dumb cop.'

Jed puffs up his chest, nods, proud. He looks over at Weiss, probably hoping he shares the sentiment.

'And I do believe the street is where I'm needed,' Noise says. Then the door at the back of the room opens, and closes, and Noise is gone.

The collective exhale in the room is heavy with whispers from the guys in the back. 'At least Fiore made it interesting,' Giantolli says.

Flagherty goes to the podium and reorganizes his papers, and most likely his thoughts. 'Enough,' he finally says to the chatter, though he waits for it to die. 'As a result of last night's shit storm, you might want to take notes.' He reads through his own: 'Stay in your beat. Notify the watch commander if you so much as think about crossing Lawrence Avenue. And, gentlemen, let's try to skip the confusion about who's doing whose paperwork.' He looks right at Jed. 'I don't want any more fuzzy interpretations of investigational protocol. Read your manual on downtime if you're unclear.'

Weiss knows why that last bit was directed at Jed: last night, while he was stuck eating cheese for dessert with Monica, Jed and Noise tripped a burglary alarm and swiped a TV. Jed was supposed to seal off the perimeter for the detectives once he secured the so-called crime scene; instead, he let the store owner into the building, which screwed up everything. Not everything, exactly, since no one got caught. The screwup, as far as Flaherty knows, is in the paperwork.

The theft was Jed's 'initiation.' Weiss doesn't know if all cops go through it and he doesn't know whom to ask; all he knows is that he's supposed to be next. He feels the burrito he had for lunch turn in his stomach.

'Giantolli and Sikula,' Flaherty says, 'at twenty-two hundred hours I want you to join the 2024 beat car, backing up the guys in the twenty-third. They got a concert letting out at the Aragon, and they're expecting a bunch of potheads from the suburbs.'

'Rock on,' Giantolli says.

'Anything else?' Flaherty asks the rest of the guys, half of whom are already out the door.

Weiss has so many questions, but he never asks; given enough time, he thinks, the answers always present themselves. He can only hope his are the right ones.

'Weiss,' Fiore says with a *V*. The German pronunciation sounds commanding, which is obviously the intent. He jerks his chin toward the door. '*Andale.*'

CHAPTER THREE

'Stop that guy,' Fiore says, pointing to the car in front of them, a late-model, black Nissan Stanza, IL plate SJX 409, turning right on Western. Tags are up to date; driver's doing the speed limit.

'Why?' Weiss asks, rolling up close behind the vehicle to get a look in the back window. Looks like a male driver, one passenger.

'Because I said so.'

They've been driving circles around the neighborhood the whole shift, Fiore has blown off nearly every possible stop, and now he's looking for trouble? Weiss doesn't ask; Fiore has a knack – nose like a bloodhound, the guys say. Lately, Weiss thinks the only feature Fiore shares with a dog is his breath.

Weiss flips on the light bar and moves in so close he can see a flash of the driver's eyes in the Nissan's rearview mirror.

'How much you want to bet this shitbag is up to something?' Fiore asks, though Weiss knows he doesn't want an answer.

The driver steps on his brakes: the taillights work. The Nissan pulls to the curb ahead of a row of parked cars in front of a closed antiques store. Weiss is barely stopped behind the car when Fiore opens his door and jumps out.

'Stay here. Run the plates.' Fiore slams the door and advances toward the Nissan.

'Stay here. Run the plates,' Weiss repeats, with attitude behind it. He's starting to feel like a chauffeur. His ass is asleep, his hamstrings tight. In the last moments of daylight, he realizes he hasn't been out of the car in close to three hours. In another five, he hopes things will change. He's tired of being treated like a boot.

He punches SJX 409 in the MDT.

Outside, Fiore approaches the Nissan's driver's side window like he knows the people inside. Does this guy have any fear? He positions himself just in front of the side-view mirror. 'How you doing?' Weiss can read his lips, and he knows that condescending smile.

Weiss shuts off the air-conditioning and rolls down his window. It's cooler out now, and he's tired of the icy, recirculated air in the car. There was a burst of rain earlier, just enough to tease the grass and leave the metallic smell of warm, wet asphalt in the air. He wishes he'd been able to get out in the rain; feel it on his face.

Ping – the computer alerts that the LEADS list is up. Weiss scrolls through the record. Name: Ambrozas, Jurgis. Six pack: white male, blond/blue, 6'1, 170 lbs, DOB 12/03/1976. Residence: 1432 South Halsted #3F, on the other side of the Loop, past Greektown, past UIC. Vehicle: Nissan. Registered. License: temporary; valid. Criminal record: none.

So now what?

Cars pass, crossing into the oncoming lane to get where they're going. Weiss wonders how many of those drivers they could have stopped just the same.

He watches as Fiore opens the driver's door and a guy who matches Jurgis Ambrozas' description gets out. Weiss opens his door and stands behind it, waiting for action. Ambrozas is taller, lankier than Fiore, but he slouches, so the two meet eye to eye. Fiore asks Ambrozas something, and Weiss can tell Fiore doesn't like the answer. He flips Ambrozas around and pushes him up against the car's back door.

Fiore motions Weiss around to the passenger side, says: 'Make sure she doesn't go anywhere.'

Weiss edges around the Nissan. Given the circumstances, the urge to draw his gun feels ridiculous.

'What else are you hiding from me?' Fiore asks Ambrozas, whose resigned expression carries the slightest hint of a smirk. Fiore pats him down as Weiss approaches the passenger window.

There, a blond woman with a black scarf tied around her head stares up at him. Through her old-fashioned features: same possible smirk.

Weiss taps on the window; her gaze falls.

He opens the door. 'Step out of the car, ma'am.'

'I better not find out you're lying to me,' Fiore says on the other side of the car.

The woman gets out, and she's tall: eye to eye with Weiss. 'He has done nothing,' she says in her best English. Weiss smells her powdery perfume, a scent he remembers from last fall – the time he waited for Leah to try on sixteen different bras at Victoria's Secret. The whole store smelled like it: they called it

Angel-something. Leah bought something less than angelic.

'Put her in the squad,' Fiore says. 'We're gonna search the vehicle.'

'We will do what you say,' the girl says to Weiss. 'We always do what you say.' The words sour her smirk and Weiss suddenly feels like he's wronged her.

'I'm sorry, ma'am,' he says, sheepish. 'I'm sure you have nothing to worry about.' He takes her arm, feeling warm skin through the sleeve of her blouse, a wrongfully intimate connection. She does not resist him.

'Do you have anything in your pockets?' She doesn't answer. He lightly pats her shoulders, her arms, and very lightly her torso ... one long leg at a time, her thin ankles. Her tennis shoes remind him of his mother's old white nurse-clogs.

'Turn around, please.' She does. A blond curl peeks out from under the back of her scarf. Her shirt is too short, and only partially tucked; the seam of her pant leg is unraveling. Everything about the girl admits fault. But not guilt. Not necessarily.

Weiss stands up. 'Okay, come on.'

He escorts her to the squad and puts her in the back. She's barely seated when Fiore throws Ambrozas in from the other side and slams the door. Weiss feels bad about shutting her in there on the hard plastic seat.

'What's happening?' he asks, trying to catch up to Fiore, who's on his way back to the Nissan. Fiore doesn't answer, just goes back to the driver's side door and begins the search.

Fiore's ransacking the center console when Weiss

sticks his head in from the passenger side. 'The driver, this car – both came up clean on LEADS.'

'The driver's got alcohol on his breath. Says he "only had one beer" at the Cubs' game.'

'So why don't you get him to blow?'

Fiore takes the keys from the ignition. 'Because I know this asshole,' he says, 'and he's not telling me everything.' He tosses the keys to Weiss. 'Search the trunk.'

Weiss walks around to the back of the car and pops the trunk. Inside, a laundry basket, whites mostly. An overnight bag he doesn't want to go through. A spare tire. God, he thinks, a guy can't even have a beer at a baseball game.

Weiss rummages through the bag, finds a pretty risqué nightgown he'd rather not show the rest of the world, and then a box of rubber gloves. He doesn't want to put the two together. In the outside pocket he finds a box of alcohol swabs.

'Weiss.' Fiore appears. 'Fuck it. We got nothing.' He waits for Weiss to get out of the way and closes the trunk.

'What about the breathalyzer?' Weiss asks.

'Forget it, it's not worth it.'

'So what's our PC?' Weiss knows he'll have to cite it in the report.

'I have probable cause,' Fiore says.

'What, that he's an asshole?'

'Just because you were born into this doesn't mean you inherited the smarts, Weiss. You act like you know everything out here and you're only asking to be proven wrong.'

Weiss bites his lip, since he wonders if Fiore's the asshole.

'Go get Ambrozas,' Fiore says. 'I'm going to have a quick word with the girl.'

'But, Jack, how are we going to write this?'

'We aren't.'

Back in the squad, driving in the same circles, Fiore cranks the AC. Weiss thinks about asking him what the fuck that stop was all about, and why they didn't document it. Then again, it was good to get out of the car, and the less paperwork the better. It wasn't really a chore frisking that woman, either. He wouldn't say he was attracted to her, though that one blond curl might turn up somewhere in his dreams.

He looks over at Fiore. The guy's been quiet all night. He stares out the window, pulling on his mustache, probably in the middle of some mental diatribe, angry with whomever.

'Do you know that girl, who was in the car?' Weiss asks.

Fiore doesn't answer; just keeps pulling on his mustache. Weiss thinks the guy must have a story he won't tell for every gray hair on his head.

Weiss turns east on Foster to make another loop. All the shops are closed now, and traffic is light for a Tuesday night. Must have been the rain, chased everyone home. He shifts in his seat; no matter which way he sits, it's hell on his tailbone. His bladder could use a little relief, too.

'Mind if we hit the Hut? I have to take a leak.'

'I don't want pizza. Go up to Fluky's. A sausage sounds good.'

Fluky's isn't in their beat. It isn't even in their district. Weiss is sick of driving this route, though, and he isn't buying the theory that if they go around again, they'll find something they missed the time before.

While they're waiting at a red light, Weiss wonders if it'll rain again. Maybe it'd postpone his initiation tonight. Putting it off doesn't mean it won't happen, but at least he'll have more time to make it right in his head. He shifts in his seat again, turns his air vent toward Fiore.

'She's a whore,' Fiore says finally.

'The girl? A whore, you mean—'

'You don't want to know.'

'Why not?'

Fiore doesn't answer, as if Weiss is supposed to garner some piece of prophetic wisdom from his silence, his distant gaze.

Weiss makes a left on Western. 'Fluky's it is.'

CHAPTER FOUR

'Go through the drive-thru,' Fiore says when they get to Fluky's.

'I have to go to the bathroom.' Weiss hates to tell him again.

'Go through the drive-thru. Then you can park and go in.'

Weiss passes the red-shuttered restaurant and turns into the north lot, where the drive-thru line circles. Will he ever get out of the car for more than a pit stop? 'What do you want to eat?' he asks, feigning indifference while his bladder presses heavy against his groin.

'A polish. Fries. And a Coke. Large Coke.'

The Cutlass Supreme in front of them pulls up to the menu board, its back end low, customized. The driver, a black kid, maybe eighteen, wears a mesh baseball cap high on his head. Weiss watches the bill angle back and forth as the kid collects orders from his passengers and relays them to the intercom. Two passengers in the backseat sit low, the crowns of their heads barely visible. Weiss catches the whites of a set of eyes that peek at them through the back window.

'Act natural,' Fiore says, a good guess as to what

the kids are saying to one another. Weiss watches for a telling squirm or a curious move.

Fiore runs the plates. The Cutlass comes up clean.

Weiss takes his turn at the intercom: 'A polish with everything, a hot dog, mustard only. Two large fries, two large Cokes.'

A girl repeats the order, her voice tinny over the transom. Weiss drives forward.

In the Cutlass, a slow bass beat kicks in, probably from a set of subwoofers in the trunk. The female passenger in the front seat lifts her arms and moves slightly, like the music forces her, or restrains her. Weiss hears Busta Rhymes punch lyrics over an intermittent, reverbed keyboard. The car rattles each time the bass drops.

'Quiet tonight,' Fiore says.

Weiss knows he's talking about the Job.

The kids in the Cutlass take forever to get their money together – who owes what for what – and when they finally pull away from the drive-thru window, Weiss is anxious about his trip to the john. At the window, a teenaged girl with tanning-bed skin greets them, her smile real customer-friendly. Her braces are a different white than her teeth.

'Hi, officers.' She looks starstruck, a reaction Weiss still isn't used to, though he's learned that the sum of his badge and his smile is greater than its parts. 'Ketchup? For your fries?' The girl asks like she's offering herself.

Weiss turns to share the love with Fiore, but Fiore's got his eye on a maroon, mid-nineties Mustang parked on the opposite side of the lot, facing Farwell Avenue.

'Ketchup?' Weiss asks anyway.

'Did you get a look at that Mustang when we drove up?' Fiore asks, reaching for his baton and the door handle at the same time. 'Drive through.'

'What?'

'I said drive through.'

'Sorry,' Weiss says to the girl, large Cokes left sweating in her hands.

He pulls forward and Fiore says, 'Go out to the street. Park curbside. No lights.'

'What did you see?'

'Had you been paying attention when we pulled in, you would have seen a young girl come up from the Citgo and get in on the passenger side.'

'So?'

'So we're police officers. We look for shit. Run the plates,' Fiore says. He's out of the squad before Weiss can put it in park.

The Mustang is sitting in the second spot from the street, an empty space next to it and an unoccupied Toyota pickup on its far side. Weiss can see that the driver's side window is three-quarters down, and the cherry of a cigarette brightens, smolders, flits in and out of sight. The Mustang's plate is in plain view. Weiss punches the number into the MDT, making a conscious effort to relax so that his bladder will, too. He wonders what PC Fiore will claim for this stop. He thinks about pissing in Fiore's empty coffee cup.

Fiore makes his way around the base of the big Fluky's sign. Its high-voltage spotlights buzz over the street din. The light falls away quickly in the lot, and the front seat of the Mustang is shadowed by the Toyota. Fiore approaches the Mustang from the back and walks up casually along the driver's side, probably to get a read on who's inside before he announces himself. Weiss wonders if it'll turn out to be another asshole Fiore knows.

Ping – the MDT alerts and Weiss skips over the basic info because his eyes are immediately drawn to the LEADS hits: domestic violence, criminal conduct by a gang member—

'Show me your hands!' Fiore barks. 'Now!' He's fallen back ten paces from the Mustang and gone down on one knee, gun aimed at the driver's window.

Automatically and all at once Weiss is out of the car, on his radio, moving toward the Mustang, gun drawn to cover Fiore. 'This is 2031, we need backup immediately at 6821 North Western Avenue—'

The dispatcher says something that sounds like a question but Weiss is busy processing the scene: nobody on foot in the lot, but cars rounding the drive-thru could be in the line of fire. The Toyota on the other side could work for cover. He's got to stay back, keep civilians away.

'2411 and all surrounding units, respond.' The dispatcher comes clear over both their radios.

'He's armed,' Fiore shouts to Weiss.

Weiss sidesteps around the back of the Mustang, keeping his distance, looking in through the back window and out through the eyes in the back of his head – his senses – he's hyperaware, his gun forward, attention everywhere. He scans the lot for other suspects, other victims. He hears himself radio the dispatcher: 'Suspect is armed, sitting in his car. LEADS showed two strikes.'

He hears the business of the drive-thru: the intercom, the cars advancing. And farther out, the sounds of the street; the movement of traffic angling around a city bus. He tunes out the periphery, honing in on Fiore's command:

'Get your fucking hands up! Out the window on the roof.'

Weiss sees the man's fingers crawl up on the roof, spreading out flat, curling into fists, spreading out again.

'Who else is in there?' Fiore shouts, still paces away, up on his feet now, shining his flashlight in the car's side windows, his gun still trained on the driver.

'Get a front visual,' Fiore calls to Weiss.

Weiss darts around the Toyota pickup and comes back at the Mustang from the front passenger side, shining his flashlight directly at a young girl's tear-streaked face. Her mascara is thick and running, her lipstick deep brown; her black hair is coiffed in curls matted around her dark brow, done up like so many Hispanic beauties. But in her eyes, and in her tears, he sees the innocence of this girl. Just this one young girl.

'I've got your man,' the dispatcher says. 'Vehicle is registered to one Juan Almodovar, currently on parole ...'

'Hands out the window,' Weiss commands the girl.

The girl shows her hands in the half-down window; a slender cigarette between her long, squared, purple-brown nails. Her thin arms hang in the air, left above right, shaking uncontrollably.

Weiss edges toward the window, hears the girl say, 'Juan, what's happening?'

Sirens wail, approaching from the south, drowning out the girl's voice. Two squads scream into the lot and in seconds four officers are there, guns trained on the Mustang. The blue and red lights swirl and click above the squads, precise and accusatory.

'Juan. Real slow: move your hands to the top of the glass on the window,' Fiore orders. Then, 'I'm coming to the door. Don't fucking move.' The other officers creep up from different angles. Weiss holds his position, his gun on the girl.

A short, stocky plainclothes cop wearing his star hanging from a cord around his neck approaches the passenger's side from the back and signals Weiss to move in. They reach the window together, Weiss providing cover as the plainclothes cop holsters his gun and says, 'Don't move, Melia,' his voice reasonable. Weiss sees the small-caliber pistol in the center console, right there in the open.

'I'm gonna open this door on three, Juan,' Fiore says on the other side of the car. 'Don't you ever take your fucking hands off the window or by God, you will be a dead man.'

'What are they gonna do?' the girl pleads with wet black eyes.

'Eyes on me,' the plainclothes cop says, real nice this time. 'Hands on the window.'

On the driver's side, Fiore steps up to the door, two other cops in tow. 'One. Two.'

And on 'Three,' Fiore opens the door and the other two pull Juan out of the car by his hands, his arms, his torso. They spin him around and push him down and the cuffs are on before his face hits the pavement.

Juan coughs the air out of his lungs.

'Juan?' the girl whimpers, craning her neck to see him, her fingers curled around the window.

The plainclothes cop's friendly disposition wanes. He opens the door and pulls the girl to her feet. 'Little Melia, always getting into trouble.' The indifference in his voice is like a weapon, so Weiss backs off, holsters his gun.

The cop pats her down. 'You know you aren't old enough to be hanging around with Juan, don't you?'

Melia crosses her arms, indignant. 'I'm having his baby.'

'What are you, fifteen?' the cop asks.

'Next week.'

'And you and Juan, been together ...'

'Since he got out of jail.'

'I'll bet your parents are proud.'

'It was a bullshit rap.'

'Isn't she lovely?' he says to Weiss.

Melia's glare stops him from answering.

Another squad arrives, and a Hispanic officer in a black GANG UNIT T-shirt approaches. 'Zeke,' he addresses the cop in plainclothes.

'Ramos,' Zeke says, a hello.

'Melia,' Ramos says.

Melia ignores him. She's on her tiptoes now, trying to get a look at Juan. They've moved him: he's sitting on the curb, legs splayed out. Looks like he's unsuccessfully bargaining with the officer standing watch.

The rest of the boys are poking around the inside of the Mustang.

'Officer ...' Ramos pinches Weiss' star to get a look at the name below. 'Officer Weiss. Nice grab.'

Fiore comes up, pats Weiss on the back. 'He didn't grab anything but his dick. You want to take that potty break now, Weiss?'

Weiss completely forgot he had to go and now Fiore's making him look like an ass. 'I'm fine,' he says, knowing this is about control.

'You guys can head out,' Zeke says. 'We'll take the collar.'

'Don't want us impinging on your diligent operation, eh?' Fiore says.

'Or cutting in on your dinner hour,' Zeke says. 'You did come up here for a hot dog, didn't you, Fiore?'

Ramos says, 'Quit the cockfight, boys. We all know what's what. I've been wanting to have a little talk with Melia anyway.'

'Fine by me,' Fiore says. 'You all seem to be intimately acquainted anyhow.'

'It's interesting you say that, Fiore.' Ramos folds his arms. 'Because I don't think Melia has any idea who she's acquainted with.'

The fear wearing off, Melia curses Ramos under her breath.

'What's that, Melia?' he asks. 'You want to look at some photographs? You want me to show you what he did to his last girlfriend?'

'It was a bullshit rap,' Zeke says.

Melia puts her hands on her hips, her chin up,

ready for a fight, but all the officers except Weiss completely ignore her. Weiss feels like an asshole when she looks at him and his smile doesn't get him anything but the finger.

'Right back,' Ramos says, headed for his squad.

'Guess we'll split,' Fiore says to Zeke. 'We got a long night ahead.'

'Fuck you!' Melia yells on a high of pent-up conviction. 'Let me talk to Juan.'

Zeke takes her arm. 'Juan's going to be unavailable for a little while. See, he might have been impressing you, carrying around that little six-shooter, but it's a violation of his parole.'

'You know why he's on parole, right, Melia?' Ramos asks when he comes back with a three-ringed photo album. He flips it open, shows a page around.

The picture makes Fiore gag.

'What the hell is that?' Melia asks, denial ruling.

'That is Juan's last girlfriend's face.'

'You're lying,' she says, awareness creeping into her voice.

Ramos turns the page. This time Weiss has to look away.

Ramos says, 'That's her *puta*, Melia. Juan was real mad.'

Melia's face runs an emotional gamut that ends with disbelief. 'He would never.' But the tears in her eyes say he would.

'Well, don't think I'm in the mood for a sausage anymore,' Fiore says. 'Let's go, Weiss.'

CHAPTER FIVE

'I liked it better when we met at the lake,' Jed says. He stuffs a wad of Skoal between his cheek and his jaw and kicks up the dirt around home plate.

'I liked it better when you didn't have an opinion,' Noise says. He puts his foot up on the bleacher step, twists to stretch his spine.

'It's a ballpark,' Fiore says from the top bleacher. 'Weiss should feel right at home.'

Weiss comes around the corner, having finally relieved himself behind the dugout. They're at East River Park, on the edge of the beat, taking a break from patrol – or more correctly, taking a few available minutes to ready Weiss for his initiation.

'Weiss, catch.' Jed tosses him a dirty tennis ball he found stuck in the chain-link fence. Weiss throws it back with impressive accuracy, but Jed dodges it.

'Nice one, Pagorski,' Fiore says.

'I'm not gonna touch that ball. He didn't wash his hands.'

Noise lights a Kool 100. Weiss smells the sweet, poisonous menthol smoke as he climbs up to the top of the bleachers and sits next to Fiore.

'So you got a taste of it tonight, Ray?' from Jed.

'Hardly,' Fiore answers for him. 'Those guys in the twenty-fourth are fuckin' soldiers. By the book. Our only job is to make arrests and we walked, no collar.'

'Someone else handles their problems,' Noise says, 'makes them look bad.'

'What makes them look bad is that they've got armed parolees getting poon in the Fluky's parking lot,' Fiore says. 'It's a family establishment. We were trying to get some dinner.'

'Good polishes up there,' Jed says, spits in the dirt.

Fiore nods a shut up, continues: 'I see the girl—'

'Unit 2024 respond,' the dispatcher's voice cuts in over Weiss' radio. They wait for her exchange with Twenty-four to make sure they won't be called in.

Noise blows a stream of smoke into the night air. Weiss watches it rise and float, quiet and thick in the humidity, like a specter.

'Twenty-four, go ahead,' from the car.

'Backup request at a traffic stop at Lake Shore northbound at Bryn Mawr …' Weiss turns down the radio; they won't be needed.

'So you saw the girl get in the car.' Jed picks up Fiore's story.

'She was barely old enough to be in high school. And they're in the car making out, whatever. I don't know if she's hooking, or running away, or some pedophile's got her on a leash. So I tap on the window, just curious, and the first thing I see is the guy's revolver. In plain view. Like it's nothing.'

'No fear,' Noise says.

'Fuckin' gangsters,' out of Jed's mouth, before he spits.

Fiore summons Noise with a two-finger wag; Noise climbs the bleachers.

'They found a sawed-off baseball bat, Imperial Gangster insignia carved into it, under his seat,' Fiore says, taking Noise's cigarette for a drag. 'He said it was a gift from the girl.'

'So thoughtful.' Jed again.

Fiore takes another drag of the Kool 100, hands it back to Noise. 'The girl was so young, no fuckin' clue, until Ramos shot the stars out of her eyes. Showed her pictures of the guy's last victim.'

'Breaking the news: worst part of the job,' Noise says.

'What's worse was watching her defend the shitbag,' Fiore says. 'She loves him; he'll take advantage of that. He'll tell her lies; she'll learn to be disappointed. And you can bet she'll stick by him until one of them winds up dead.'

Weiss thinks of Melia, arms crossed in the parking lot, loyalty her defense. 'I hope the girl makes it.'

'If you're worried about the girl, Ray,' Jed says, 'you should have gone into social work.'

'He didn't have a Chinaman at DCFS,' Fiore says, referring, as they always do, to Lieutenant Don Weiss.

'I didn't have a Chinaman, period,' Weiss says. 'I got my star on my own.' He's taken endless flak over his father's position in the department since the day he put his last name on the application. His dad didn't help him get the job; in fact, his dad is the reason he has to prove himself tonight.

Weiss cracks his knuckles.

'You anxious about something?' Fiore asks.

'Enough with the drum roll.' Noise flicks his cigarette away, looks at Fiore. 'Let's hear the plan.'

CHAPTER SIX

Fiore tells Weiss to park on the southwest side of Lincoln just past Argyle Avenue. Argyle breaks a few blocks over and picks up again here, running one-way west; this means traffic only comes from two directions instead of four, and only one from behind.

In the squad, Weiss looks at the clock. It's just shy of 11 p.m. Behind them, Argyle is residential, dark, and quiet. Weiss wishes he could have parked there.

Fiore hands Weiss a thin, glossy catalogue. Weiss holds it near the window to look at it by the streetlight. On the cover, some woman's bejeweled finger points to the text: *Rytoi Jewelers ... specializing in the art of redesign.*

'I dog-eared it. Page six.'

Weiss flips to the page: rows of pricey rings feature various gems.

'Josephine likes rubies.' Fiore points to a stone-studded gold ring. 'Something nice like that. It's our anniversary.'

'You're going to give your wife stolen jewelry for your anniversary?'

'It's the thought that counts.' Fiore takes the catalogue, looks at page six. 'If they ever paid us enough to afford this kind of thing …' He stops before he says anything candid. 'How's your girlfriend?'

'Mine?' Weiss is surprised by the question. 'I don't have one. Technically. Currently.'

'Been in love before?' Fiore asks.

'I guess so. I don't know.'

'Ah, you're a kid. You can get away with playing the field. But I'll tell you this: there's no worse feeling than disappointing the woman you love.' He closes the catalogue and tucks it into the visor along with any hope of Weiss pursuing a conversation. 'Anyway, pick up something for your next girlfriend, maybe. They have a pretty good selection in there; I don't think you can screw it up.'

Actually, Weiss thinks, *this whole thing is pretty fucking screwed up*. He doesn't want to steal anything for anyone. But what choice does he have? The way he sees it, both his options are unpleasant. One: commit this petty crime. Feel like an asshole, yeah, but finally be 'in' – and quit taking heat. Two: forget it. Take the high road, tell Fiore to fuck off. Let Fiore's 'disappointment' infect all the other guys in the district, and turn into doubt; count on a cold-shouldered career. And get used to being the 'Lieutenant in training.'

There is a third option: he can quit this thing altogether. He didn't get his star because of his dad; he got it because he wanted to connect with him. The Lieutenant's life revolves around the Job, always has; Weiss just wants to be in the orbit. And now, if Weiss wants 'in,' the law – the very thing his dad stands for – has to be broken. Is it worth walking away from? Would his dad understand?

'That's it right there.' Fiore points just down the street on the right, where a red-lettered electric sign says RYTOI JEWELERS in fancy script. The storefront has one small display window that juts out from the building; it's empty.

'We'll drive down to Ainslie. You get out at the alley; I'll take the squad, circle around.'

Weiss looks at the clock again: eleven exactly. He has to decide.

Fiore gave him the rundown at the park, and this thing seems like a no-brainer. The directions are clear: bust the back door lock using the fireman's axe Fiore put in the trunk. Using the back of the axe like a hammer, bend the drop pin and move the steel folding gate. Open the door, remembering that the movement sets off the silent alarm, and security is on its way. Get the surveillance tape – you don't want to be on camera – stick it in your pocket, and get rid of it later. Then get the stuff advertised in the catalogue, page six. Use the axe once more to break all the glass displays – make it look like a real smash and grab, and a real pain in the ass to figure out what's missing. Get out of the building, dump the goods in the trunk. And then, start the investigation.

But what if there's a witness? Some kid riding his bike. A bum finishing a Dumpster dive. Another business owner, back because he forgot his daily planner, sees Weiss in the alley.

'Second thoughts, Weiss?'

Even though he didn't eat at Fluky's he feels like he has heartburn. What if he can't find the surveillance equipment? Or it isn't a closed-circuit system, like

37

Fiore says, and everyone and their grandmother sees him on a newsreel tomorrow morning. Fox News breaks the story: an officer caught in the act.

'Hellooo? Officer Weiss?'

'Yeah,' he hears himself say. Fiore wouldn't risk a bad racket. And he says these Eastern Europeans won't spend the money on hefty security. Weiss has to trust him. That's what this is all about.

Something nice for Josephine. She deserves it after who knows how many years with Fiore. Hell, Weiss feels entitled to some kind of reward, and it's only been six months. But Weiss has never even met Josephine. Aside from just now, Fiore rarely talks about her. Like so many other things, he says Weiss won't understand. He's partially right, since Weiss doesn't know how a woman in her right mind could stand the guy.

Weiss looks at the storefront, dark and vacant. The sidewalk is empty. A few cars zip north on Lincoln, paying no mind to the squad with its lights off. And then, for more than a moment, everything is quiet.

Weiss looks over at Fiore, hoping for some kind of nudge. He could go over the part about how the jeweler marks everything up a hundred percent. Make him feel like Jed, make him believe this is his 'in.' He could at least make the chance of getting caught sound improbable.

Instead he says, 'I'm not into pep talks.' He pulls on a pair of gloves and gets out of the squad.

Weiss grabs his gloves, gets out, and catches up with Fiore on the sidewalk in front of the jewelry store. 'Josephine likes rubies?'

'Yep.'

Headlights appear from the south. Fiore stops, stands there by a couple newspaper boxes and a garbage can.

As the car passes, Weiss turns away, hoping to hide his face. The storefront door and display window are made of shatterproof glass – the kind that looks like someone put chicken wire between the panes. Must be part of the security system: breaking the glass trips the alarm, and the chicken wire is an obstacle.

Behind him, Fiore knocks over the hefty, grated metal garbage can. Weiss turns a gasp into a chuckle as its contents spill out onto the street. He's anxious, but he doesn't want Fiore to know.

Fiore picks up the garbage can.

'What the—' Weiss starts and without time to finish jumps out of the way as Fiore heaves the garbage can over his head and throws the can at the glass door. It strikes waist-high and sticks in the wire once the heavy base has gone through.

So much for deliberation.

Fiore takes hold of the can and pulls it back toward him, sets it on the ground, and turns to Weiss, offering his first actual smile all night.

'I think I'll take a drive around the block. Meet you out back, say, five minutes?'

'Fuck you, Jack, this isn't how we planned it.'

'A good cop can always improvise,' Fiore says, using both hands to push Weiss toward the opening.

'This is crazy, Jack—'

'Leg up,' Fiore says.

'No.'

'Weiss, either you're going in, or you're going in. Don't embarrass yourself.'

Fiore pivots, heads for the driver's side of the squad, gives Weiss one last look before he gets in and drives off.

Another pair of headlights appears, from the north this time, and Weiss has to get the hell out of sight or he's fucked.

He swallows the lump in his throat and pulls on his gloves. He puts one leg through the hole in the door, pivots, and backs in, pulling his other leg through just as the car passes.

Inside, Weiss' feet feel light on the carpet. The room is soundless; even the street din stays just outside the hole in the door. The air is too cold, like in the car, and it seems thin. He feels the sweat on his upper lip.

This is all backward, he thinks; now he's got to handle it in reverse. He has to get the jewels, then trash the place, then get the surveillance tape – the camera must've captured Fiore throwing the can. And now its eye is on Weiss.

He looks around. Glass cases as long as coffins sit to each side; one at the back. The security camera is rigged above another case on the back wall.

He forgot his flashlight and can't see what's what without peering into each case, using the patches of light that come in through the hole and the display window from the streetlight out front. The case on the right is full of watches; the one on the left holds chains, necklaces, rings – wait, no, those are charms. Would Fiore settle for a charm? He scans the stuff from left to right, working his way to the back of the room.

In the back case there are the rings, men's and women's, displayed on delicate white mannequin fingers. He can't tell which ones have rubies but decides Fiore's going to have to take what he can get and he better not complain because he's the one who fucked this thing up from the start.

Without the axe, Weiss has to find something else to break the cases' glass. He jumps over the case on the right and finds a stool on wheels, thinks this is going to be messy.

He brings the stool down on the case of watches and surprisingly the glass doesn't even crack. He hoists the stool over his head, turns, and goes for the case opposite, all his weight thrown into it. This time the stool drops through the case with an anticlimactic crunch. He pulls the stool back. A necklace is caught on one of the wheels. He gives the case another overhanded strike, decides he's short on time, and moves to the back.

This time, he uses the stool like a baseball bat and knocks the glass on the side into the display. Good enough, he thinks. He reaches in among shards for the jewelry, glad he has gloves. He pulls rings from their white fingers and holds them up to his face, trying to distinguish their colors. In the shitty light he can't tell green from red so he thinks fuck it, takes five or six and shoves them in his pants pocket, glass remnants included.

He realizes he still hasn't caught his breath so he stands there a moment, getting the details straight.

Page six rubies. Cases smashed. What's that smell? He's surprised, in the cold conditioned air, that a faint, rank odor finds his nostrils. Must be dirty ducts. Or old carpet.

Weiss hears a clanging noise coming from the back room: it has to be Fiore hitting the steel gate in back. Relief washes over him, like after he's thrown up, and his uniform is damp all over, sweat-through – maybe he's what smells.

No matter: he's got to stick to the plan. Page six rubies. Cases smashed. Time to get the tape.

He jumps over the back case and pushes a curtain aside, enters the room. It's pitch-black, and more musty. Light switch? Yeah, right, and Fiore will tell everyone he's scared of the dark. He feels along the wall that runs flush with the security camera. He finds two electrical cords. Fiore said the camera is connected to the rest of the kit through the wall, so he follows one cord down to an outlet, then tries the other. It continues to the floor, runs along the baseboard, and up again – to another outlet.

Fiore pounds on the back door again, yells something Weiss can't make out. He takes a step forward, toward the noise, and his kneecap jams into what must be a metal desk. The pain shoots up through his hip and he resists the instincts of his vocal cords so all that comes out of his mouth is a strained hiss. After a moment he feels his way around the desk, favoring his knee, and finds the back door. He locates the handle, unlatches the dead bolt, feels like he's escaping. He turns the handle and pushes, but the door won't open.

He wonders: how the fuck do I improvise with a steel door? He recalls the original plan: bend the drop pin and move the folding gate. The gate's outside, which means that the door has to open in. He pulls the handle and it swings open, lighter than it seems. Fiore's standing there, shining a flashlight in his face; Weiss waits for some smart-ass comment.

'Jesus,' is all Fiore says.

'I don't have my flashlight. I couldn't see anything – I didn't get the tape.' Weiss crouches down to release the drop pin from the inside. He pulls up on the pin with both hands; it won't budge.

'Jesus,' Fiore says again. He's looking at something behind Weiss but Weiss is busy with the pin and explaining—

'I'm sorry, you threw me off, going through the front.' He leans back, puts weight into it, tugs, and the pin releases. He steps to the right to pull the gate open, grips the leading edge …

'We're in deep shit, Weiss.'

'What?' Suddenly his chest feels tight.

'We've got ourselves one hell of a crime scene.'

Fiore steps inside, past Weiss, throwing the beam of his flashlight on a very still, very dead man. His body is splayed in an unnatural position on the floor, and the blood on his chest seems fake, but his clouded gray eyes stare at a very real hell. His mouth is half-open, like maybe he'd been pleading for his life until his final breath.

Weiss doubts he'll feel relieved, but he throws up anyway.

CHAPTER SEVEN

Fiore doesn't make fun of Weiss for tossing his cookies. In fact, he doesn't say anything at all; instead, he turns on the lights, disappears into the front room. Probably cleaning up Weiss' mess.

Good thing, because Weiss froze up like he was the one who kicked. He leans against the back door, his hands on his knees, staring at the body. It's less than three feet from the outlet where he gave up his search for the video equipment. A few more steps and he would have tripped over, maybe onto, the body. Weiss presses his lips together; the thought stings his eyes.

The guy has liver-colored skin at the backs of his shoulders. The rest of his flesh is almost as white as his wife-beater, but more cold; more blue-white. Weiss has never seen a dead body like this. There've been bodies, sure – overdoses, old folks, accidents. But this one, this life ended midsentence, the body left to rot, is absolutely criminal.

The place seems perfectly still, like the dead man, though Weiss can hear Fiore moving around in the other room, radioing for backup. Weiss stares at the man, waiting for his chest to rise or fall; waiting for his hand to twitch, or his eyes to blink.

From somewhere in the room, Weiss hears Fiore say, 'Why don't you go outside, get some air.' Then, 'How about you go out to the squad, pop the trunk?' His tone is strangely considerate. 'Maybe you want to brush the glass off your pants.'

None of these suggestions gets Weiss' body to cooperate. Then, Fiore comes over, steps around the puke, and squats down in front of Weiss.

'What do you say you do something with this?' Fiore holds the videotape in front of Weiss' nose and he snaps out of his daze, and into a panic.

'Fuck, in my pants, the rings—' He stands up and goes for his pocket, but Fiore grabs his forearm—

'That's where they'll stay.'

'No way. They're going to know we were here. They'll think we killed that guy.'

'Are you out of your fucking mind?' Fiore grabs Weiss by the back of the collar and pulls him out the back door.

Weiss can't lift his head as Fiore drags him, stumbling across the pavement.

'What the hell are you doing?' Weiss asks.

Fiore stops, stands him up at the back of the squad, turns him around so they're face to face. 'You want to know what I'm doing? I'm covering your ass.'

Approaching sirens penetrate the humid air in waves. Backup is less than a minute away, Weiss thinks, and the evidence is in his pocket.

He swallows, his throat dry, and looks Fiore in the eye. And for the first time, he notices something, but not the usual sarcasm and scrutiny that characterizes Fiore's face. He sees something else: it's alliance.

'Look, kid, everything's gonna be fine. I checked the place. You were careful. You didn't disturb the body. They look for hair, fibers, whatever, we were in there searching the place. Securing the scene. We're fine.'

'They're not going to believe I went inside! I threw up all over the entrance!'

'Weak stomach. Doesn't keep you from pulling it together now, and pretending you did your job.'

'The stool. Footprints. Sweat: they're gonna know—'

'They're only gonna know what we want them to know. Just keep your mouth shut and do what I tell you.' Fiore pops the trunk, dumps the videotape. 'I'll walk you through the report. We got no trouble; we don't know any more about the dead guy than we did before we found him. That's for the investigators.'

'They'll think the burglary and the murder are connected.'

'Not connected to *us*.' Fiore emphasizes the word as he closes the trunk.

'Jack, this is fucked. I don't know if I can do this—'

'*This* is what you were trained for, Weiss!' Fiore's face grows hard again, his patience waning as the sirens blare; they're around the corner—

Fiore takes hold of Weiss' collar again, spins him around, and lays him out facedown on the trunk of the squad.

Then Weiss feels thin, cold metal press against his temple. He can't believe Fiore drew his gun. It can't be his gun. Still, Weiss shuts his eyes, shakes involuntarily.

'Does this scare you?'

Weiss won't say yes.

'It should.'

Weiss focuses on his breath. Tries not to shake. This is about trust; he knows it.

'Open your eyes. Come on. Get up.'

Weiss pushes himself off the hood, stands up, straightens his star – the only thing that keeps him coming back for more of this shit. A fire engine rounds the corner on the south side of the alley, stops; its width requires a five-point turn.

Fiore stands there, holds up the object he held to Weiss' head: a metal ballpoint pen. 'Our most powerful weapon,' he says. He points it at the jewelry store. 'For that guy in there, the truth was a bullet. This is our truth: whatever we write in the report.'

From the north, a squad appears, barrels down the alley, screeches to a halt.

Fiore clips the pen to Weiss' shirt. 'Hell of a graduation, huh?'

In front of the store, Weiss guards the barricade tape to keep onlookers from interfering with the hole in the glass door. The garbage can has already been bagged, taken for evidence. A few curious neighbors have come and gone, satisfied with Weiss' explanation of the break-in; Weiss figures Fiore stuck him here so he'd have time to get the story straight.

A half hour later, the only person left hanging around is a girl, maybe eighteen, a wanna-be of some kind. She's unkempt, probably symbolic of the mess inside her head, just the kind of person who would linger. Weiss tries to pretend she isn't there.

'So have you ever killed anybody?' the girl asks, eyeing Weiss' gun.

'No, ma'am.'

'Shot someone?'

'No, I haven't.'

'Do you like carrying that gun? Does it make you feel powerful?'

Powerful, she says. Like Fiore and his pen. Weiss turns and looks inside: the place is lit up, crime scene specialists are taking photos, measuring angles, dusting for prints.

Jesus, he thinks, *they're going to find traces of me.*

'It's late,' he says, suddenly uncomfortable, hoping to get rid of the girl.

'Is this neighborhood dangerous?' she asks.

'No more than the next.'

'Weiss.' Fiore sticks his head through the hole in the door. 'Detective's here, wants to talk to you about the report. Pagorski's coming around to relieve you.'

Great, Weiss thinks, feeling the rings in his pocket. Maybe talking to the girl wasn't so bad after all.

'I've never seen you before,' the girl says. 'Are you new?'

'Relatively.'

'What would I have to do to see you again, get myself arrested?' The girl's attempt at humor isn't lost on Weiss.

'I wouldn't,' he says and hands her his card. Even though it doesn't give her any information aside from his name and badge number, he wonders why he's showing interest. Makes about as much sense as agreeing to watch over your own crime scene.

'Thank you, Officer Weiss,' pronouncing it *Weece*.

When Jed approaches he says, 'Hey, Ray. What's with the groupie?' Like she isn't standing there. Confidence stolen, the girl crumples Weiss' card in her hand and crosses the street without looking back.

'She's just a kid,' Weiss says.

'What's a kid doing hanging around a strapping young single police officer?'

'I didn't ask.'

They watch her disappear into the dark on Argyle Street.

'You know what they say about those young ones, Ray: they know more about love than girls our age.'

'I don't want to know where you're going with this.'

'You tell her you're a sensitive guy? That you cry at chick movies? Does she know you just lost your dinner over a dead guy?'

'I'm never going to hear the end of that, am I?'

'Nope. But don't worry: we're taking care of it. They're waiting to ID the body, but they think the vic's the store owner – a Lithuanian guy, been doing business here for years. The suspect didn't walk off with much, as far as they can tell. Detective figures it was a burglary gone bad, but the guy's been dead awhile and the alarm just tripped, so the timing's off. I heard her say she's gonna look into the owner's accounts, see if there are any special orders, big items missing ... motives for murder.'

Weiss stares at the ground, feeling the rings in his

49

pocket, wondering if his pants are loose enough, hoping nothing is visible through his dark blues.

'Seriously, man,' Jed says, 'don't sweat it. It's not like you killed the guy.'

'Thanks. That makes me feel so much better.'

'If you ask me? My gut says the murder was personal. And that's what they're going to focus on, Ray: murder. Not a couple of missing earrings.'

'I better get over there.' Weiss ducks under the tape at the same time Jed does, switching positions.

Jed holds out his hand. 'Congratulations, buddy. We're finally *us*.'

'Yeah,' Weiss says, lingering weariness clouding the statement. His handshake is firm, however brief.

'Have fun with that detective,' Jed says as Weiss heads up the street. 'I'd like to.'

'You're the other one?' Sloane Pearson says without looking up from her notepad.

'I'm Officer Weiss.'

'The one who puked.'

'I have a weak stomach.'

Pearson finishes scribbling some detail on the pad and sets her eyes on Weiss. She sticks out her free hand. 'Sloane Pearson, Homicide.'

'Hi,' Weiss says, feeling dumb for being so casual. 'Hello.'

'I don't have much for you tonight. Your report is pretty clear ...' Without acknowledging his smile, she rearranges some of the papers she's got spread out on the hood of a squad, looking for something specific.

She's got to be a few years older than he is and he can tell she's mature in all the ways he's not: a steadied brow, watchful eye, a patient face. She probably knows more than he does about just about everything.

And her body isn't bad either, leaning over the squad, tucked into a run-of-the-mill pantsuit, a little skin in all the right places. Good hair, probably better out of the ponytail, and her ass …

'Okay, officer,' she says, waving the report around to get his eyes where they should be, 'you went over this more than once and everything's correct?'

'I did.' And now she's holding the report breast-level. Is she testing him? Weiss makes certain eye contact.

'Then we're finished.' She tosses the report on the hood, flips her ponytail over her collar, and makes for the store's back door.

'Detective?' Weiss says. She stops, turns, raises her eyebrows for a silent 'what?' – for probably the thirtieth time in as many minutes.

Weiss still feels stupid, but he asks anyway: 'Do you know who that is in there? The guy who was killed?'

'I don't. Freaked you out, did it?'

'I'd just like a name to go with the face when it pops into my head in the middle of the night.'

'It *is* the middle of the night.'

Weiss takes that as a good-bye, but she's still standing there, studying him.

'The guy didn't have any ID on him,' she says. 'We think his name is Petras Ipolitas. We're trying to locate a family member. The guy who owns the salon next door said this store wasn't open for business today. That's all we have.'

'Ipolitas.'

'Go home, have a beer, try to forget about it. There are far worse things.'

'Worse than going home and drinking alone?'

Pearson shows just enough of a smile to make it interesting. Then she takes off, leaving Weiss with five gold rings and no good way to ease his guilty conscience.

CHAPTER EIGHT

Weiss asked Jed to grab a beer, but Jed wasn't interested since he wanted to get home to his new wife and take another shot at knocking her up. Weiss' plan B: dropping by his ex's new apartment. He'd wanted to wait until she contacted him, but it's been nearly three weeks since he helped her move, and he hasn't heard a word. Maybe she's playing the same game he is. Somehow Leah always wins.

Weiss drives up Broadway feeling like the crime scene is in the backseat, afraid if he looks in the rearview mirror, he'll see Ipolitas' face. He isn't into karma, but it's better than guilt. So maybe Ipolitas had it coming. Either that or he was one unlucky guy, getting robbed by one man and killed by another on the same day.

Broadway turns into Sheridan; Weiss continues north and turns right just past Loyola's campus. It's after two, and he hopes Leah's up studying. He could have called. But she would have told him not to come.

He parks in the red zone at the dead end by the lake, turns on his hazards, and gets out of the car. The sky is clear now, and the half moon gives the lake a silver stripe. A damp wind blows, invites Weiss to stay outside for a minute, breathe the air.

But he can't appreciate the moment like a normal person. His senses are too sharp, his body too conditioned; now every person, every sound, every shadow is suspect. Nothing is routine. The soft tick-tick-tick of his hazards is the only rhythm that feels right.

He scans his peripheral vision, realizing he doesn't feel quite himself because he isn't carrying his gun. It isn't something in his brain that's changed; it's something in his bones.

He approaches Loyola Tower's entrance and rings Leah's apartment, 11A.

The intercom crackles. 'Hello?'

'It's Ray.'

No response.

'Leah, I need to talk. Just talk.'

'About what?'

'Come on. I had a bad night.'

The door buzzes. That was easier than usual.

Weiss walks to the back of the building and takes the swing-gate service elevator up to the eleventh floor. Leah shares her place with Jen, a nursing major who assured Leah she'd spend half her time at the library and the other at her boyfriend's. Weiss hopes, for Jen's sake, that it's true. He can attest to the fact that Leah needs her space.

Her apartment is a clear shot at the end of the hall from this elevator and she's waiting in her doorway when he lifts the gate and steps into the hall. He hates it that she's evaluating his approach. She looks at his shoes. Waits to smile.

'Hey,' he says, wondering how she still manages to make him feel self-conscious after four years of should-we or shouldn't-we, especially since he's the one who decided on shouldn't the last time.

'What's up?' she asks, like she's talking to her brother. Her brother is a jerk.

Weiss sizes her up as he gets closer. She's wearing men's boxers, rolled at the waist, and a strappy top he remembers peeling off of her more than once. Her dark curls are up in some kind of twist, showing off her shoulders, her neck. And she's wearing a necklace he's never seen: a pink tear-shaped glass charm on a silver chain. He hopes it's something she picked up from work at Field's.

When he gets to the door, he touches her arm to gauge where she is on the affection scale tonight. She doesn't respond, doesn't even raise her eyes to meet his; sometimes she does this so he'll make the move. With a seed of doubt around her neck, though, he isn't in the mood to play games.

He sticks his hands in his pockets, says, 'I found a body.'

'Gross.' She doesn't sound impressed, or interested. Still, it gets him in the door.

He follows her to the futon, where she wraps a blanket around herself and resumes her position among scattered notes and textbooks. She doesn't make room for him to join her.

'Place looks nice,' he says. Since he helped her move from her last apartment, she hung some of her paintings on the living room walls. One, of a naked woman – or a guitar, or a wooden rhinoceros, depending on your level of appreciation – reminds him of when she started college as an art major at Columbia. The year she turned nineteen, and decided Weiss was too simple. The same year he enrolled at DePaul to prove her wrong. Like their relationship, though, his stab at a respectable education didn't quite work out.

'So what happened?' Leah pulls her feet up under the blanket. Behind her, on the windowsill, Weiss notices a pair of valentine-red candlesticks he remembers she used to light when sex was an occasion. They're burned lower now.

Weiss refuses to sit in the rocking chair across the room, the one they'd used once upon a time in ways that he remembers too fondly, so he moves her books and sits on the other end of the futon. The title sitting between them: Wesley's *The Theology of Love*.

'What are you studying?'

'I'm writing a paper on Christian marriage.'

Marriage: one of the bullet points in her breakup outline. 'So you're discriminating against gays,' Weiss says, to divert the topic.

'You're not funny,' she says, stowing a pen in the spiral of a notebook. 'The Jesuits are big on forgiveness. I'm writing a counterpoint.'

'Of course you are.'

'Why did you say you're here, again?' asks the ever-patient ex.

'I found a dead man.'

'I don't understand; it's not like you've never seen a body.'

Weiss wants to tell her about the whole night: the robbery, the murder investigation, the false report – and about Fiore – but he doesn't want to see her sweet, smart-assed expression turn. Any hint of disappointment in her eyes reminds him of every mistake he's ever made. And in that respect, he knows what Fiore meant about loving a woman. He can't tell Leah what he did.

'I just felt different,' he finally says. 'It hit me. How screwed up the job is.'

'So what, now you don't want to be a cop anymore? You want to quit, chalk it up to a learning experience?'

Weiss knows she's trying to bait him. To make him react.

'Don't be mean,' he says.

'I'm just playing devil's advocate.'

'He doesn't need one.'

'What do *you* need, Ray?'

I'm a pussy, he thinks; I need a hug.

Weiss looks at her, bundled in the pink kitty blanket, always cold. No matter how she tries to push him away, to be flip or indifferent, he can still see glimpses of the old Leah. The Leah who made him want to be a better person; not the one who wanted him to be someone else.

When he moves *The Theology of Love* and the other books to the floor, she doesn't stop him. She does say, 'Ray, maybe you should talk to your dad about this.' But her voice is soft, suggesting otherwise. Suggesting no talk at all.

A curl falls from the twist around the edge of her

face, teases her eye. He raises his hand to brush it away—

'Ray,' she says, clutching the blanket around her, a defense that doesn't stand a chance. He moves toward her; her notebook falls to the floor and the pen slips from its spiral. He puts his arms around her and the blanket and pulls her to him and kisses her, feeling her body tense, and then give in. The blanket falls away easily. He takes her face in his hands then, kissing her just as he wants to. Her fingertips tickle him through his T-shirt, nervous, reacquainting.

He's aroused, but the physical feeling isn't what's driving him. He wants her to react to him; to show him she's affected. He holds both her arms tight, controlling, and moves to kiss her neck. He wonders if her eyes are closed, enjoying this. Or if she's going along with this because it's familiar. Or if she wants him at all.

She unbuttons his fly, and he quits wondering.

He pulls at her necklace, the silver chain with the pink charm from who the fuck knows. He brings her face to his and kisses her mouth hard, anger interfering. He lifts her shirt and touches the skin of her slender waist and her breath catches, quickens. He wants to rip off her rolled-up boxers and fuck her right there, to prove to himself he can. He wants to pull her on top of him so she'll have to show him what it is she wants. *She'll* have to prove that she wants him, too.

He feels her hand on him, warm, hesitant. He smells her hair; tastes the juicy gloss he kissed from her lips. Breath heavy, all senses wanting, he opens his eyes.

But when he looks at her, he sees that he has to stop.

Her face is hopeful, searching for some way to connect with him. This way, any way. Even by a lie.

Her hand slips out limp from his jeans. 'What's wrong?' she asks, though she knows. This means something different to her.

He puts both feet on the floor, buttons his fly. He can't fuck her; he can't even be honest with her. And maybe he never has been.

'You said you needed to talk.' Emotion withheld in her voice; the words enough to do the job.

'I'm sorry,' is a stupid thing to say.

'Fuck you,' is no better, but she has cause to say it.

He gets up, apology unaccepted, and lets himself out, the tiniest part of him hoping she'll cry once he's gone.

When Weiss gets home he knows he won't be able to sleep. Before he was a cop, he'd have been able to turn on ESPN, crack open a Bud, and unwind, chasing the events of the day away without much effort. Now, every day builds upon the next, his experiences making him better, harder, smarter than the day before. He no longer unwinds; he rewinds.

TV is a distraction. He needs something to hold his attention. Something tactile; something that requires concentration. So at three in the morning, he goes down to the basement to clean his grandfather's .38 Special.

He had used the basement for storage, mostly, and

he shared the washer and dryer with Nick, the guy upstairs, until he moved out at the beginning of July. Since Nick left, Weiss spends more time here. The concrete floor and ground-level windows keep the place cool, even on the hottest August days. He likes the space, the simplicity; the pull-strings that light bare, seventy-five-watt bulbs.

He unlocks his steel storage cabinet, its three-point locking system essential, especially now that he knows how easy it is for crooks to get around more casual safety measures. He takes a case from the top shelf and sets it on a card table along with a brass wire brush, a cleaning rod, cloth and cotton, Hoppe's gun cleaner, and a bottle of Turtle Wax.

He sits in a folding chair and sets his mind to business. He flips the cylinder out to the right, exposing the chamber end of the four-and-three-quarter-inch barrel. The barrel is bored with a slight taper toward the muzzle – for superior accuracy, his dad told him; a little bonus in case Weiss turned out to be a lousy shot.

He's running the brush back and forth through the barrel, loosening the residue, when Ipolitas' image interrupts the routine. He wonders if the guy lived a good life before he died. If he had any regrets.

Weiss doesn't know what he regrets. He always wanted to make his dad proud. And he always liked the idea of being a cop. Why should he be sorry about that? Every profession has its scams. A guy he worked with at Skokie Township had a bunch of people caught up in a pyramid scheme. Even when Weiss was a bartender, the boss was trying to pull one over on the Seagram's distributor. He had to pick a game sometime, didn't he?

He saturates a cotton swatch with Hoppe's and attaches it to the rod, his mind working at a faster clip than his hands. He inserts the rod into the barrel, collecting loose residue and leaving a film of protective oil. This gun killed three bad guys in Cincinnati. They were bad guys, weren't they?

He uses a swatch of Turtle Wax to clean the six cylinder flutes. His hands are slow, like his grandfather's might have been. Slow and careful. But his own hands remind him that he stole from a dead man.

When they left the crime scene, Fiore and Weiss stopped to destroy the videotape. Fiore drove them over to the north branch of the river, a couple blocks from the baseball diamond in East River Park. Weiss pulled all the magnetic tape out of its case and set it on fire. Fiore crushed the case, tossed the pieces in the water. On the way back to the station, they went over their story once more, and Fiore assured Weiss everything would be okay. Then Fiore took the rings and predictably bitched about the selection. Asshole.

Weiss flips the gun's cylinder shut and brings his attention back to the task at hand. This is his favorite part: polishing the outside of the blued steel barrel, the hammer, the trigger. He handles the weapon so delicately that the term *deadly* seems inapplicable.

Finally, Weiss eases the gun back into its case from the oiled cloth, careful he doesn't leave fingerprints, because the salt and sweat from his skin will etch into the metal, leaving imperfections over time.

He regrets the fact that his actions tonight might someday do the same. He never intended to tarnish his star.

CHAPTER NINE

The dream is always about the same. Weiss started having it shortly after he got out on the street when one Terrence Mann, a thirty-three-year-old day trader from the Mercantile Exchange, drove his Lexus SC into a milk truck. Terrence hit the side of the truck just so the N of the DEAN logo was deformed, looked like DEAD. Weiss and Fiore were first on-scene. Fiore blocked off the intersection, dealt with the truck driver, and sent Weiss underneath to find out if Terrence was alive. He was; he told Weiss so between wet breaths, his internal injuries getting the better of him. Down on his elbows in the middle of the street, Weiss listened to Terrence talk real enthusiastically about the strength of the dollar. Then, quite abruptly, Terrence said he didn't want to die. That was the last thing he said. Weiss never saw his face.

In the dream, Weiss is standing in the same intersection. He's supposed to be directing traffic, but the bones in his forearms are crushed; he can't lift his arms. And he can't stop Terrence, cruising through the intersection on his way to an unstoppable, deadly encounter with the milk truck. Terrence's face is always different, always worse.

In this dream, his face is Petras Ipolitas'.

Weiss jerks awake to someone beating on his back door. He rubs his eyes, makes his first yawn a good one, to shake the dream. The clock reads ten to seven. Jed's early, and he isn't patient.

Weiss throws on a pair of mesh shorts and a Packers T-shirt, knowing the latter will incite the usual argument. He laces up his New Balances, stops in the kitchen to slug half a bottle of orange Gatorade, and opens the back door.

'You look like shit,' Jed says, now sitting on the top step, 'which I could understand, if we'd been able to celebrate last night. Nothing like a murder to put a damper on our drinking hour.' He stands up, lifts Weiss' chin for inspection. 'How come you have bags under your eyes, man?'

'I was up late.'

'Don't say Leah.'

'I won't.'

'I don't want to have to kick your ass.' Jed steps back, boxes the air: a mean hook, a swift uppercut. He's sweating through his long-sleeved thermal and sweatpants. Probably because it's already seventy degrees.

'What's with the getup?'

'I could ask you the same thing,' Jed says, eyeing the green and yellow helmet on Weiss' shirt. He punches Weiss' shoulder, skips down the steps. 'Let's get this over with. I'm starving.'

They jog east on Irving Park, taking it slow, warming up. Weiss' knees feel pretty good though the right one is a little sore. He sucks in the morning air easily, his lungs strong. Jed keeps up with him, though it's apparently more of an effort. His legs are massive and his feet fall flat, indiscriminately, on the pavement. Reminds Weiss of a duck.

They cross at Clark Street, cut into Graceland Cemetery, and head north. The path around the graves is quieter, the air less polluted than on the surrounding streets. Usually Weiss picks up the pace here, but this morning he doesn't want to leave Jed behind. After last night, he doesn't want to run alone.

Jed would probably make some comment, call Weiss a *gnojek* for running too slow, or point out the irony in being worried about a dead guy – if he could catch his breath. Instead Jed keeps trucking, one foot in front of the other, head forward, death as irrelevant as the headstones in his periphery.

Funny, Weiss thinks, I'm the one keeping up with him.

This is how it's been though, since the day they met. One drops the ball, the other catches – juggles if he has to. Better than brothers, Weiss thinks: willing accomplices. Like when Weiss covered for Jed after he crashed his car, driving him around until he could afford a new one – which was a long damn time, since he already owed payments on Katy's engagement ring. Jed never said thank you; then again, Weiss still owed him a substantial amount of money for the bet that Katy'd say no.

They bonded in the academy, outsiders waiting to get in, sharing the drive, and the struggle. They found strength in each other: getting smart from one's mistakes, picking up the other's slack, thinking alike despite completely different brains. And different backgrounds: Jed, with no doubts, wishing he had Weiss' family connections; Weiss, with too many questions, envious of Jed's faith in the system. Through it all, each enabled the other to see the bright side.

Now, they can bicker and bullshit to no end, but they know that when it comes down to it, there's no fucking around. So Weiss knows Jed won't rile him about last night, and Weiss isn't going to bitch about the fact that they're practically walking around the cemetery.

The Red Line train peeks over the east wall, spilling noise onto the grounds as it hustles toward the Loop. Weiss watches the train as they run toward the wall, watches lives slip by, going from one place to the next.

How stupid we are, Weiss thinks; we just keep moving along, oblivious, until something stops us.

They turn, running south now, past enormous tombs that overlook a tree-lined pond. Strange, Weiss thinks each time they run this route, that dead people in the middle of a city have such a nice view. Minutes later, when they pass George Pullman's gravesite, Weiss remembers the Christmas when Santa brought him a model train.

Weiss was six. His dad was drunk after too many hot toddies, and he couldn't understand his youngest son's interest in trains. 'You want to be like George Pullman?' he asked, to which Weiss replied, 'I want to be the police.' The comment ignored, Dad sat Weiss down by the fireplace and told Pullman's story.

Weiss rolled the shiny Lone Star locomotive back and forth on the hardwood floor while his dad rambled on about historical stuff that doesn't matter much to a kid: a long-winded story about a rich man without a generous bone in his body. Pullman invented the luxury railroad car and created a monopoly, then pulled his trains from the tracks during a depression, leaving the city and his own workers with 'jack shit' – the profanity sticking in Weiss' boy-mind.

Then his dad leaned in real close, his breath warm with brandy, to tell the part that gave Weiss nightmares well into puberty: when Pullman died, his family encased his coffin in a block of concrete, covered it with railroad ties, and buried him eight feet deep – in the middle of the night – to protect him from vengeful workers. Weiss' dad said, 'The truth was? They did it so the son of a bitch couldn't get up and come back.' Weiss stopped his toy in its tracks. His dad got up to make himself another drink, said first, 'I guess it just goes to show you'll pay for your crimes somehow.' Weiss never asked for another train.

'Fuck this,' Jed says, winded. 'Let's cut through.'

When Weiss hesitates Jed says, 'Come on, ya pansy,' and heads into the grass, making a staggered path between graves.

Weiss follows, figuring Jed's right: he is being a pansy. He's hung up on a dead stranger. Just like when he was a kid: the nightmares have always been about someone he never knew.

They maneuver around headstones and return to the paved loop at the Eternal Silence statue, where they're supposed to do push-ups. Jed hits the deck; Weiss stands there, for once affected by the figure of the haunting woman in stone. Her face is obscured, weathered by time, but Weiss is pretty sure she's looking at him.

Jed drops his knees to the grass and looks up, waiting for Weiss. 'Dude, you're starting to worry me. You're too uptight. Maybe you should call that detective.'

Jed's surprising perceptiveness encourages Weiss. He gets down on the ground, facing Jed, in plank position. 'You think she knows anything about Ipolitas?'

Jed's face screws up into a question mark from his eyebrows to his shaved hairline. He has no idea what Weiss means. 'I'm just saying, I think you need to get laid.'

Perceptive? Yeah, as dirt. Weiss gets on his knees. 'Jed, do you realize that a person was killed and I could be traced to it?'

Jed sits back on his heels. 'You have people looking out for you.'

'Oh yeah? What if there's evidence. What if they figure out I robbed the place. Who's going to look out for me then?'

'You don't think we can handle it, you can always call Daddy.'

'Fuck you.'

Jed rises to his knees. 'Maybe you *should* take some heat,' he says, now eye to eye with Weiss. 'Because I don't think you appreciate what we have. What *you* have. I think you're fuckin' spoiled.' Then he drops to the ground and pounds out push-ups until the muscles in his arms quit. After that, he drops to his knees and forces himself to do more.

Watching Jed struggle, veins pulsing in his temples, arms trembling, Weiss understands his own mistake: he can't argue with faith. Jed came from a home with no father at all. He fought nature and lack of nurture to get this job, and he found a place to fit in. For Jed, doubting the Job is impossible; and coming from Weiss, it's an insult.

Weiss gets down and counts out forty push-ups before he says, 'Maybe you're right.'

When Weiss gets home he realizes his cell phone is out of commission, and it doesn't take a detective to figure out he failed to give his dad money for the bill. He could punch himself for forgetting again; this means he has to drive up north today, and pretend everything's great.

He got the phone a few years ago, part of some family deal his dad purchased when he was going to DePaul. Weiss was making decent cash bartending at Gamekeeper's, but he didn't keep a bank account because he needed financial aid. He also needed a phone, because his roommates didn't have a landline – cable Internet and all that. So, the Lieutenant did him a favor, and got this phone plan. He renewed the contract last year, claiming Weiss couldn't beat the price. Weiss suspects this is a way for his dad to keep tabs on him, but he would never say it out loud.

The phone is the one thing his parents still take

care of now that he's on salary, and on track for a pension. It's also the one thing the Lieutenant won't bend the rules about: Weiss doesn't pay on time each month, the phone might as well be a tin can.

Weiss doesn't have to be at work until three, so he gets his act together and drives up around lunchtime, a strategic move. It's Wednesday, which means the Lieutenant is at work, and his mom's probably waiting for the cleaning ladies to finish up so she can get over to the North Shore Performing Arts Center where she works part-time in the ticket booth. The Lieutenant hates that she works at all now that she's retired from nursing, but she likes to get out of the house, and she gets to see all the shows for free.

Weiss figures if his mom is still home she'll be in too much of a hurry to grill him about his first and final date with Monica. He hopes he'll be able to drop off the check and see what's in the fridge without having to explain why he looks tired, or stressed, or underweight. It's not that he doesn't want to see his mother; it's just that he doesn't want to see her today.

He takes McCormick Boulevard up to Oakton, the city spreading itself out, the streets opening up, buildings given a little breathing room. Heading west on Oakton, he counts out eight streets that begin with K, the very same thing he used to do as a kid when he rode his bike home from little league games at James Park. Kenneth, Kilbourn, Kolmar ... the ninth K, two miles from the park, is Kenton Avenue. Home base.

The house, a one-story ranch in a row of similar one-story ranches, sits on a tree-shaded lot a block away from the Central United Methodist Church. His mom is the only one in the family who attends services there; when his dad was promoted and got his weekends off, he said he deserved at least one day a week when he didn't have to ask God for help. During football season, he'll even go so far as to take His name in vain.

Every day, the *Sun-Times* runs a pithy one-word description of the weather on the front page. Today it said 'iffy.' Weiss always wondered who comes up with that one word. When he gets out of the Cavalier, he wonders how they always get it right. The clouds are tiny and spread like someone tossed them across the sky; they move quickly, like there's something bigger to follow. Humidity makes the air stagnant, but every so often a sharp wind steals a few leaves from the trees. With a good six hours of sunlight left, the day could go either way. *Iffy*, he thinks. Exactly.

He walks around the side of the house and lets himself in the back sliding door with the key 'hidden' under the kid-riding-the-turtle statue – an obvious choice. Security has always been absurdly lax here. Probably because everyone knows it's a cop's house.

In the living room the air feels stuffy, and the familiar smell of home is competing with some berry-clean air freshener.

On the mantle, his mother has rearranged the photos: his older brother Billy's new mug shot is center stage, an 8x10 head-and-shoulder, suit-and-tie picture that makes him look distinguished, like a real businessman. Makes the photo of Weiss in uniform, now thoughtfully placed to the side, look like a kid in a costume. Weiss hates the picture anyway. His hat is crooked.

'Hello?' he calls on his way into the kitchen to see what's for lunch. He's not going to dwell.

His mother usually keeps the place stocked, so the contents of the fridge are disappointing. He takes inventory: a chicken carcass, the leftover meat probably waiting to be put in a casserole; a block of reduced-fat margarine and a half-empty gallon of skim milk; a drawer full of lettuce, etc. The pantry's no better: a couple cans of low-sodium tomato soup, high-fiber cereal, fat-free pretzels.

Jesus, he thinks, a pretzel like a knot of wood in his mouth: my parents are becoming old people.

His flips through the queue of mail and unpaid bills on the counter, finds his phone bill. The clock above the stove ticks toward one. He decides he'll write the check and stop at Taco Bell.

He's sitting at the kitchen table filling out his account register for $57.84 when he hears the garage door open. He curses the timing, but hopes it's his mother – and that she's back from the grocery.

The spring hinge in the door to the garage creaks as it uncoils and the Lieutenant comes in, a greasy brown bag in his hand. The door slams shut on its own.

'Raymond. This is a surprise,' the Lieutenant says, his tone carefully polite.

'I didn't expect you, either,' Weiss says.

'I'm passing through. Didn't want to eat at my desk. Did you tell your mother you were coming?'

'I couldn't.' He hands the Lieutenant his check for the phone bill by way of explanation.

The Lieutenant puts the brown bag on the counter and when Weiss smells something deep-fried, he immediately determines what's inside. 'Poochie's?'

'If I share it with you, will you keep it a secret?'

'How come?'

'Your mother's on this heart-healthy kick. She thinks she's going to prolong my life by making me eat cottage cheese. It's gotten so that I'm afraid to come home for dinner.'

'Did you get fries?'

The Lieutenant nods. 'There's some Diet Coke in the garage.'

Weiss runs out and gets two pops from the minifridge in the garage, tonic water being the only alternative. When he returns, the Lieutenant is sitting at the kitchen table, his coat off, an Italian beef and cheddar fries divvied up on paper plates. He didn't wait for Weiss; he's already eating.

Weiss sits down and tears into his half of the sandwich, thick bread soaked by the meat and soft peppers. The fries are stuck together with coagulated cheddar, salty and sharp. The Diet Coke tastes like shit. Neither of them speaks until the food is gone.

The Lieutenant wipes his mouth with a thin paper napkin. 'You're in a spin,' he says, something he'd tell Weiss as a kid when he sensed stress, like Weiss' brain has been through the wash.

'Busy,' Weiss says, folding his paper plate in two, stuffing it in the brown bag.

'Have you been sleeping?'

'Dreaming.'

'We all have them. They'll get better, or you'll get used to them.'

'I know,' Weiss says, wanting to say that knowing doesn't help. Wanting to say he is spinning, maybe even out of his own control.

'You think the dreams are bad, wait until you see a guy you put in jail doing his thing out on the street a week later, a chip on his shoulder with your name on it.' The Lieutenant gets up, pours his pop in the sink. 'It's next to impossible to make headway in this job, and it's hell on your conscience.'

'You made headway,' Weiss says.

'Imagine my dreams.'

The Lieutenant sits again, looks out the front window, his blue eyes reflecting. 'I was up at the crime lab this morning, Raymond.'

Weiss stares at the greasy Poochie's bag, afraid to make eye contact. Why is the Lieutenant directing the statement at him? Has some evidence turned up at the jewelry store? Does he know something about last night? Weiss' knuckles feel swollen, but he resists the urge to crack them.

'What were you doing up there?' Weiss hopes he sounds nonchalant.

'Routine appearance.'

'Oh.' Weiss breathes a steady sigh of relief to ease his guilty conscience.

'I ran into one of the commissioners,' the Lieutenant says. 'I know he was there to push a political agenda; he wants to reallocate money for a park project. I also know the lab needs help. There is

evidence – boxes of it – sitting in the hallway, unpro-
cessed. And the commissioner comes up and ignores
the evidence, literally, and shakes my hand and says
"Congratulations, keep up the good work, the crime
rate in Cook County is at an all-time low."' The
Lieutenant looks at Weiss, his attention unnerving.
No matter that he's talking about something
completely unrelated to Weiss' initiation crime; Weiss
feels like he's been caught. He sits up straight like he's
always been told to.

'The crime rate isn't any lower,' the Lieutenant goes
on. 'The commissioner just rearranged the numbers to
meet his needs. And I'm not supposed to argue,
because I've got to answer to him when the crime rate
goes back up. Makes me mad: a man in my position
shouldn't have to sacrifice self-respect to get respect.
And policing by numbers? That's not headway.' He
checks the clock over the stove and gets up. 'I have to
get back down to the office. Are you going to hang
around for your mother?'

'I'm on at three,' Weiss says.

'Another time, then.' He puts on his coat, picks up
the Poochie's bag. 'Can't say I'm one to ignore
evidence.'

'Did you say anything?' Weiss asks when the
Lieutenant's at the door to the garage. 'To the
commissioner?'

'Of course I did. I told him to shove his agenda up
his ass.'

On that note, the Lieutenant exits, letting Weiss
believe that maybe they just made headway.

CHAPTER TEN

Weiss gets to work precisely at three, no longer early, but certainly on time. He parks the Cavalier and sees Fiore across the lot, checking the equipment in the trunk of the squad they'll use. He waves Weiss over.

'Get dressed. We're taking a ride down south.'

'Where?'

'Guy we found last night? I know who killed him.'

'Aren't they sending the detective?'

Fiore eyes Weiss incredulously, zips up his range bag. 'Would you rather ride with her?'

Weiss hustles into the station. He isn't sure Fiore was planning to wait for him in the first place, so he doesn't waste a second.

Fiore drives, and Weiss wishes he'd argued against it. He weaves in and out of traffic, cutting into the right turn lane at Kedzie, speeding through the intersection, cutting back between other drivers and parked cars. At the red light at Pulaski, he inches up so close to the Chrysler in front of them, Weiss is sure he'll tap the rear end. He goes fast, stops fast, and gets them to the Edens Expressway in five minutes. It should take ten.

'So how'd you find this guy – the suspect?' Weiss asks, knowing the how is more important than the who.

'Snitch. Used to help me out when I was down in nine.'

Fiore never says much about his time in the ninth district, so Weiss figures that part of the conversation is over. Just as well, since Fiore's doing one hundred in a fifty-five, and he should keep his attention on the road. Weiss grips the roll bar, pretends he's enjoying the ride.

Two minutes later Fiore merges onto the Kennedy headed toward the Loop. The reversible lanes are headed out of the city, but by some stroke of luck, inbound traffic is light. Fiore lets off the gas a little.

'Bet you're feeling pretty relieved about this,' he says.

'I guess that I am,' Weiss says, though the relief in his voice is because Fiore's slowed to a reasonable seventy mph.

'We nail this guy, nobody's going to be looking at us.'

Weiss looks out the window, agreement withheld, because they've still done wrong, and it's Fiore's fault.

After a moment, Fiore says, 'I'm sorry, you know, for getting us into this shit.'

Weiss nods, tries to remember if he's ever heard Fiore apologize. He can't think of a single instance.

'If it's any consolation,' Fiore says, 'Josephine loved the ring.'

Fiore steps on the gas and they shoot through Hubbard Cave. Traffic doesn't slow until Fiore gets stuck between two tanker trucks that are also trying to merge onto the Dan Ryan. Weiss tunes out Fiore when he starts bitching at the rigs and other cars and the transportation system in general over the delay.

From this angle, the city looks backward to Weiss, since he grew up on the north side. As soon as the Sears Tower dominates the left side of the skyline, Weiss can't call it home.

When Fiore gets past the jam, he picks up the radio. '2031.'

'Go ahead, Thirty-one.'

'Is Miss Pearson on this channel?'

Weiss anticipates the response.

'Detective Pearson,' she says, emphasis on 'detective.' Apparently Fiore already found a way to annoy her.

'We're about ten minutes from the location,' Fiore tells her.

'Well, you're going to have to sit tight, because I'm waiting on the warrant.'

'What, you want us to go down there, take the guy out to a late lunch? Give me a break.'

'I'm doing the best I can,' Pearson says.

Fiore hangs up. 'Broads.'

Fiore has enlightened Weiss more than once about the distinction between women and broads: both complicate life, but broads lack sufficient reason to do so. Weiss figures the complication of Pearson's warrant outweighs its reason. Still, he wouldn't call her a broad.

Fiore exits at Thirty-first Street and heads west. He passes Halsted, turns left on Morgan Avenue into the

Bridgeport neighborhood. Weiss feels like he's in another city entirely. There's a disassociation from one building to the next, from one block to another. An old home's sturdy edifice is stripped and covered by a second-rate façade. A brand-new building is empty, only a leasing sign in the window. A street is blocked by parked dump trucks, but no workers. Signs of progress, but no promise. It's like everything planned here has already happened, or never will.

Fiore passes a brick-faced building on Morgan. A Pabst Blue Ribbon sign hangs between a wood door and a barred window, the only indication that the place is a bar. He turns the corner and parks the squad out of sight from the entrance.

'You ready?' Fiore asks.

'What about the warrant?'

'The guy is in there, having a nice cold beer, watching Euro-soccer or some shit, and he probably has the murder weapon in his pocket. You aren't thirsty?'

Fiore opens his door, pulls his nightstick from between the seats, and slides it into the ring. Then he gets out of the car and, without looking back for Weiss, rounds the corner to the bar.

Weiss grabs his nightstick and gets out of the car. His heart races. He shoves the stick in his belt, thumbs the button on his holster, and catches up to Fiore just as he's opening the bar door.

Weiss steps inside behind Fiore, who moves forward and scans the left side of the room where half a dozen men sit on stools at the bar, their afternoon in front of them. The only guy who looks up from his beer has a yellow-blond mullet, the likes of which Weiss hasn't seen since hair bands quit teasing their manes in the late eighties. Weiss isn't sure the look works for him like it does for a rock star.

The bartender greets the officers with a smile that says he's got nothing to hide. Weiss scans the other side of the place, captures images of men's faces when they look his way from two-top tables. One with a face pocked like he slept on popcorn ceiling material. Another with hollow eyes who looks like he hasn't slept at all. A construction worker, behind them, with forearms like Popeye's and a week's worth of labor on his skin, under his fingernails. Each man in the middle of a beer or a meal or a story that doesn't invite interruption. Weiss backs off; he doesn't know who he's looking for, anyway.

'Let's get a table,' Fiore says.

'Anywhere you like,' the bartender offers, his vowels harsh. Reminds Weiss of his Polish neighbors.

'I have to hit the john,' Fiore says, probably to check for the suspect. 'Order me a bottle of their best champagne.' His jokes are rarely meant to make people laugh.

Weiss picks the table at the very back of the bar and sits so he can see everyone. He moves the second chair around to the corner so Fiore won't bitch about the seating arrangement when he returns; neither one can stand to sit with his back to the action.

Weiss keeps his eye out for anything beyond the usual paranoid glance as he takes a menu from between a bottle of ketchup and a napkin dispenser.

The menu is covered in plastic that is covered in

something sticky. It says SKYLARK on the cover. Before he opens it, a girl who's too young for her tired face shows up to take his order.

'Seven-up for me, coffee for my partner,' he tells the girl, who doesn't bother scribbling it on her order pad.

'Special today is blynai,' she says, and heads for the bar.

Other guys' meals don't give any indication as to what blynai is. Whatever's left on the construction worker's plate is disguised by gravy. Weiss opens the menu, scans lunch: cold beet soup, sauerkraut soup. Meat dumplings; oven-roasted duck. Kugelis and eggs.

He closes the menu, tucks it back in by the ketchup, and thanks God for Poochie's. He hopes Fiore isn't hungry.

Fiore comes back, repositions the corner chair, and sits. 'Nobody in or out?'

'Nope.'

'There will be.' He takes a paper napkin, wipes the table in front of him. 'See that guy at the end of the bar? The one with the big head?'

Weiss picks him out right away: he's sitting next to the guy with the mullet, his head roughly twice the size in comparison. It sits on his body real close to his shoulders, like his neck gave up.

'I see him.'

'That's Remy Stolarski. "Shitfer" they call him, since there's nothing going on in that humungous noggin. He tries to be a good guy, church-going and all that. But a while back he fell in with some guys, got into trouble. He tried to run a scam to pay his bookies by taking cash from the offerings at St. Mary's of Perpetual Help – think he took the name literally. Anyway I went to mass one Sunday, marked a couple bills, collared him right in that very seat he's occupying now.'

The waitress comes back, drops off the coffee and soda. 'You eating?'

'Nah,' Fiore says, 'but get Shitfer a beer. On me.'

She tosses a straw on the table for Weiss' drink and goes back to the bar.

Fiore takes a sip from his mug, makes a face. 'Jesus am I glad to be out of the ninth. They can't even make a decent cup of coffee in this part of town.'

At the front of the bar, Shitfer nods his huge head, toasts a full beer to Fiore.

'What'd you do that for?' Weiss asks, about the beer.

'Never hurts to be friendly.' Fiore tries the coffee again, his face prepared in a scowl.

Weiss sticks the straw in his drink and sucks up a syrupy mouthful. He wishes the place had music. Or the game on the radio.

Two guys at a table next to the construction worker talk to each other in a language that sounds Russian, though the last time Weiss heard Russian was during some action movie where the bad guys were KGB. He tries to pick out a word or two, guess its meaning from the intonation, but it's no use. Weiss couldn't pass high school Spanish; he doubts he could even translate Pig Latin.

As Fiore stirs NutraSweet into his coffee, the front

door swings open. Weiss squints, trying to make out details of the lanky figure in the sunlit doorway. The man has one foot inside the door when he stops, steps backward, and flees.

'Never hurts to be right, either,' Fiore says. Then he gets up and rushes out the front door.

'Guess I'm picking up the check,' Weiss says to no one in particular. He leaves a ten on the table and follows Fiore.

Weiss gets outside just as Fiore tackles the guy, gets him on the ground, and holds him in a headlock. Weiss can't see either of their faces but he hears Fiore say, 'Weiss, find his car.'

Weiss looks up the street, then down, scanning the parked cars, wondering how the hell he's supposed to figure out which one belongs to the guy – whoever the guy is. As usual, Fiore expects him to *know*, proving once again he doesn't know shit. Thankfully, no one's come out of the restaurant to watch him screw up.

'I have not done anything,' the guy says, squirming under Fiore's weight.

'Why'd you run, then?'

Should have made mental notes on the way in, Weiss thinks. He doesn't know what was parked where. Now what? Should he run all the plates on the street? Find the one with the warm hood? Maybe just ask the guy.

Then Weiss sees a late-model, black Nissan Stanza parked on the other side of the street, and it starts to make sense. 'It's across the street …'

'You didn't do anything, Jurgis, then I suppose you won't mind me taking a look in your car.' Fiore pulls him up by the back of his shirt so he's sitting upright on the pavement. 'We have an informant who says you've been a bad boy.'

'How much did you pay him?'

'Are you being a smart-ass?'

'No.'

Fiore looks at Weiss. 'Then I think he's offering to cut a deal with me. What do you think?'

Weiss shrugs: he knows Fiore's manipulating the guy, but he's not getting into it.

'Only deal you can make with me,' Fiore says, 'is to give me your keys.'

Jurgis curls his lips around his teeth. Even after the struggle, he's so pale it's a wonder there's any blood running through his veins. He looks up at Weiss, but Weiss offers no consolation.

'Come on, Jurgis,' Fiore says. 'Make this easy.'

Jurgis reaches into his front pants pocket, his hand bloody, scraped on the pavement during the altercation. He hands the keys to Fiore without looking at him.

'Put him in the squad,' Fiore tells Weiss. 'Bring it around front here.'

As Fiore heads off toward the Nissan, Jurgis asks him, 'Am I under arrest?'

'I hope so.'

Weiss isn't sure whether Jurgis takes that as a yes or a no, so he moves in quickly, helping him up from the ground and escorting him around the corner to the squad before he starts asking about his rights.

'I have done nothing,' Jurgis says.

'Then I'm sure this will be cleared up.' Weiss opens

the back door, lets Jurgis make his own way in and get his knees into a decent position, thinking: *It never hurts to be friendly.*

Weiss gets in the driver's seat and backs the squad around the corner, then flips a bitch that puts him right behind the Nissan. The trunk is open, and Fiore stands there, arms crossed, looking at whatever's inside.

'I was at the Cubs game,' Jurgis says from the backseat.

Fiore comes around, gets in on the passenger side, sits, fixes his gaze on the open trunk in front of them. He doesn't say anything for so long that Weiss wonders whether he's discovered something too gruesome for words or come up completely dry.

An unmarked car rolls up past them, parks in front of the Nissan. His eyes set on the trunk, Fiore says, 'You lied to me, Jurgis.'

'I did not.'

Detective Pearson gets out of the unmarked car, approaches the squad like she already knows what's what.

'You lied to me again,' Fiore says, 'and now I don't think I'm going to bother to ask which one of those guns in your trunk you used to kill Petras Ipolitas.'

CHAPTER ELEVEN

'Officer Weiss,' Pearson says when she sticks her head out of the interrogation room. 'Suspect says he'll only talk to you.'

Weiss sits up straight, feels the bones in his ass against the hard wooden bench. They've been sitting here for almost two hours waiting for the detective to talk to them; he's starting to miss the squad's barely cushioned seat. He looks over at Fiore, who's been reading *The Onion* and hasn't so much as snickered once – until now. 'Lucky you,' he says as Weiss gets up.

Pearson steps out of the interrogation room to meet him. She pulls the door closed, stopping just before it clicks shut. 'He's scared,' she says, her voice low. 'I need you to bring him out of his shell.'

'How?'

'I don't know, but I feel like I'm on a bad blind date in there. I can't get a line on him. I can't even get him to tell me what I already know. I hate to say this, but I need a guy on my side.'

'What about Fiore?'

Pearson holds her solicitous expression almost perfectly, except for the flare of her nostrils. Weiss can tell she's resisting the urge to look over his shoulder at Fiore when she shifts her weight and uses him as a blinder. 'He says he'll talk to *you*,' she says, professionalism intact.

'When he confesses, you going to make me go home and drink alone again?'

'Isn't one bad date enough?'

Weiss steps back, clenches his jaw like he's been hit by an unexpected blow. He thought she was interested.

'Let's go in with urgency, see how it plays out,' Pearson says, all business. She pushes open the door.

Jurgis Ambrozas is sitting in the closet-sized interrogation room smoking a cigarette fast, like he's nearing a deadline to get through the pack on the table. Under the fluorescent lights, the guy is a ghost, as dirty-white as the smoke he exhales.

'Okay, Mr Ambrozas, I've done you plenty of favors this evening,' Pearson says, her thumb at Weiss. 'Now it's your turn.' She sits in the folding chair across the table from him.

There are no other chairs, so Weiss stands behind her. He tries to put on a friendly face, but he's still irked about getting shot down. His smile feels fake, so he opts for a more natural, pissed-off look.

Pearson fixes her eyes on Ambrozas, puts her hands on the table like she's bracing herself for her own speech. 'You know as well as I do that eventually you're going to tell someone the truth,' she says. 'Maybe not me, maybe not Officer Weiss. But someday, you'll tell a friend or a cousin or some guy at the Skylark, and they're going to tell someone else, and it'll come around. The point is, eventually, I'm going to find out the truth. I can find out from someone else, or I can find out from you, now. The choice is yours.'

Ambrozas looks up at Weiss, then at the video recorder, tells it, 'I was at the baseball game.'

'And then?' Pearson says.

Ambrozas sets his eyes on Weiss, takes a drag of his cigarette, blows quick smoke in Pearson's direction.

'Listen, Jurgis,' Weiss says, 'we're not saying you weren't at the game.'

'The tickets, they are in the car.'

'And we're looking into that,' Weiss says. He steps to Pearson's right, sits on the corner of the table, turns his back so she's not in the conversation directly. 'We're going to need a little more than a ticket stub to prove your innocence.'

'I thought, in this country, you had to prove my guilt.'

'The weapons in your trunk might do that for us,' Pearson says.

Weiss keeps his attention on Ambrozas, lets her statement settle between them like it's obvious and yet not the point. Then he asks, 'What was your relationship to Mr Ipolitas?'

'I only know of him.'

'You're on a temporary visa, yes?' Pearson says. 'A tourist?'

Ambrozas nods once, stubs out his cigarette.

Weiss wonders why she completely changed the subject. Is this about control? Letting him know she's in the driver's seat?

That's it, he thinks: *the driver's seat*. Yesterday's stop. Ambrozas was driving. 'If you're a tourist, how come you own a car?' he asks. 'How come you have a driver's license?'

Ambrozas pinches the bridge of his nose with his forefinger and thumb, like the truth is up there, making him congested.

'These inconsistencies don't help your case,' Pearson says.

'I want to be legal,' Ambrozas says to Weiss. 'I want to apply for a green card. But they say to wait three months, so my intentions are not in question.'

'Too late for that,' Pearson says.

Weiss glances over his shoulder, annoyed by her snide interjections. No wonder she's single, if she can make a guy feel solidarity with a suspected murderer. Back to Ambrozas: 'Jurgis, are you working, here in the States?'

'No.'

'Are you saying no because it's illegal?'

'No. I do not have a job.'

'How come you want to stay?'

The unspoken answer puts tears in Ambrozas' eyes. 'Please, I have done nothing wrong. I was at the Cubs game—'

'How do you know Ipolitas was killed while you were there?' Pearson cuts in.

'On the news, they said—'

'Okay, okay, Jurgis,' Weiss says, getting up. God damn Channel Two for their up-to-the-minute alibis. God damn Pearson for being so pushy.

Weiss leans against the wall, backing off because Pearson won't.

'How about you tell us who went with you to the game,' she says. 'Maybe they'll have some answers.'

'I will not cause trouble for someone else,' Ambrozas says, the words making his jaw tight. His eyes become hard, full of frustration, maybe fear.

'That's very noble of you,' Pearson says. Weiss wishes he could tell her to shut up, but it would probably only hurt him on the replay.

'Nobody's going to get in trouble,' Weiss says. 'All we need is someone to corroborate your statement – to back you up.' Weiss remembers the woman who was with Ambrozas: the curl of golden hair, that angelic perfume … 'What about the woman? Was she the one who went to the game with you?'

Ambrozas takes another cigarette, taps it on the table, waits for a light. Weiss doesn't have one; if Pearson does, she isn't sharing.

'She might be able to help you,' Weiss says, unless Fiore's statement about her being a hooker was correct, in which case she'll be about as helpful as Ambrozas' wallet is fat. Not exactly a reliable witness, or a credible one, either.

'Officer Weiss and I are going to be turning in our report in the next hour,' Pearson says. 'Do you want your name to be the only one on it?'

Weiss thought she knew the urgency bit wasn't working. 'What Detective Pearson is trying to say—'

'You don't have to say it for me, officer.' The chair's metal legs scrape the linoleum tile as Pearson pushes back from the table. She stands up, looks down on Ambrozas. 'If you aren't going to tell us anything, the fingerprints on the guns will.'

'Those are not my guns,' Jurgis says. 'I did not know they were in the trunk – I allowed you to search it! I am being framed. They want me deported.'

'I wouldn't worry about that just yet,' Pearson says. 'You aren't going anywhere until we find out who those guns belong to and whether or not one of them's a murder weapon.'

She gets up, stings Weiss with her eyes, makes her professional exit.

Weiss stays where he is, knowing he has about ten seconds before someone else comes in to take Ambrozas away.

'You wanted me in here. You said you'd talk. Give me something. Who's the woman?'

Ambrozas studies the unlit cigarette. 'I have to protect her.'

'From who?'

Ambrozas flips open the top on the cigarette pack and puts the fresh one back, tosses the pack on the table, looks at Weiss. 'From you.'

'I don't understand. Tell me where she is,' Weiss says. 'I'll make sure she's safe.'

Giantolli opens the door, his mouth making the entrance first. 'Lithuanian consulate was notified but it doesn't sound like they're going to make a move tonight. Bail's a million.' He takes the cuffs from his belt, maneuvers around the table to Ambrozas. 'Would you like a gangbanging or non-gangbanging room this evening? We have a special rate for murderers who use Visa. Oh, but I guess your visa's no good.'

Ambrozas hangs his head as Giantolli cuffs him.

Weiss knows there's nothing he can say: Ambrozas is done talking.

'Are you some kind of magician?' Pearson asks when Weiss comes out of the interrogation room.

'What's the punch line,' he says without curiosity, off her sarcastic tone. She walks with him down the hall, briefcase in tow.

'You tricked him right into telling us absolutely nothing.'

'Maybe there's nothing to tell. Maybe he didn't do it.'

'I admire your optimism,' she says, but not like she means it.

They reach the staircase that leads up to the offices and down to the locker room and stop, ready to go their separate ways.

'Thanks for your help,' Pearson says, and turns to go upstairs.

'The guy's got no record,' Weiss says to her back.

'In the U.S.,' she says over her shoulder.

'No motive,' he calls out.

'That we know of,' she says.

'He has an alibi.'

Pearson stops, turns around, and addresses him from five steps up. 'There were more than thirty-eight thousand people at that Cubs game. You think I'm going to waste time figuring out if he was really there when he won't even make it simple and tell us who he went with?'

'He did agree to let us search his trunk.'

'Sure he did. Everyone cooperates with Fiore.'

'Ambrozas is protecting someone.'

She comes back down the steps, holds the handle of her briefcase with both hands in front of her. 'Officer, let me clue you in on something. Bad guys don't think like we do. They don't rationalize their crimes, they don't seek forgiveness, and they certainly don't protect each other. This isn't a movie. There's no resolution. He did it, he didn't do it, it still happened, and I have to keep up, pick up, and move on.'

'What if he didn't do it? Shouldn't you at least consider other suspects?'

Pearson shifts her weight like her briefcase is heavy. 'You think this is the only case in the city? Someone else is out there getting murdered as we speak, and the file will be on my desk in the morning, along with cold cases, appealed cases, the possible OD on Ravenswood and the guy who floated into Montrose Harbor yesterday, none of which offer any probable suspects or solid evidence. In this case, we have a suspect, we have evidence, and we don't need to complicate matters. We'll wait for ballistics.'

Weiss thinks maybe it isn't her briefcase that's heavy: she's got to be carrying some of that weight on her shoulders. When she turns to acknowledge a detective who passes them by, Weiss notices the subtle line where her makeup stops under her chin.

'There's no doubt you're doing your job, detective,' he says, feeling a little sorry for her and, because of this glimpse of vulnerability, feeling considerably more attracted to her. 'I want to help you. On this case.'

'Great,' she says, her smile offering a number of possibilities.

Weiss smiles too, a dumb one for sure, but he has no other way in mind to bridge the awkward silence.

Then Pearson says, 'You want to help me, you write a thorough, detailed arrest report.' And Weiss realizes she wasn't considering the same possibilities.

Pearson turns and climbs the rest of the steps to her case-crammed desk, leaving Weiss to wonder how he's supposed to write the truth this time.

CHAPTER TWELVE

Weiss puts on his street clothes thinking a trip to Eddie Bauer on his next day off wouldn't hurt. He wonders if Eddie Bauer is still cool, decides he'll ask Leah when they make up, which they always do. She was pretty much responsible for his entire wardrobe when things were serious. Safe to say most of it's out of fashion by now.

Not his shoes, though. He picked out his black Puma Frankenclydes all on his own, and they've lasted longer than any relationship.

He sits on the bench between lockers, counts the cash in his wallet, debates another drive-thru dinner. He hates grocery shopping. Especially at night.

Jed comes in, stripping off his uniform before he's through the door. 'Hey, Ray,' he says, 'what a fuckin' day. Let's get a drink.' His pants are around his ankles by the time he gets to his locker.

Weiss is glad this morning's tension is unnoticeable; still, he asks, 'Don't you want to get home to Katy?'

'Nah. She started walking down the beach in soft focus this afternoon.' Since Katy went off the pill, Jed hasn't referred to her period the same way twice.

'And the world awaits another Pagorski,' Weiss

says, knowing the jokes are smoothing over any hard feelings.

'I don't get it,' Jed says. 'I've been screwing her brains out.'

'Maybe you should ditch the tight sweatpants.'

Jed peels off his undershirt, grabs himself through his boxers. 'Everything's tight when you're a real man.'

Weiss stands up, shoves his wallet in his back pocket. 'Did you get dinner? I have to eat something.'

'I could eat. Let's go to Brownstone.'

'A pitcher of Bud Light and a large sausage pizza,' Jed says to the waitress between sports highlights on the flat-screen TV above him. Weiss wonders when it happens: that unnatural shift in the male brain that makes some score more important than scoring. *A shame*, he thinks; this waitress deserves some appreciation: her long, streaked hair, the masterful display of her cleavage, the short skirt; her *Playboy* mouth, open ever so slightly as she writes down the order.

'You got it,' she says, and she's about to walk away when Weiss stops her—

'That's for him. I'd like the chicken Caesar and a Newcastle.'

She adds Weiss' order to the ticket and smiles just for him.

'Who orders salad at a bar?' Jed asks, like his order is perfectly normal. They're at a high table for two, hardly big enough for the both of them. A guy in the booth to their right lights a cigarette and its smoke drifts. Weiss moves his chair, waves his hand at the smoke, and stares the guy down, hoping he'll get the point.

'Ray, you've been something else lately,' Jed says, his eyes on the TV until a commercial. 'I have to ask: do you think you might be gay?'

'Yep.'

'I knew it. My own best friend is a friend of Dorothy.'

The waitress brings their beer and Jed practically snatches his pitcher from her hands. He pours a glass too fast and ends up with mostly head, and slurps at it like a thirsty dog. Weiss hoists his bottle, toasts the waitress: a *cheers* to civility.

'So, Ray,' Jed says, pouring more carefully now. 'Seriously. What's happening with that detective? Is she hot for you or what?'

'Hardly.'

'Fiore says she is.'

'Fiore says a lot of things. Not all of them are true.'

'What's that supposed to mean?'

Weiss takes a sip of his beer, thinks about the right way to say, 'The arrest this afternoon. It was bullshit. I mean, Fiore stopped this guy Ambrozas yesterday for absolutely no reason. He was clean. And we didn't document the stop.'

'Wait, you're saying you *want* to do unnecessary paperwork?'

'We collar him today, and all of a sudden he's a murderer.'

'How does that make Fiore a liar?'

Weiss hears the defensive edge in Jed's voice and decides to take it easy. 'I'm saying it's coincidental that Ambrozas is our suspect. That's all I'm saying.'

Jed takes a second helping of foam, says, 'If I were you, I wouldn't be using my three-quarters-of-a-college-degree to come up with a theory about it. The average shitbag pops up in the system more than once. And I'll tell you what: if you think a guy's up to something you can stop him two times or two thousand times.'

'I don't think this particular guy killed anybody.'

'Who cares? If he didn't, he'll walk Monday morning. Ray, you should be shining Fiore's shoes since he found a suspect. Would you rather watch your career go down the tubes for some jewelry his wife'll never wear out of the house? That was a serious fuck-up, and he covered your ass.'

'It was his fuck-up. He made me steal the jewelry.'

'Come on. He didn't make you do anything.' Jed puts down his beer, runs his hand over his buzz cut, looks Weiss in the eye. 'Ray, I stole a television nicer than I'll ever own. I took it to Noise's house, I set it up; I waited for the cable guy, for Christ's sake. And I didn't so much as raise an eyebrow over any of it. You know why? Because who gives a shit about a TV? This is about loyalty. We're all in this together now, and we have to take care of each other.'

Weiss doesn't offer any sort of 'amen.'

Jed says, 'I gotta hit the can,' gets up. 'Get yourself another beer and quit acting like you handed down the death penalty. It was just an arrest.'

Weiss feels the strange ache of envy as he watches Jed make his way to the back of the bar.

*

The four Newcastles have dulled Weiss' senses and he's glad Brownstone is just a few blocks from home. It's after two, and Jed offered to give him a ride, but Weiss decided he needs the walk. The air is cool and humid: autumn is challenging summer. His favorite time of year is when summer gives up.

The neighborhood seems quiet though the subtle vibe of the city is all around him – that feeling that things are happening just out of sight, around the corner, behind closed doors. For once, he doesn't really care.

He flips open his cell phone to see if he's got service yet. No luck. He scrolls through the numbers, stops at JAMEE, the waitress with the *Playboy* mouth. He hits delete; it was too easy. JED is the next name on the list, and probably the reason Weiss bothered getting the waitress' number in the first place. Yes, another episode in the 'proving himself' series.

He scrolls to LEAH. He would call her if he could. He owes her an explanation. He knows she wouldn't answer, but he'd call anyway, just to document the effort. Why he keeps making the effort is anybody's guess. Does he love her? He has no idea. He closes the phone, keeps walking.

The four Newcastles may have dulled his senses, but after talking to Jed, his problem with the Job has become crystal clear: it's too easy.

A crime is committed, evidence collected, suspect found. Once it's off the street, the whole package is tailored by the system, and the court decides how it's wrapped up. Weiss has nothing to do with it. He doesn't have a say when it gets complicated. All they want him for is the collar, simple as that. So it isn't his job to find out who killed Ipolitas, or why. And if he feels like a jerk for arresting Ambrozas, he should have become an attorney, so he'd be on the other side of the system.

He wonders if DePaul would take him back.

He wonders why he always thinks he can do better.

He approaches his two-flat on Leavitt. The building is dark except for a faint light upstairs. Hal, the landlord, has been paying special attention to the place since he has to rent the top floor again. He's holding out for a tenant who will stick around for longer than a semester and take care of the place. Nick, the latest ex-tenant, was a college kid with daddy's money and no maid. He and Hal were at opposite ends of the attitude spectrum to say the least. Hal asked Weiss for his assistance on moving day, and it wasn't because he needed help with the heavy stuff. Now that Nick's gone, the windows are washed, the common areas clean, the entrance a welcome mat short of an invitation. Weiss can't complain except that it seems like Hal's always lurking around, even though he lives in the suburbs.

Weiss lets himself in, hits the john, and then the black leather couch. He's glad he went out and had a few; he's loose enough to shut off his brain for a while. Even if he did arrest the wrong man for murder.

In the morning, he thinks as he drifts off to sleep. *It'll all be more complicated in the morning.*

CHAPTER THIRTEEN

Weiss opens his eyes, taking in the muted morning light and the buzz at his front door. Through the windows that face west, he sees low clouds. Forecast calls for a chance of rain with a possible headache. He is awfully thirsty.

The front door buzzes again; Weiss sits up. He slept on the couch, a hard, vacant sleep that requires some recall now as to how he ended up there. He remembers the Newcastles; he remembers walking home. He doesn't remember dreaming.

Buzzzzz. Through the glass panes in the double-door entryway, Weiss sees Hal standing outside. He could wait in the shared entrance, but he's out there looking up at the sky, his thumb on the buzzer. He sips from a plastic travel mug. Looks like he just jogged over from the 1980s: black and purple nylon pants cuffed at the ankles, a gray T-shirt advertising THE WISCONSIN DELLS, a gold rope chain around his neck. The eighties were probably his prime.

Weiss opens the interior, then the exterior door and stops short of a good morning when he notices the shovel at Hal's feet.

'No pets. That's in the lease.'

'I don't have any pets,' Weiss says, wishing he were fully awake and more appropriately irritated by the accusation.

'I'm showing the upstairs at nine o'clock, and it looks like you turned the god damned yard into a dog park.' What Hal lacks in style, he makes up with eloquence.

'I don't have a dog, Hal.'

'I'm showing at nine.' He picks up the shovel, hands it to Weiss. 'Come on, give me some help. Before it rains.' Then he excuses himself, heads up the stairs to the empty unit. Weiss puts on his shoes and goes outside.

Hal wasn't kidding: there is dog shit all over the lawn. No way one dog could have left it, or even a pack of dogs. It looks like someone dumped a trough from the local pound in the middle of the yard. The presentation is truly sad, like a sand castle after high tide, though the sour, sulfuric odor certainly gets the original idea across. The odds that this was done on purpose are as sure as … well, Weiss is sure. And here he thought going through the initiation meant he wouldn't have to take any more shit.

Weiss looks up the street, across, and down like whoever left the mess will show himself, laughing hysterically of course, and probably snapping a picture. Flecks of rain hit Weiss' face. Thunder echoes from a few miles west. Yeah, he thinks, this is hysterical.

He heads for the gangway to get a garbage can.

*

After the thunderstorm, the mayor decided to hold an impromptu press conference about turning part of Rosehill Cemetery into a conservatory, another superfluous part of his plan to clean up City Hall's image. Flagherty cuts roll call short because half his patrollers are requested for the event.

Though Weiss had been operating on the assumption that this morning's shit was a prank, the short roll meeting nixes his chance to find out which joker left the surprise yard work. He was counting on the guys to rile him about it, like they did when Giantolli took a permanent marker to the inside of his hat, leaving a black ring across his brow that was visible for a week. And he thought for sure the other night's vomiting episode would merit some kind of childish gag – Pepto-Bismol poured into his locker through the vents, at least. But for whatever reason, nobody's said a word, which means Weiss'll have to wait it out. *Bastards*, he thinks: *this isn't what in is supposed to be like*.

Fiore opts to go to the cemetery, which means Weiss gets to patrol alone for a few hours. He resists the urge to hug Carol, the veteran dispatcher with a pack-a-day voice, on his way down the hall. Weiss' luck may have been down this morning, but a Fiore-free afternoon balances the scales.

Weiss is on his way out through the revolving door at the station's Lincoln entrance at the same time Detective Pearson is on her way in.

'Hi,' he says through the glass.

She doesn't say anything.

Weiss pulls back on the push bar, stopping the

wings' counterclockwise movement. Pearson is directly across from him, trapped.

'Hi,' Weiss says again.

She gauges her response, and her smile stops short of amusement. 'Officer.'

Weiss pushes forward, allowing Pearson to enter the lobby. He continues around until he's inside again, too.

'Detective,' he says. 'I just wanted to ask …'

She turns, legs together at the knee in a slender, stiff black skirt, and waits for the question. Her hair is up; her pearl earrings match her creamy satin blouse. Weiss feels like he's trying to flirt with the smartest, most sophisticated girl in school.

'About the case,' he says. 'The Ambrozas case.'

'Unless the truth fairy flew in and left the ballistics report on my desk, nothing's changed.'

'How long do you think it's going to take?'

'Days. A week most. The state's attorney on the case usually schedules a manicure and a makeover when she gets one like this, because the press will be all over it. As soon as she's ready she'll push the evidence through the lab before the case loses any momentum. And before the Lithuanian consulate has a chance to complain.'

Weiss nods to Giantolli and Sikula when they come out the secured door and make for the street. Giantolli wags his tongue between his index and middle fingers. Weiss hopes Pearson doesn't turn around.

'What about the car?' he asks. 'Did they find the Cubs tickets?'

'Honestly, if you think that's going to save him, I'll find you a cape and call you Captain Obvious.'

'Here I come to save the day!' Giantolli sings, his arms up like a superhero. Weiss watches him fly through the revolving door.

'Feel free to team up with Robomouth,' Sikula says, following Giantolli out to meet Noise in a squad curbside.

Weiss turns back to Pearson. 'What about the guy who was acquitted, in L.A., because he was on camera at the Dodger game?'

'It's true: you rookies get your street smarts from the tube. Forget the cape. I'll write you some bad dialogue and you can pretend you're on *CSI*.'

'What about the girl?' Weiss asks.

'You know, officer, I don't understand. Usually, if you boys make a mistake, one of you'd hold up the rug for the other to brush it under. I'm surprised Fiore hasn't duct-taped your mouth shut yet. Why are you so interested in this case?'

Weiss' smile is his tongue-tied answer.

'Is there an ulterior motive?' Pearson asks, the playful implication in her tone turned critical by a frown. 'What is that? That smell ...'

Weiss takes a step back, embarrassed, thinking the odor from this morning's yard work was stuck only in his nostrils, now afraid he brought it with him somehow.

'Oh, no,' Pearson says, kicking back her heel to check the bottom of her leather shoe. 'Did I step in something?' She goes over to the rubber mat in front of the standard entry doors, wipes her feet.

Weiss backs away. 'I don't smell anything,' he lies. Then he pushes through the revolving door before the detective decides to sniff around about anything else.

CHAPTER FOURTEEN

The thing about the Job is, there's no time to get hung up on what happened, even a minute ago. Something always supercedes it. Before Weiss can locate the source of the smell, he's on his way to a domestic violence call, and it's time to worry about other people's shit.

The call, on this lovely, rain-soaked afternoon: one Rhonda Ailers of 5323 N. Claremont, unit six, blames her black eye on one Joseph Ailers, of the same address, who apparently hit happy hour as well, and drank enough Early Times to take him through the weekend. When Mr Ailers exceeded his limit and went home, he had an alleged altercation with his wife, then fell fast asleep on the couch. This made Mrs Ailers considerably more agitated, as he was obviously no longer in the mood to argue.

Cut to Weiss' arrival. He rouses Mr Ailers, who is none too happy about it, if that's a surprise – adding alcohol to the mix inevitably increases the chance of arrest exponentially, and Mr Ailers is agitated to the power of ten. Good thing he's skinny, and at this point about as coordinated as a twelve-year-old in high heels.

As Weiss escorts a very displeased Mr Ailers out of 5323 N. Claremont to the squad, Mrs Ailers suddenly decides she got her facts wrong. The 'real' story, she declares: Weiss stormed into their home and used his authority to beat down a good man. A good man who was only trying to relax after a hard day at the job site. And also, she says, Weiss called her a bitch.

In Mr Ailers' state of sleepy, whiskey-riddled confusion, he decides his peach of a wife is telling the truth, which in turn makes Weiss the root of the problem. Luckily, because he is already in handcuffs, Mr Ailers can only assure Weiss that his intention to kick ass is compromised not by the restraints, but because he has to piss.

When Mrs Ailers hears this, she revises her story again, and this time her husband will rot in jail; by her stretch of the imagination, Mr Ailers is only defending her because he has something to hide, something involving his inability to get it up.

Weiss doesn't know how Mrs Ailers got her black eye; however, he thinks the real root of the problem is this: Mrs Ailers is indeed a bitch. There's no law against a woman changing her mind, though, so he takes Mr Ailers to the station, figuring the drunk tank is the only place he'll be able to sleep it off in peace.

Weiss books Mr Ailers and drives over to meet Jed and Noise at Broadway Grill. It's impossible to miss the place: the brick façade is covered with aluminum siding on the ground floor; the red, white, and blue flashing lights that wrap around the building's corner are as bright and tacky as amusement park signage.

Inside, Jed is halfway through a cheeseburger and fries; Noise has pushed his half-eaten slice of pizza to the end of the table.

'I was gonna order you a burger,' Jed says to Weiss, 'but I was afraid you turned vegetarian. Noise, I think Ray took that sensitivity training to heart. I think he's been pussified.'

Noise slides out of the booth, says, 'I have to make a call.' Weiss doesn't consider the statement a response, but partners don't often verbally answer one another. Or, another, more plausible explanation: Noise heard him, he just opted not to listen.

Jed watches Noise go, waits until he's outside, and takes what's left of his pizza; Weiss takes Noise's spot.

'Some days there's just no pleasing that man,' Jed says, doing his best impression of a woman, which to Weiss sounds more like a gay man from the deep South.

'What's the matter with him?' Weiss asks.

'He's pretty sensitive for a six-foot-four black man who carries a gun. He doesn't like to be fucked with.'

'Who's fucking with him?'

'You know the place we took the TV from? Lucky Mike's? I guess the owner is all upset about it. Says we had a deal. Anyway the whole thing started a pissing match between Noise and Fiore – who's in charge, who deals with who. Noise said he thinks it's getting personal.'

Wait a minute, Weiss thinks. 'What do you mean, they got a deal with Lucky Mike?'

'Noise called it an "arrangement." I guess we work with some businesses, you know, handling problems off the books in exchange for discounts, free stuff.'

'Did Noise call it "illegal," too?'

'Come on, man. We're just working with the community. And if there's no call to nine-one-one, there's no crime reported, and there's nothing to add to the statistics. Everybody wins.'

'It's about numbers.' Just like the Lieutenant said.

'I don't know, I'm no good at math.'

'Is this is a regular thing? I mean, guys do this, in the district? In the whole department?'

'I wouldn't say that. I don't think the superintendent's office would say that. Then again, I don't think it's something they're going to focus on in the crackdown, do you? It's not that big of a deal, man. I mean, it's nothing to go crying to Daddy about.' Jed picks up the pizza. 'Think about it: all the free meals? You think that's because I got a nice smile?' He shoves the slice in his mouth.

'What's Lucky Mike going to do?' Weiss asks.

'I don't know, call the cops?' A ridiculous grin takes over Jed's mouth, shows the skin from a hot pepper stuck between his two front teeth.

Weiss wouldn't call this camaraderie, but if Jed knows things he doesn't, he has to ask: 'Has Noise said anything about what happened at my place?'

Jed holds the slice poised at his mouth, concern delaying another mouthful. 'Huh?'

'Someone dumped a bunch of shit in my yard last night. I thought you guys might know something about it.'

'Hey, man, after all the beers we had, I'll admit, I pissed in someone's yard. But I didn't shit in yours. Couldn't tell you who did.'

Weiss stares him down, no smile to speak of.

Jed shoves everything but the pizza's crust in his mouth, chews, moves it all to one cheek. 'Ray, there's more than one dog in the city. You're paranoid.'

'There are a million dogs in the city. I just don't believe that they all congregated in my yard last night.'

'So you think it was one of the guys? A joke?'

'If it was a joke everyone would know about it. No one's said a word.'

Jed picks up his Coke, patiently sucks soda through the thin straw, swallows.

Weiss leans in, says, 'I think this has something to do with Jurgis Ambrozas.'

Jed shakes his cup, rattling the ice. 'Oh, man, next you're going to be telling me your theory about the black helicopters. You arrest a guy and now you think there's some conspiracy against you?'

'Everyone knows I think the arrest is bad. Everyone knows I talked to Pearson. I think they want to shut me up.'

'You think it's because you made a stink about arresting the wrong guy.' He chuckles at the stupid pun. 'You want to find the culprit and charge him with wrongful defecation.' That one makes him laugh.

'I'm serious about this, Jed. Someone is trying to send a message.'

Jed lifts the plastic top off the cup, tilts his head

back for ice, says first: 'Maybe they're trying to tell you you're full of shit.'

Jed's radio squelches. 'Unit Thirty-two to dispatch,' says Carol, her pack-a-day voice coming through the static. Jed puts down the cup, pushes his food aside, and depresses the transmitter on the radio clipped to his chest.

'Thirty-two go ahead,' he says, quick and low.

'Thirty-two, I have a robbery in-progress at Smith Gas Station, 2034 West Lawrence; Thirty-two and surrounding units, respond.'

Jed gets up quickly, saying, 'Thirty-two on our way.' A single wave at the fry cook and he's out the door.

Weiss calls in on his radio, 'Thirty-one responding.' He follows Jed, and there's no time to think about what happened, even a minute ago.

CHAPTER FIFTEEN

Weiss is first on-scene at the gas station. He pulls the squad between pump number two and the Mini-Mart, throws it in park. He unbuttons the leather strap that holds his gun in its holster as he gets out and, using the squad as a shield, radios: 'Thirty-one on location.'

Carol says, 'Thirty-one, you're too late. Victim says the suspect fled north on Seeley.'

Just then the victim, a female clerk wearing a cheery yellow uniform and a furious face, comes barreling out of the Mini-Mart. 'Did you see him? You had to have seen him. He ran up that way, maybe a minute ago.' She points the cell phone in her hand north on Seeley Avenue, a residential street that runs one-way south.

'Are you okay?' Weiss asks, taking out his notepad as he rounds the squad.

'Aside from the fact that some tweaker just took off with everything in my register? And that you're going to stand here and ask me stupid questions while he gets away?'

Over the radio, Jed chimes in: 'Thirty-two we'll take a ride around Winnemac Park. Do we have a description?'

Weiss tucks away the notepad, walks away from the vic like he's listening to classified information and not what she just told Carol, who says: 'Hispanic male, approximately five foot ten, two hundred pounds. Shaved head, goatee, white shirt; tattoo on the back of his neck, possible gang insignia.'

'That narrows it down,' Jed says. Right.

'Twelve here, en route,' Giantolli cuts in. 'I just love gangbangers. ETA about a minute.'

Weiss looks up Seeley at all the buildings, all the parked cars, the alleys, stairwells, basements, garages, places to hide. Time doesn't help him, either, not to mention the fact that it's getting dark. If Jed and Noise are on the other side of the park, there are three blocks between him and backup. Three blocks, one tweaker.

Weiss walks back over to the vic. 'Was he armed?'

'No, he just asked for the cash real politely.'

Weiss keeps his expression even, waiting for the real answer.

'A knife,' she says. 'I had a couple hundred in cash in the drawer and I'm not about to lose my life over this crappy job.'

Weiss scans the street again. This time, what his eyes assumed were leaves blowing across the pavement some fifty yards ahead change shape. For some stupid reason he looks up at the trees. Like money falls from them.

He radios, 'This is Thirty-one. Dispatch, victim says she's fine. Get Twelve to secure the scene. I have a line on the suspect.'

'Ten-four.'

'I'm lucky he was just thirsty,' the vic says.

'What?'

'When I was on the phone,' she says, 'he came back. He took a Red Bull out of the fridge and drank it right there, like he didn't even care I was on the phone with the cops. I thought he was going to kill me.' She stands there, arms crossed, gaze far off. The whole thing's just now hitting her.

There's something about a traumatic experience, Weiss thinks, *that brings out the beauty in a woman.* He can appreciate a crack in the armor. But blame Terrence Mann, because Weiss has never been good with aftermath, no matter the damage.

'A couple of officers are on their way to meet you,' Weiss tells the vic. 'They're just a few blocks away. Will you be okay here by yourself for just a minute?'

She nods, though he isn't sure she heard him; she's off in what-if land.

'Wait right here, and make sure no one goes inside.' He leaves her outside the Mini-Mart and the squad in the fuel lane and follows the paper trail up the street.

All the streets are one-way here: a block ahead, Ainslie runs west; the traffic on Seeley runs toward him. He looks for anything moving against the grain.

A few bills litter the sidewalk at the corner of Ainslie, where a brick apartment building announces itself to the street without so much as a patch of grass for a welcome mat. Nowhere to hide right here, unless the suspect's inside one of these places, which means he lives here, and that makes him a gangbanging, tweaking, stealing moron.

Weiss picks up the bills. Two blocks between him

and backup now. He looks both ways on Ainslie, again, for backward movement. Anything that doesn't go with the flow. Like the crow that flies from a telephone wire to the grass on its right. Like the woman across the street, walking her yappy Pomeranian that turns, circles, darts every which way on its leash.

Like the guy up the street who just materialized from behind a rhododendron and takes off running, away from Weiss.

Weiss doubts shouting 'Police!' will convince the guy to stop and explain why he was hanging out behind a bush. He stuffs the bills in his pocket and works his way into a sprint.

The guy's got fast feet for such short legs, especially since they're encumbered by baggy pants, but he never looks back, just goes full-speed ahead toward Argyle. As Weiss gains on him, he sees the ink on the back of the guy's neck below the faint line of his shaved head: old English lettering. Weiss guesses he isn't carrying groceries in the plastic Jewel bag clutched in his left hand. He's got to be the tweaker.

On the run, Weiss radios: 'I've got a visual, southwest side of the park. He knows I'm on him.' The tweaker crosses Argyle and slows just a little, like he's out of breath or unsure where to go.

'Thirty-two here, we're on the north side of the park,' Jed says. 'We'll come around.'

The tweaker opts for a straight shot northeast through the open soccer field in Winnemac Park and he picks up the pace. Weiss speeds up when he sees a group of high schoolers that shouldn't get involved on the other end of the field.

Then, when Weiss closes in and he's within spitting distance, he pulls his Mace. 'Stop!' he orders.

He doesn't expect the tweaker to turn around, but he does and he flings his knife. Weiss darts to the left, but the knife hits him anyway. It bounces off Weiss' thigh handle-first but it might as well have gone through because it demands a reaction, and the split second it takes to look is all the guy needs to drop the Jewel bag and tackle Weiss, taking him down in an instant.

Weiss sprays his Mace at the tweaker's face but it only incites aggression. Weiss has to throw the can out of reach when he feels the guy's prying hands at his belt, his billy club, his gun holster. The guy laughs like this is a friendly game, his eyes cranked open by whatever drug he's on. If his response to the Mace wasn't enough indication, Weiss is sure the guy is high if he thinks anything good can come of fighting back.

Their hands tangle, grappling for Weiss' gun. With barely any leverage from his position on the ground, Weiss knees the tweaker in the groin and rolls away, but he comes back too quickly, like a rabid dog, and again all hands are after the gun.

This time, though, Weiss is on his stomach, and he's able to wrestle the gun away and whip it, with a swift flick of his arm, a good ten feet from reach, farther than the Mace. When the tweaker gets up to go after one or the other or maybe even the money, Weiss grabs him by his jeans that hang low, near his knees. The tweaker topples backward, but like a cat, he turns to land on his hands and knees, on top of Weiss. He's agile, he's amped, and he's fucking mad.

The tweaker thrashes around, trying to get away, but Weiss holds him there, first by his shirt, and when that stretches and rips, by his arm – his left arm, unfortunately, because Weiss soon learns he has a mean right hook.

Backup has to be close, Weiss thinks, as the tweaker delivers blunt punches to his head. Weiss can't let go; he'll be dead if he lets go and this guy gets his gun.

Weiss turns his head to avoid the tweaker's fist, but the guy keeps at him, punching him in the ear. Weiss can't tell if he hears sirens or it's all in his head now. That's when he opens one eye and sees the squad, lights and sirens blazing as it rolls up … slowly … and stops. Why are they hesitating? Is Weiss' brain slow, is everything slowing down around him? Is Jed slow to get out of the car?

Weiss closes his eye, feels the hot sting of open wounds, anticipates the next blow, and the next. He holds on and keeps holding on, he's not going to let this fucking guy go, not even when he hears Noise and Jed approach, shouting commands, their words imprecise, like he's listening from under water.

Suddenly, the assault stops. Weiss thinks he hears other sirens. He sees the light on the other side of his eyelids, but he can't open them.

Then, as he lies there, he tries to make out the words Noise says, muffled, though close to his ear: 'Stop your shit.'

CHAPTER SIXTEEN

The ambulance transports Weiss to Swedish Covenant. His injuries aren't life-threatening – they're not even bad enough to get him his own room – but someone at the hospital has to look him over. He's been stuck for over an hour on a cot in an all-purpose sick room, privacy provided by a cordoned curtain and a paper robe.

Now that the shock of the incident has worn off, Weiss is pretty sure he's okay, since he finds himself checking out the nurse who's finally showed up to examine him. She sizes him up, consults his chart. Her name tag reads J. YOON.

'Tell me your name,' she says. *Bossy*, he thinks; imagines her in a black leather getup. Maybe underneath that lab coat.

'Your name?' She is sharp, set on the task at hand. Like a dominatrix.

'Ray. Weiss.'

'Any nausea, dizziness, headache?'

He waits for her to look up from his chart with her focused, almond eyes to say, 'Headache.'

'Raise your right hand, wiggle your fingers.'

He does.

'Okay. Can you turn your head to the left?'

He can, but slowly. The muscles in his neck feel swollen, pulled taut.

'Does that hurt?' she asks.

'A little.' Tough guy.

'Turn to me. Follow my finger.' J. Yoon raises her right hand, moves her slender index finger back and forth, then toward his face, away. He tries to follow, but he's distracted by the way she watches him, like she's observing more than his visual acuity. He gives up on this part of the exam and sets his eyes on her beautiful, symmetrical face.

When the moment could be awkward, J. Yoon doesn't miss a beat. She leans toward his left shoulder, whispers, 'Can you hear me?' Her hair smells nice. A tease.

'Yes, I can hear you.'

She leans to the right, whispers in his other ear, 'Repeat after me: elastic, street, Cuba, massage.'

'Sounds kinky.'

She sits back, allows herself to smile. 'I think you're going to survive.'

This must happen to her all the time. He wonders if she's smiled for anyone else today.

'I'll have the doctor give you some anti-inflammatories for the pain and swelling,' she says. 'You should contact us if you have any changes in sensation ...' – she refers to his chart – 'or fatigue; dizziness, confusion ...'

Weiss could handle those symptoms if she were the one taking care of him. Cue the sultry porn sound-track—

'... or if there's any fluid drainage from your nose, mouth, or ears. I'm not talking about the wounds we patched up; those might seep while they heal.'

Okay, not so sultry.

She sticks her pen in her lab coat pocket, runs her hand down her smooth, black ponytail. 'We will contact you, if need be, pending the results of your assailant's blood test. There's an officer waiting to take you home. I'll send him over and we'll get the discharge paperwork ready.'

And just like that, J. Yoon is off to make another man feel better.

Weiss lies back, wondering how bad his face looks. He hopes no one's talking about medical leave. When Sean McKinney got attacked by that junkie from Boys Town last month, he had to take the cocktail and sit out a week because the junkie refused to test. Weiss hopes today's tweaker will test, and test negative. AZT isn't exactly cough medicine.

'Look at you,' Fiore says on his way around the pale green curtain.

'Don't tell me: somewhere between bad and worse.'

'You should see the other guy.'

'He was on something. The Mace didn't even faze him.'

'Don't worry. He's fazed now.'

'What'd they do with him?' Weiss assumes the tweaker got more than a talking-to once they reached the station.

'Rubber room,' Fiore says.

'Will he test?'

'He'll do whatever we tell him.' Fiore rubs his

thumb and fingers together. He seems nervous, the way his eyes flit around the room. 'Hell of a way to get a day off, kid.'

'They're taking me out?'

'Sarge switched you with Suwanski. You're off tomorrow. You'll ride with Schreiber Monday night.'

'That's good.'

'For you, maybe. You don't have to ride with that Polack.' Fiore looks like he's uncomfortable, or unhappy. Weiss is sure he has some negative comment on the tip of his tongue. Probably pissed because he was stuck at the mayor's speech, missed all the action.

'Let's get out of here,' he says. 'I hate hospitals.'

Fiore drives slow on his way to Weiss' place, like he's on patrol, except he isn't. Seems like he's waiting for Weiss to say something; to rehash what happened this afternoon, either to take or to place blame. But the painkiller Weiss took has already made its way through his empty stomach, and he's more inclined to enjoy the silence, the darkness, and a little relief.

It's not so strange riding in the squad off the job; the smells, the sounds, the tension in the air is familiar. Weiss doesn't mind any of it. He feels safe.

'I hear you're dealing with some shit,' Fiore finally says.

Familiar, yes, but no longer safe. 'Jed told you.'

'We spoke.' Fiore turns up the air-conditioning, adjusts the vents so they blow at his face. He stops at a red light, maintains his forward gaze. 'Is there something you want to say to me?'

'I wasn't accusing anyone.'

'I'm not talking about the shit; only thing I'll say about that is you deserved it.' He steps on the gas too hard. 'I'm talking about your big mouth.'

Weiss starts to sweat. He closes his eyes as he tries to remember what he said to Jed that would've tripped Fiore's switch. He can't pin it. *Change in sensation, fatigue* ... He asks, 'What'd I say?'

'You're going to start a war, kid, and you're already losing soldiers.'

Weiss tugs at his collar. 'Look, Fiore, I'm going to need something more straightforward than a metaphor. I just got my ass kicked and my head is swimming.'

'That wasn't straightforward enough?'

'You mean ...' What was it Noise said? *Stop your shit*. Jesus. 'You mean, today, Noise and Jed ...' He can't say it out loud: they let him take the beating.

'Give me a break, Weiss. You're one of us now; we protect each other.'

'They were there,' he remembers now, on the ground, watching the squad approach, slow motion. 'They didn't intervene. Not right away.'

'Are you out of your fucking mind?' Fiore says, turning the wheel hard. He pulls over on Irving Park and jams the gearshift into park. 'You're really something,' he says, his voice unchecked. 'Me? I kind of hoped you got some sense knocked into you today. But Jed – Jed went out of his way to cover your ass. And you're such a fucking pussy, you blame him for your own weakness.'

'You're right, I didn't mean it—'

'And you insult him, you insult all of us, with this Ambrozas bullshit.' The last words hit Weiss with spit. He knew it: this is about Ambrozas.

'Come on, Jack. We arrested the wrong guy. Shouldn't we be looking for the right one?'

'No, we shouldn't be, you idiot, because Jed's the one who put the guns in Ambrozas' trunk!'

'Why … ?' Weiss can't think what to ask. He feels like he was punched in the head again. Heat rises from his skin and the air-conditioning feels like ice. *Dizziness, confusion …*

'I'm gonna lay it out for you plain,' Fiore says, 'and then we never had this conversation. You got me?'

Weiss only realizes he's nodding after Fiore starts talking. 'I know Jed told you about our arrangements with certain businesses. Ipolitas was one of the men we worked with. A bottom-feeder, I know, and I'm not proud to say we need assistance from guys like that. But he's helped us make some pretty significant arrests.

'It's not so much a one-hand-holds-the-other scenario as it is a system of checks and balances – we put him in check, he balances. But when Ambrozas showed up in the mix, Ipolitas asked us for a favor. He asked us to get rid of Ambrozas.'

'You mean—'

'No, I don't mean "get rid" of him.' Fiore beats him to the assumption. 'I mean arrest him. Send him back to where he came from.

'So I got my eye out for Ambrozas. We're all waiting for him to come out of the woodwork. Except when he does, he tells me Ipolitas is the one who's the problem, and he tells me a few unsettling details that sound about right. This he-said, he-said thing is like some kind of soap opera now, and I don't know which bad guy I hate more. So I decide we have to show Ipolitas who runs the show. But when we go to Ipolitas' place, well, you know it wasn't such a happy ending.'

'So Ambrozas *did* kill Ipolitas?'

'If he didn't, he knows who did. The only thing I know is that Ambrozas set us up to walk in and find his body.'

'Why did Jed plant the guns?'

'Did you hear what I said, Weiss? We were set up. You want to wait for the knockdown? As soon as Jed heard, he took care of it. No questions asked; he covered our asses.'

'I don't understand why Ambrozas wanted to talk to me after we arrested him.'

'He was trying to play you, kid. Trying to put ideas in your head so you'd go after his case and fuck yourself. He knows you're new to the game.'

'He said he was being framed,' Weiss says, replaying Ambrozas' words without his conviction.

'Who gives a shit? You had one job and that was to arrest him. You want to keep at this? You want to go tell the state's attorney that your best friend planted evidence? Tell her you wrote a report for a robbery-homicide that left yourself out as a suspect? Mistakes have been made and documented. You documented them. You want to wind up in jail, or you want to let this scumbag Ambrozas take the rap?'

His mouth is open, but Weiss can't think of a damn

thing to say. He had been so stupid, thinking he was smarter than everyone else. And he let himself get trapped.

Fiore pulls back out into traffic. 'Ambrozas is a shitbag and his arrest sends a message to all the other shitbags and that is: don't fuck with us. And the message you need to get through your head, right now, is to keep your fucking mouth shut.'

The conversation ceases for the rest of the ride. Fine by Weiss; his head feels like an aching balloon, light from the painkillers, spinning with information.

When Fiore pulls up to Weiss' place, Weiss gets out of the squad, assuming 'good-bye' is a given, but halfway up the walk, he realizes the squad hasn't moved. When he turns, Fiore's behind him, standing in the yard, right where the dogshit had been dumped. The look on his face says he either smells the remnants or he's disgusted with Weiss.

He steps up, studies Weiss real close, the same way he does with suspected drunks. Then he backs away, takes an important breath, says, 'Serve and protect.' By his tone, Weiss half expects a secret handshake, but Fiore's hard cop-face doesn't invite so much as a response.

'That's what we're supposed to do, right? Serve and protect?' The way Fiore says this doesn't invite an answer.

Weiss waits for him to make his point, but instead, he turns and makes for the squad. So apparently that was it: serve and protect.

Great, Weiss thinks: philosophy from a decal on the squad door. What the hell does he ever mean?

He watches as Fiore drives away at a slow, unsettling pace, like his eyes are on the rearview mirror, watching back.

Weiss goes inside. He makes his way around the kitchen mechanically, his stomach the only thing compelling him to stay awake. Thoughts drift in and out of his head like scattered mantras: Serve and protect. Keep your mouth shut. Don't fuck with us. Jed is an idiot.

He puts noodles in a pot of water, lights the stove, watches the noodles bend as the water comes to a boil.

He doesn't know how he let all this happen. They told him the initiation was no big deal, but now that he went along with it, he's stuck, a link in a chain that grows more tangled and terrible by the second. The only thing he knows for sure: Jed's a link, too. So now what?

The scattered mantras ping-pong around his head.

Don't fuck with us. If Ambrozas goes to trial, it's up to the courts – not the cops – to rule his fate. But if Ambrozas isn't talking, his defense attorney will focus on the evidence instead of the crime. The evidence. Where it was found, and where it came from. The guns. That Jed planted.

Jed is an idiot. Yes.

Keep your mouth shut. Have to.

Serve and protect. Yes.

He forgot to set the kitchen timer so after an estimated ten minutes he strains the cooked spaghetti and dumps a half jar of Ragú into the pot, stirs. Wishes he had some Parmesan. Wishes Jed wasn't such a god damned follower. Wishes he had the first clue about how to fix this. But the truth is, all he has in front of him is a bowl of overcooked noodles and a brain that feels about the same.

He sits at the kitchen table and eats by the light over the sink. The medication made his mouth dry and the noodles taste chalky. The ice cubes in his water are freezer-burned, the water itself sulfuric.

Or maybe the bad taste in his mouth is because of Fiore.

The front bell rings. Weiss stops; the spaghetti twirled around his fork slips back into the bowl. From the dim kitchen through the living room, he sees his father's skeletal frame in the doorway. This afternoon's trouble must have made it around, and up the ranks.

Weiss didn't have the cojones to fess up earlier and he definitely won't now. But there's only so long a guy can hide from his father. He dumps what's left of the noodles in the garbage, thinks about the best way to break the latest news to the Lieutenant.

'Raymond,' the Lieutenant says when Weiss opens the door, a hello. Even by the yellow porch light, his eyes are that trust-me blue.

'Hi, Dad.'

'Your mother wanted me to make sure you're okay.'

'I'm okay. Do you want to come in?'

The Lieutenant looks at his son like it's a trick question. Then he says, 'It's late.'

To Weiss, this is a trick answer, making him the one to decide. 'Come on,' he says. 'I'll grab a couple beers, we can sit out back.'

The Lieutenant nods, good answer; follows his son inside.

'Furniture looks good,' the Lieutenant says, referring to the black leather couch Billy donated when he got married over the summer. The Lieutenant is also referring to the fact that Weiss didn't have a couch beforehand.

'It's comfortable.'

'Have you seen the stuff Tracy picked out? For the house?' The Lieutenant is now referring to the living, dining, and bed sets Billy's wife bought from some high-end store in Barrington for their new fairway home at Bull Valley Country Club. The Lieutenant's enthusiasm belies the fact that he doesn't give a shit about furniture and he's never played a single round of golf. His enthusiasm is all for William Weiss, CFP, CEO.

'I'm sure it's great,' Weiss says, continuing on into the kitchen and swiping two Buds from the fridge. He feels intimidated. Under the microscope. This isn't like lunch yesterday. This isn't like home.

The Lieutenant takes a beer from Weiss as he passes through, opens the back door. He steps out to take in the night air, like it's different on this side of the house. Weiss puts a kitchen chair outside. The Lieutenant sits, uncaps his beer, and looks out over the yard, the alley, the darkness.

Weiss stands behind him, waiting, not breathing, feeling the familiar discomfort of the times he was a kid in trouble.

'Raymond,' the Lieutenant says, 'if you tell me that what happened today was someone else's fault, I'll stand by you.'

Weiss uncaps his beer and takes a long drink, knowing years of interrogating suspects makes the Lieutenant an expert in phrasing things to force a certain reply. Weiss can't blame anyone else, and they both know it, which means he's supposed to admit he's at fault. But he's not going to play the game the Lieutenant's way just yet, so instead of coming clean, he asks, 'What if it was my fault?'

The Lieutenant lets the question hang long enough to become a confession. Then he takes a long swig of Bud, turns on the chair so he's straddling it, looks up at Weiss. 'Now I'm sorry about what happened to you today, and I can understand your embarrassment.'

But, Weiss thinks.

'But,' the Lieutenant says, 'I want to know why I'm hearing that some people think you deserved it.'

Weiss looks at his beer. The words cut hard, and he has to take a drink to resist a knee-jerk response. He wishes he knew exactly whom the Lieutenant is referring to in this case.

'I know you, Raymond. You're a smart kid, and you probably know more than most, and that's exactly the problem: knowing doesn't count in the Job unless you're sitting at a desk. It isn't about your brains; it's about your guts. Your instincts.' The Lieutenant uses his free hand to jab Weiss in the rib cage; not to hurt him, but to make his point.

'Being "right" isn't going to save your life,' he says.

'Being a guy who's willing to sacrifice your life for your fellow officers – that might. So if you're going to use your head, figure out how you're going to get these guys to respect you. Because if you're on the street without respect, you're just another asshole with a gun.'

At that moment, Weiss considers telling the Lieutenant that the reason he always wanted to be a cop was to get *his* respect. To say he clings to his star because when his dad wore it, it was a symbol for all that should be right in the face of all that was wrong – at home, on the street, in the world.

The Lieutenant's blue eyes challenge Weiss to say anything at all.

He doesn't.

The Lieutenant finishes his beer and stands up to inspect Weiss' black eye. 'Go see your mother when your face clears up.'

Weiss steps out of the way. Without a good-bye, the Lieutenant puts his bottle by the sink, makes his way through the kitchen, into the living room, and out the front door.

Weiss would throw his beer bottle against the wall. He'd knock over the kitchen table and everything on it and kick whatever hit the floor across the room. He'd rip his brother's stupid leather couch to shreds, run outside and scream at the world, get in his car and drive and drive. Hell, he'd fight his own shadow. He'd do all these things if he hadn't heard some version of that speech, the Lieutenant's lecture, a hundred times over.

And for the hundred and first time, he can't deny

that some of what the Lieutenant said was correct. Weiss needs the guys to respect him. And he doesn't want to be another asshole with a gun.

But there's a problem with the speech this time: according to his father, the Lieutenant, Weiss is supposed to go by his gut; but no matter what he thinks, something in his gut isn't sitting right. He wishes it were the spaghetti.

Tomorrow's Friday, not his usual day off, but the first of three. Weiss hopes he'll wake up with a little clarity, a way to come out of this with his star and some sense of self-worth. Right now, as he crawls into bed, his head aching, he's pretty sure it's going to be impossible to do both.

CHAPTER SEVENTEEN

Weiss' cell phone rings again and again and in his dream Terrence Mann, his face like Jurgis Ambrozas', is trying to hand it to him. When Weiss finally locates it on the floor where it landed after he knocked it off the nightstand, he looks at the display. It says 6 MISSED CALLS. He scrolls through the numbers and they're all the same: Jed, Jed, Jed, Jed, Jed, Jed. Every two minutes or so. Fucking guy, he's nuts if he thinks Weiss is working out this morning.

Weiss flips the phone shut; at least it's back in service.

He lies in bed, head fuzzy, trying to kick in his mental replay. He remembers the fight with the tweaker, and how things only got worse after it. He's thinking about what the Lieutenant said when the phone rings again.

'What's the word, Fancy Boy?' Jed says when he answers. 'You get your ass handed to you and now you don't want to come out and play?'

Weiss rolls over. Dried blood on the pillowcase; the Band-Aids now adhered to his wounds. His neck is stiff, like every vertebrae has teamed up against his mission to move. 'I think I gotta take a day off.'

'I figured. Come down to the Abbey, I'm waiting on sausage and soda bread.'

'Soaking up last night's four-to-four?'

'They couldn't pay me to leave my barstool.'

Weiss wishes he'd been there, drinking with the guys after the shift, telling stories. He wonders if, last night, they were telling stories about him.

'Come on, I'll order you some eggs.' Jed hangs up, and the time appears on Weiss' phone's display: 11:23 a.m. He'd better get at it.

The Abbey is pretty quiet, the calm before the Friday happy-hour storm. Jed's got a corner table against the brick wall and the window in the pub. He's busy shoveling hash browns into his face when Weiss sits down across from him, takes a piece of soda bread.

'There he is, Mr Fantastic,' Jed says through a mouthful.

'What is it with you and the nicknames?' Weiss takes a bite of the bread, realizes he's starving.

'I'm trying to find a name that sticks,' Jed says. 'I don't think it's that one. How's your face?'

'You're the one calling me fantastic.'

Jed smiles, a smile Weiss doesn't recognize. Reminds Weiss of when he was a kid and one year, after summer went by, his best friend wasn't his best friend anymore. Something intangible happened. Something changed. He won't let that happen now.

Weiss puts his elbows on the table, says low, 'Jed, Fiore told me what you did.'

Jed wipes his mouth. This isn't news. 'You don't have to thank me.'

The waitress, a woman Weiss pegs for Irish by her claddagh ring and her FAI WORLD CUP shirt, sets an order of fried eggs, rashers, and sausage in front of Weiss. Jed eyes the full plate, takes the piece of bread he's owed.

Weiss looks out the window, wonders how to proceed. On the street, members of a rock band unload their amps and equipment for tonight's show, looking less than rockin' in the noon sun. A guy in black jeans and a sweat-through black T-shirt that reads THE COST looks low on patience as he tries to dislodge a bass drum from a hatchback's wheel well. The kick drum pedal juts into the head and it bows, nearly enough tension to tear it.

Weiss unwraps his silverware, puts his napkin on his lap. 'I'm worried. About the consequences.'

Jed picks over a lonely grilled tomato, the only thing left on his plate. Weiss knows he isn't considering eating it, but he is considering something. Maybe he realizes the severity of the situation, but just in case, Weiss spells it out: 'Jed, this could come back to us.'

'No it won't.' Jed pushes his plate away, throws his napkin on the table like it ends the conversation.

Outside, another band member joins the bass-drum release effort from the backseat. His help causes an adjacent speaker cabinet to roll out of the hatchback, hit the pavement, and spill its guts, ceasing to provide sound for The Cost tonight.

Weiss looks over his shoulder to make sure no one's in earshot. 'Where'd you get the guns?'

'Don't ask me that.'

'I have to,' Weiss says. 'If any one of them can be traced, we could be, too. Ambrozas could go to jail on false evidence. What if he's innocent?'

'He isn't innocent.' His voice is sincere, but he crosses his arms; defensive, defending.

'Did you think this through, Jed? Do you realize how serious this is? Were the guns stolen? Registered? Traceable?'

'I'm not an idiot.' Jed sits back, writes off the concern with that unfamiliar smile. 'Look, Ray. It was just a stall tactic, to take the focus off you and Fiore. I'm not accusing a guy of murder or anything else. I'm just helping people to see that you didn't have anything to do with it.'

'You think I did?' Now Weiss is defensive. He taps the tines of his fork on the edge of his untouched plate.

'Ray, let's put a few of the puzzle pieces on the table. *You* went into that jewelry store. *You* stole some stuff. *You* shot the guy when he startled you, *you* threw up all over the place after you killed him, and *you* were the first officer on-scene. Do those pieces fit together to make an accurate picture? No. But some detective, some lawyer, or some jury might think so.'

'That's ridiculous.'

'I think so, too. I also think it's ridiculous that you think I dumped dogshit in your yard, and that I let that junkie get a few punches in before I pulled him off of you.'

'I never said that.'

136

'Thing is, Ray, people hear things; they believe what they want to believe. I personally don't believe my police would go against each other. This job's nothing without loyalty. That's what I believe.' He raises his arm, makes a check mark in the air for the waitress.

'Do you know where the guns came from?'

'They're orphans.'

'You aren't going to tell me.'

'I don't think I am, no.' Jed drops a twenty next to Weiss' plate and pushes back from the table. 'I have to go to the station, follow up on a couple reports. You want to know about the guns, you want to poke around the case, you want to fuck me up, that's where I'll be. Enjoy your eggs.'

Jed gets up, no smile on his face at all. He takes a couple steps back, pivots, and leaves Weiss sitting there, knowing something intangible just happened.

CHAPTER EIGHTEEN

Weiss finishes his breakfast alone and decides to walk home even though the Abbey is a good mile away and it's so hot outside he can smell the coal tar roofs cooking on Grace Street. He had decided it best to spend his first day off like any other, catching up with all the things he'd neglected during the workweek, but at this point he just wants to go home and put things off some more.

He walks up to Irving Park so he can get across the river. On the other side of the street, in Horner Park, softball teams congregate around the diamonds to start the weekend with a little friendly competition – and a lot of beer, judging by the cases of Miller Lite a couple guys in gold EAGLES jerseys empty into coolers by the bleachers.

Weiss thought about joining the Sergeant Association's 16" slow pitch team this season, but he still feels the sting of his senior year shoulder injury that ended any hope of playing college ball. He loves the game; he doesn't want to taint the memories by making it a hobby now. Still, he misses suiting up. The restless air in the dugout. His teammates, like brothers; his mom in the stands. Bumming sunflower seeds. His Big League Chew, as cool as tobacco. And waiting his turn to get out there and swing. Make the team proud.

Weiss' cell buzzes in his pocket, snaps him out of the nostalgia trip. He checks the number and he can tell by the exchange it's from somewhere in the station. Maybe Jed's calling, to clear things up. Or maybe there's been a break in the case. Shit. It's too soon for ballistics, isn't it?

Weiss tells himself to stop thinking like a guilty person. It could be Flagherty, wants to change the shift again. Or someone in admin, needs to update his mailing address. Maybe it's about the junkie's HIV test.

None of the possibilities comfort him.

'Hello?' he answers.

'You still interested in the Ipolitas case?' Pearson asks. At the sound of her voice, his pace picks up to an anxious clip.

'I didn't think you'd ask.'

'I'm not asking – not officially. But I had an interesting conversation with one of the vic's clients today, and I'm starting to think you may be on to something. I don't think Ambrozas is our man.'

Weiss' breath is caught in his throat. If she keeps investigating, will she be on to them?

'Are you there?' Pearson asks.

'Yeah.' He crosses Campbell Avenue, oblivious to traffic. 'I don't know if you heard about what happened yesterday, but—'

'The fight? Oh I heard all right.'

'—but I'm not exactly making a name for myself right now.'

'You are. Just not one you'd appreciate.'

'I don't think I'll do myself any favors helping you.' But Weiss has to, he has to help her nail the right guy so she won't find out about Jed, or the thefts, or his own part—

'So what?' she asks. 'The whole bit, sticking up for Ambrozas, was a cover? I don't like being lied to, officer.'

Weiss is afraid he just jumped feetfirst into hell.

'Hello?' Pearson says.

Keep your mouth shut, he thinks.

'Weiss,' she says, 'take a joke, would you? I saw the way you were looking at me yesterday.'

'Oh.' He gets it: she thinks he's interested in her.

There's a pause on her end, like she's hiding a smile, or maybe waiting for someone in earshot to walk away from her desk. 'Listen,' she says, voice softer now, and rushed, 'the state's attorney won't make a move until we get the ballistics report Monday. I got one of the lab techs to talk to me and he said all the guns are different, so we should be able to narrow things down by caliber alone. But get this: the serial numbers were scratched off every one. And, they couldn't get a single print on the guns, or anywhere. The whole trunk was sprayed down with WD-40.'

'That's one way to clean a gun.'

'And also a way to set someone up.'

'Ambrozas could have been trying to cover his tracks,' Weiss offers, knowing it was Jed, covering his.

'By transporting illegally tampered weapons, one of which may have been used to commit murder?'

'I guess that wouldn't be too smart.'

'The court won't see this case until Monday,' Pearson says, 'so Ambrozas is spending the weekend in the can no matter what. What I'm thinking is: if you're right, and someone else killed Ipolitas, we can use this window to get ahead. Explore other possibilities.'

Shit, Weiss thinks. Possibilities.

'Why me?' he asks.

'You volunteered.'

And he said Jed was the idiot.

'You know Moody's Pub?' she asks.

'On Broadway, yeah.'

'I'm cutting out of the office early this afternoon. Meet me there, say, three o'clock, and we'll put our heads together?'

Weiss doesn't have a choice. 'I can be there.'

'Let's not put out an APB about this. I don't need any more clever harassment from your barely upright coworkers.' Pearson hangs up without explaining, but he can imagine.

By the time he gets back to his place, Weiss is a sweaty, stinking mess. He strips off his soaked-through T-shirt, his shorts. He didn't shower last night or this morning, and his skin has held on to the distinct smell of the hospital. The combination of stale coffee and urine and bleach is attached to his aura. He peels off the Band-Aids on his face and ear; the day-old adhesive is another displeasing odor. His socks smell like the station's locker room and his boxers? Nothing worse than neglecting the boys. He can hardly stand himself.

He gets naked. The shower is a religious experience. He closes his eyes, lets the tepid water run over his head, down his torso. He usually shaves in here, but he'll have to let his beard grow until he goes back to work Monday, because the last thing his face needs is a razor. He soaps from the top down thoroughly: scrubs his ears, behind his knees, tops of his feet. The soap burns his face where the Band-Aids used to be. He stands, his head under the stream of water, until the pain subsides.

When he gets out of the shower he feels anxious. He looks in the mirror: the bruises and cuts make him look tough, though he doesn't feel that way. His ear feels like it doesn't belong to him, as sore as it is when he brushes through his dark brown shag – trendy, he thinks – only because he hasn't had time to get it cut. Pretty soon Flagherty will make him go to the barber, or Fiore will give him enough grief to talk him into it.

He surveys the clothes in his closet, his mind on this afternoon's affair. He has no choice but to do this thing with Pearson. He hopes he'll be able to find out what she knows and point her in another direction, away from the guns. If he can't, he has to help her find out who killed Ipolitas so she doesn't find out about the rest.

He buttons up his best short-sleeve J. Crew and forces himself to wear jeans instead of shorts. He puts on his Pumas. It's hot, yeah, but he knows Pearson will still be in work garb and he doesn't want to show up, some asshole in sandals. He sprays some Hugo Boss on his collar, just enough to suggest he bothers, and calls a cab.

A vacuum of cold air sucks Weiss up the steps into Moody's. Pearson is already sitting at one of the heavy wooden booths, a file folder and a half-empty schooner of beer in front of her, a fireplace crackling to her left. Ninety degrees outside and she picks a pseudo-ski lodge. Go figure.

First thing Weiss notices is that she hasn't gone to any lengths to impress him. Her hair is tied back, as usual, but now frizzy wisps at her hairline compromise the style. Her white blouse is wrinkled from all-day wear, presumably under the suit jacket that's stuffed into the corner of the booth. And he's never seen her wear glasses. They're thin-framed and sleek, but glasses just the same.

He's deciding on a compliment as he approaches, but he hasn't got one by the time he sits. 'Hey,' he says anyway, 'you look ...' smart, he doesn't say, because it won't sound like a compliment.

'Hey,' Pearson says back, takes the schooner in both hands and drinks. Most of her fingernail polish is chipped away.

'You look stressed,' is what he comes up with, deciding flattery would be a stretch.

'You look like you lost the fight,' she says.

Weiss opts for a silent touché and slips further into the booth.

'Sorry,' Pearson says. 'I get like this after I'm stuck

in the office all day. The bureaucracy at that place makes me want to join NOW.'

'What'd you expect? You're in a boys' club.'

'No I'm not. You only get to be a member of the club if you break cases, which is next to impossible when said club is in charge of assigning those cases, and ninety-nine percent of the time they give you shit.'

Weiss catches the bartender's eye and points at Pearson's schooner, holds up two fingers. The plain-faced bartender nods, his movements instantly prioritized. He tosses his dishrag aside, uses one callused hand at the tap and the other at the register.

Weiss leans back, puts his attention on Pearson, hoping his interest will disarm her.

'What?' she says.

Weiss takes a peanut from the basket on the table, cracks it open, throws the shell on the floor. 'This is the one percent. You want to jump on this case, to get in the club,' he says like a know-it-all. He tosses the nuts in his mouth.

'Fuck the club. This is my job.' Pearson pops a peanut into her mouth, shell and all. Her glasses make her eyes look bigger, and she's reading his reaction.

Weiss shifts in his seat. Turns out he's the one feeling disarmed.

Pearson chews her peanut and leans forward, hands around her beer, says, 'I don't know you, Officer Weiss, but I know this: I've tried, more than once, to give a street cop the benefit of the doubt. And more than once, it's been a mistake. So I want to know up front: have you been, are you, or will you be trying to prevent me from doing my job?'

'What do you mean by that?'

Pearson takes off her glasses, her eyes still big. 'Are you going to fuck me over?'

Weiss wonders if she can see him clearly enough to know whether or not he means it when he says, 'No.'

The bartender delivers the round; Pearson pushes her schooner aside to make room for the new one. Weiss takes a drink from his, tastes pear. He was looking forward to a beer; she must have ordered some kind of cider. His mouth puckers but he drinks it anyway, because he doesn't know what to say.

He eyes the file folder on the table. He came here to get information, but it looks like he's going to have to give to get. He puts down the cider and lightly touches the rim of his swollen ear, hoping to start with sympathy.

'Detective, I'm not sure what it is you want to hear. You're right: you don't know me. And you probably can't come up with an acceptable reason for my interest in this case. You conclude that I must have some agenda. I get that, because, hell, everybody lies. Everybody has an agenda. What I don't get is this: I'm the one who said Ambrozas was innocent in the first place. So how is it that I'm going to fuck you over? As far as I'm concerned, you're the one who has the agenda. You're the one who called me.' Weiss quits there, thinking Pearson already prepared a response.

Instead, she stares at her cider, her gaze resigned, like she's been told something she already knew and never wanted to.

Weiss sips his cider, waiting her out. He wonders what truth, if any, she sees in his face, and how much more he'll have to tell to sway her.

Then, Pearson pushes her schooner aside and puts on her glasses, magnifying her concession. 'A guy turns up dead. Shot to death. We want to know who did it, we have to know more than how and when. We have to reconstruct the last days of his life. Find out where he ate his last meal, what he ate, when. Look through his mail, check his phone records, talk to friends, family, whoever saw him last. We have to get to know him. Who he was when he was alive.'

She slides the file folder to Weiss, keeps her hand over it. 'I'm going to share this information with you because you're the one who brought it to my attention. You said Ambrozas had no motive. And since I've been getting to know Mr Ipolitas, I think there are plenty of other people who did.'

She opens the folder. 'These pages on top are invoices from Ipolitas' store,' she says. The letterhead of each reads: RYTOI JEWELERS. Address, phone number; a blue symbol of a diamond. Below the letterhead: client IDs, order numbers, handwritten estimates.

'We used the active invoices to contact clients.' Pearson moves the top pages faceup, so they're side by side with the others. 'Active invoices are for people who were having jewelry appraised, stones reset, that kind of thing. Ipolitas was supposed to have that jewelry in his possession. Thing is, some of the items were missing. A Rolex. Some diamond earrings. A set of antique garnets. And the invoices for the stuff that's missing? Written in different handwriting.' She points out the careful script on one page; on the other, a right-slanted scrawl.

'We interviewed the clients. And for every unmatched invoice, we were told the same thing: the Rolex, the diamond earrings, and the garnets – they were all left with a woman.'

'So?'

'So Ipolitas' only employee is Feliks Rainys, a thirty-two-year-old Lithuanian man who's here on a J-1 visa.'

'What's his story?'

'Haven't heard it. Can't find him.'

'What's your guess on the woman?'

'As good as yours. But get this: when we searched Ipolitas' place, we found seven unused airline tickets dating back to March of last year. All different women's names, all return trips they never took to Vilnius.'

'Back home to Lithuania.'

Pearson nods. 'No way for them to leave. He had their passports, too.'

'So you've got faces?'

'There are copies of everything beneath the invoices.'

Weiss flips through the pages to the black-and-white passport pictures. Seven women: each one younger, blonder, more naïve-looking than the one before.

'You suppose these women are still in Chicago?'

'If they are, they won't be lining up to talk to us. I told you we went through Ipolitas' mail? A couple envelopes of cash, five hundred each, no return addresses. I have a hunch Ipolitas promised the women they'd attain the American dream, blow job by blow job.'

'If the Feds get wind if this ...' Weiss feels his shoulders tensing.

'Human trafficking? Prostitution? I can't imagine they'd be interested.'

'No wonder you want a head start. You think they'll come in and take this over your head.'

'You bet they will.'

Weiss finishes his cider slowly, taking mental inventory of what he knows, from the beginning: he stole from Ipolitas. Ipolitas turned up dead. Ambrozas is arrested, on account of a tip from one of Fiore's CIs, which may or may not be true, since Fiore said Ipolitas and Ambrozas were at odds, and Ambrozas was marked as the suspect. And Ambrozas sits in jail now, thanks to Jed planting the guns. Ambrozas refuses talk in order to protect the girl with the golden curl. The girl Fiore says is a whore. A whore who could bump this up to a federal investigation. And a federal investigation that would bring them all down.

'Are you thinking what I'm thinking?' Pearson asks.

'I probably won't word it as well,' Weiss says, tipping his glass for the last drops of cider, thinking he'd better let Pearson do the talking, and hoping that she's on to something completely different.

'Dissatisfied customer,' Pearson says.

'A john? You think Ipolitas was killed by a john?'

'See if you follow this, hypothetically, of course.' Pearson holds up one of the photos, of a teenaged girl, her fresh face ready for America. 'Say Ipolitas was bringing girls over, selling their services. And let's say this one,' she looks at the name, 'Vanda Bartuska, becomes a favorite of his. He wants her for himself. He promises the good life, diamonds and steak dinners. He's older, and she doesn't love him, but it's better than hooking, right? He lets her work in his store, but then one of her old customers comes in. He's mad. He wants in on the action he had before, so he makes some threats. Vanda gets scared, she doesn't want to go back to Lithuania. Ipolitas offers other women; the john isn't interested. Fight ensues, john pulls the trigger, Vanda disappears.'

Weiss takes Vanda's photo, turns it around to Pearson. 'Or, what about this: say she's a favorite of a customer and vice versa? They're in love, she wants out, Ipolitas says no way. The customer decides to get rid of the problem. John pulls the trigger, Vanda disappears.'

Pearson takes a sip of her cider, mulling it over. 'You know what we have to do, don't you?'

'Find the women in these pictures.'

'The *woman*. Just the one who knows who killed Ipolitas.'

Weiss offers her a smile, encouraged to have a hand in this. He prays he can make it play out in his favor.

'Are you up for this?' Pearson asks. 'Tonight?'

'It is date night.'

'I figure if you charmed me, talking to a few whores will be cake.'

'I did charm you, didn't I?'

Pearson toasts her schooner. 'Keep talking. Screw it up.'

Outside Moody's the heat of the day has waned but still holds a polluted gray-brown haze low in the atmosphere. Weiss stops on the sidewalk, watches the traffic.

Pearson steps up next to Weiss, file folder in hand. She pulls her purse over her head so it hangs across her chest.

'Thanks for the burger, officer.'

Her purse strap tugs at her blouse where it's open, reveals a little lace. Weiss tries not to notice.

'My name's Ray.'

'Just trying to keep it professional.'

'You're asking me to solicit sex illegally in order to obtain information outside your jurisdiction. I think we can be on a first-name basis.'

'Just don't get your picture posted on the PPA Web site.'

'That'd be a real career move: Ray Weiss, Prostitution Patron. My face up there with all the johns.' The site, a PR move for the department, hasn't affected prostitution numbers; probably because the guys on the prowl for street whores use automobiles as search engines.

A cab turns the corner at Thorndale, comes toward them.

'You'll call me in the morning?' she asks, stepping forward, flagging the cab with the file folder.

'Sooner if I can.'

'Sloane?' he says as she opens the cab's door. 'Thanks for letting me in on this.'

'Honestly, Ray? If we crack this, I'll reconsider that date.' She gets in the cab, and as it slips in between southbound traffic and disappears, Weiss is a little bit sorry that he's playing the game for another team.

CHAPTER NINETEEN

'Hey, honey, you lost?' A black woman stuffed into a leopard-print miniskirt leans into the passenger window of Weiss' Cavalier tits first. Her plump, glittered lips are pursed in an overpracticed pout.

'Not lost, just looking.'

There are approximately five hundred women strolling Chicago's streets willing to exchange dignity for cash on any given day. Of that number, half are homeless, two-thirds are black, and only a handful are self-employed. Most of those who work south of Madison during the Bulls' off-season are financing a crack habit, further narrowing the parameters. Weiss figures there can only be so many white girls who work for a Lithuanian pimp, and he's willing to bet his new friend, here on the near west side, is familiar with the competition.

'You like what you see?' She smoothes her magenta wig. 'I'm a expert with the likes of young white boys,' which she demonstrates, both hands involved, like air-guitar fellatio. 'It's all in the grip.'

'I'm looking for,' there's no better way to say it, 'a white girl.'

'Oh, it's like that,' she says, stepping away from the

window, pout validated. 'You bring yourself down to Fulton Street but you won't stoop that low.'

'No.' To set off her reaction, he uses an aw-shucks lilt to say, 'The girl I'm looking for ... she's my sister.'

'No shit?' At the news her thick legs shift, knees bend.

'She's fifteen.'

The woman smoothes her wig again, slowly this time, without a thought of vanity. Then she presses her hands together, fingers intertwined: this grip maybe full of regret, or prayer.

Weiss instantly feels like an asshole. He hates to lie. Make a person believe in nothing; fool them into sympathy. He flashes twenty bucks, though it's no consolation. 'Can you help me?'

The woman huffs, straightens up, scans the street for other customers. The only other car sits under the El tracks, lights off, business discreet. She tugs her leopard skirt down to a reasonable inseam. 'Put your money away. I don't know nothing about no white girl. If she's on the junk she's southside. Forty-third Street. If she's clean, she's up in Wicker Park.'

'Thank you.' He puts the car in drive, ready to hit the gas, but then she leans in—

'What's her name?'

A split second of hesitation: a tell on his part. She grips the door handle like she can hold him there.

'What's your sister's name?' she demands, cocks her chin to one side.

'God damn it,' she says, opens the door, and gets in. 'Give me that money.' She removes one platform heel and rubs her arch, sighs, a minute of relief off her feet. 'Come on, give it to me,' she says. 'If I wanted to be a snitch, I wouldn't get all dressed up.'

Weiss produces the twenty. She shakes her head but takes the bill anyway, tucks it between her tits, slips on her shoe, and gets out.

'Move along, officer. You're bad for business.' She slams the door and crosses the street, looking for an honest customer.

Weiss drives up to Wicker Park, pulls over at Damen and Wabansia, opens his windows, and listens to the sounds of the street. Sometimes, just by closing his eyes and listening, he can pick up on things he'd miss if he were using all his senses at once.

Over layers of conversation from the Northside Tap's patio, he hears a couple girls spill out of Cans, a bar across the street that serves just that. They're clearly drunk, their speech loose and loud; apparently hearing is also impaired after a number of Miller Lites.

A Blue Line train rushes into the Damen El station, briefly preempting quieter conversations. When the train stops, Weiss hears a guy outside Bar Louie explaining, presumably to his girlfriend: '... I told you I was going out with Scott. Don't look at me like that....' His tone is intentionally light, which makes him sound patronizing, which is obviously what's actually intended. Weiss leans back on the headrest, marvels at the convoluted ways in which we make each other miserable.

Then, from his right: whistling. After a few notes

Weiss recognizes the tune is 'Der Komisar.' He opens his eyes, sees a Streets & San guy, maybe sixty years old, whistling while he inspects a storm drain. That he's working on a Friday night and knows an eighties one-hit wonder are brilliant facts without explanation. Weiss smiles: on the street, it's always the strange moments that stick with him.

Weiss decides he's procrastinating. Sure, he's in Wicker Park, but this isn't exactly what the hooker on Fulton Street meant. The ladies of the night don't work outside the bars around here – not because frat boys try for sex by purchasing inordinate amounts of alcohol, which may or may not be cheaper than a hooker, but because cops love the food at Northside. The ladies are careful to stay out of the way.

Weiss starts the Cavalier, heads up Damen, makes a left at Armitage. He snakes back on the one-way streets, using his eyes now to find potential dates. He feels like a creep for sensing the slightest enjoyment of the prowl.

On Cortland Street, Weiss sees a girl standing on the sidewalk like she's waiting for a cab, or maybe someone else. He drives up slow, checks her out. She's a small girl in a small shirt, her jeans hanging low so her belly shows, highlighting a few inches of waistline bulge someone told her to be proud of. She watches Weiss drive past, a challenge in her stance that says she isn't a hooker. Weiss drives on, hoping the low-rise trend is on its way out.

Weiss does this route once and decides to take his chances heading out of the city on North Avenue. He only makes it a few blocks before he sees two squads blocking a side street; whatever the reason, he's sure the prostitutes have enough sense to take their business elsewhere.

He turns around, makes his way up to Bloomingdale Avenue, follows the Metra tracks toward the river. He skips up a block when the street runs out, crosses under the Kennedy Expressway, and starts looking for loiterers when he finds the tracks again. These tracks don't get much use by way of trains, since this part of the line runs just over the river where it serves as a storage area for old railroad cars. A perfect place for high schoolers to drink beer, young love to bloom, working women to make a buck. Once in a while the cops will come around and chase them all away, but it's a big city, and no one can pay attention all the time.

Sure enough, before Weiss reaches the end of the line: bingo. Two cars in a parking lot off Elston, engines running, their drivers taking in tonight's offering: a group of ladies hanging around an alleyway.

Weiss cruises the scene, on the lookout for the local Five-O before he turns into the lot. There's only one streetlight, but the activity on the expressway provides a gray glow that fills the rest of the shadows.

Weiss counts five women: one hanging in the first car's passenger window, trying to negotiate. The second woman has already settled her deal: she gets into the second car, a Camaro, and seconds later her new boss floors it, spinning his tires before he tears out of the lot to find a less conspicuous place to park. Weiss wonders if the remaining ladies recognize the paradox.

The dust settles as Weiss drives up, rolls down his window. Two of the three women approach; the third hangs back.

'Oy vey,' the woman with washed-out blond hair and brunette roots says to the other. Then to Weiss, 'You looking for a party?'

'Of sorts.' He sizes up the women. First one, with roots: thirty, maybe a hundred and thirty pounds, built tough, Hispanic. The other: twenty under the makeup. Taller, skinnier, white. A possibility.

'My friend Angelina and I can show you a party,' the Hispanic says.

'Angelina,' Weiss says, 'where you from?'

'Wherever you want me to be from.' She licks her lips and the effect is somewhere between awkward and awful.

'I like a woman with her own ideas,' he says. 'What about your friend back there?'

'You don't want her,' Angelina says, 'she don't even speak English.'

Weiss can't believe it. 'She's exactly who I want. Call her over.'

The Hispanic, not one to take taste personally, calls over her shoulder, 'Hey, you're on.'

The third woman hesitates before she approaches. She's a slight, pale thing; jet-black hair follows her hard jawline. Black makeup around her eyes, shoulders slumped so her chest seems flat. Hard to tell how old she is, but it looks like she's lived a long time.

'Come on, Amante,' the Hispanic says, 'before the nice man changes his mind.'

Angelina coaxes her to the window.

'Take a ride?' Weiss asks, flashes a couple of bills.

Without acknowledging her coworkers, Amante gets in the car, no indication that she's actually willing, but none that she'd being forced, either. Weiss wonders how this indifference is supposed to get a guy going. Not that it makes a difference to him. When she closes the door, he makes a quick, discreet exit from the lot.

Far enough down the street to be reasonably sure no one's going to bust them, Weiss looks over at his passenger and decides to estimate her ability to communicate. He says, in his friendliest tone, 'What kind of name is Amante?'

She tilts her head, her ears catching a familiar word, but much like a dog when he learns his name, there's little progress beyond the basics. She resumes her uninterested gaze out the window.

Weiss drives back toward Wicker Park. Since he didn't see any prostitutes there earlier, he figures no one will suspect them; they're just two people on a date.

Except that they couldn't be more mismatched if a blind guy set them up. Between Weiss' squeaky-clean appearance and the girl's thrift store/sex shop getup, it definitely appears as though one is doing the other a favor. Hard to tell which, though, since Amante appears confused, maybe afraid, with every passing block.

Weiss says, 'Don't worry, I won't hurt you.'

He returns to the spot where he parked on Damen, the area still alive with the Friday-night-who-gives-a-fuck crowd. Weiss parks, and pronounces every word when he says, 'Please listen. I don't want sex. I need to talk to you about someone you may know. Petras Ipolitas?'

Her face is a mixture of disbelief and resignation. She looks out her window, like maybe she's considering bolting. Maybe she's scared; she doesn't understand why he'd take her to such a public place. Or maybe he isn't pronouncing the name correctly.

'Petras Ipolitas,' he says again. Weiss finds a gas station receipt in his center console and scrawls the name on the back. 'Here.'

Same face from Amante. Weiss wonders if she can read.

'God damn it,' Weiss says conversationally, assuming she doesn't know what he's saying anyway.

Then she turns to him and says, 'I've never heard of the guy, and I don't appreciate you taking the Lord's name in vain.' She crosses her arms, defining the look on her face: aggravation.

'You speak English?'

'Of course I speak English. I just prefer to skip unnecessary banter, particularly with catty hoes like the ones Darnell stuck me with tonight. So do you want a blow job, or you want to talk about this guy?' She takes the paper and pronounces, 'Eep-o-leetus.'

'I take it you haven't heard of him.'

'Is he in the business? Are you gay? Because I know a guy who would make your head spin, he's—'

'I'm not gay. I think Ipolitas was a pimp.'

'He isn't a pimp anymore?'

'He isn't alive anymore.'

Weiss produces a list he made from the passport

copies Pearson showed him. 'Maybe you recognize one of these names?'

A perfunctory glance, then, 'I can't even pronounce these names. I'm from Wisconsin, mister. What the hell is going on? And why are we parked here, anyway? This is trouble.'

'I want you to know I'm serious. I have to figure out who killed this man, Ipolitas, and if you know anything, you have to tell me.'

'I don't *have* to do anything.'

'You see those cops in there?' Weiss indicates two guys in uniform, dutifully scarfing burgers in the Northside Tap's window. 'They're your other option.'

Amante sinks in her seat. 'You suck.'

'Twenty bucks. Just look at the list again. I think Ipolitas was bringing these women over from Lithuania to work for him.'

Amante looks at the cops, sucks air through her teeth, takes the list. None of the names seem to register. She fans herself with the paper, thinking. Then she says, 'If we had competition on the street, Darnell would know about it. And he'd take care of it.'

'You mean, he would kill?'

'Come on, mister, you're being a bit dramatic. Darnell runs a tight ship. Competition comes around, we step up our efforts. New outfits. Less fast food. Haircuts; that kind of thing. But lately? It's a seller's marketplace. I'm falling out of my lingerie and he won't even bother to hook me up, and he doesn't need to because the johns keep coming back. Which means: there is no competition.'

'Any chance Darnell knew Ipolitas?'

'There's always a chance, mister. But I think you're cruising the wrong corner. Can I go now? Darnell will have my ass if he knows I'm sitting here shooting the shit with some wanna-be cop for a measly twenty bucks.'

Weiss isn't proud to be pegged a wanna-be, but at least he got her to talk. He slips her the twenty and she opens the door.

'Stay here a second.' She gets out, stops at a row of newspaper boxes, and lifts the door to one. Weiss half watches her, runs over everything she said, concludes he's hit a dead end.

Then Amante comes back, tosses a *Reader* onto the passenger seat. 'You ever read this rag? Back half of it is nothing but escort services. Darnell doesn't even try to compete with those.'

Weiss looks at the back page: his new angle on the investigation.

'Thanks, Amante.'

'Please, enough with the Amante bit. My name's Betsey. If you ever want a real date, you know where to find me.'

It's sometime after midnight and Weiss' eyes are heavy, the Coca-Cola no longer enough to keep his mind clear. He's sitting in the basement, the bare light down here best for late-night work, though the work this time has nothing to do with firearms.

He's looked through so many ads, at so many nearly nude photos of Kylie and Kim and Kristi, that he's decidedly numb to their suggestions. But he promised himself he'd get through the whole paper tonight, so he'd have something for Pearson in the morning.

It didn't take him long to figure out that many of the ads are repeats, or variations of the same. Kylie is also Amanda; she wants to meet you and fall in love and she also wants to talk dirty. Kim is not Candace, but they can both be reached at (888) HOT-4YOU. And Kristi? She bears a striking resemblance to Fantasia, though the two have no professional affiliation, as far as Weiss can tell.

He's made a list of numbers, weeding out the repeats and obvious wrong turns like someone called Ebony Barbie. He organizes the numbers by area code and arranges them by offering. He divides (773) and (312) area codes into two lists, and subdivides each by escort services, massages, and phone sex – which he puts at the bottom of the lists, since he doubts Lithuanian women are practiced conversationalists. He makes one last column for those he can't categorize that use codes like 'BBW' and 'GFE.' He doesn't even want to imagine.

When he gets to the last page of the *Reader*, he has nearly a hundred phone numbers logged. He's out of Coke, he has to take a leak, and the last thing he wants to do is make a single call. He isn't even sure he'll get through to anyone without having to give up his credit card information, which he's firmly decided against, having already dropped forty bucks on hookers.

He opens his mouth, a deep yawn. He folds up the

paper, vows to get up early and get back at it. He raises his arms, a good stretch; pulls on his neck, cracks his knuckles. He rolls his shoulders, relaxes all his muscles, exhales.

And then he hears a shotgun blast upstairs.

The air in the basement seems to recede, wait. He knows the distinct sound of a shotgun blast. He doesn't know the target until he hears the second concussive shot that shakes the house like thunder when it hits the front window upstairs, shatters the glass. Weiss hears the glass and most likely everything in its wake crash to the hardwood floor directly above him.

He rouses himself to cut the lights in the basement, uses the suggestion of light from the ground-level windows for guidance, feels his way back to the steel storage cabinet. He curses the three-point locking system when he fucks it up the first time. Why did he leave his .45 upstairs? He hears his own breath, quick, revealing; he knows the thick basement walls block out most of the noise above ground. Could be a car starting, a faraway siren, someone outside calling his name; he might as well be wearing earplugs down here.

He gets the lock open on the second try and reaches for the case on the top shelf that holds his grandfather's .38 Special. He takes a cardboard box full of bullets, shells he reloaded himself, from the second shelf.

He squats, places the case on the concrete floor, prepares to load the gun: something he can do with his eyes closed. Good thing.

In less than a minute he's at the basement door, gun in hand. He has to climb twelve steps: six up to a landing, turn, six more. That'll get him to the shared entryway where he can secure the scene, assess the damage. *Fuck*, he thinks, *the scene is my house.* He listens, waits, darts, and aims, gun pointed up at the landing. No one is there.

He skips up the last six steps, spins, and presses his back up against the far wall – the only solid wall, as the door to his place is on his left, the second flight of stairs in front of him, the main entrance to the right. He sweeps the space with his gun aimed then crouches below the doors' windows, out of sight.

He peers out the stained glass that surrounds the main door but he can't see shit in the dark through the beveled panes. He's not about to turn on the porch light. He checks the doorknob: it's locked, though that will make little difference to someone who's already fired a gun. He stays down, reaches for the door to his place, which he left unlocked, and turns the knob.

The door creaks, making his entrance all the more agonizing. He slips inside, stays low, gun in all directions. He left the kitchen light on, so he avoids looking there and screwing up his night vision.

He stays on the edge of the room, moves around to his right. The front window is gone, 90 percent of the glass at his feet. He can make out the rest of the damage by the streetlight: his standing lamp is busted; the hanging philodendron his mother gave him is an exploded mess of mud on the floor, the chain on the planter left dangling like an empty noose.

The room is still, except for the undecided air where the window used to be, and the crunch of glass when Weiss steps forward to get a look out the window. Only a few shards of glass still hang in the frame. Outside, Weiss' car is where he parked it. It appears intact. He remembers the red Civic in front of it, the black Expedition behind, from when he parallel parked.

Then: headlights – Weiss ducks as they approach, his heart beating, his gun-hand sweaty. He holds his breath, gets flat on the floor, his body on the glass. Why the fuck did he go near the window?

The car passes without incident. Weiss waits an extra minute, listening. Nothing.

He looks at the mess of glass on the floor. Then, a few feet away, he sees a flattened pellet. Size of a small marble. He reaches for it, presses it between his fingers. It's double-ought buck, just like they use at work.

He gets up, brushes himself off carefully, dismissing the possibility that he just tampered with another crime scene.

Weiss feels his ego swell, become accusatory. He heads for the kitchen in long, confident strides, ready to shoot, directing his gun at all angles, corners, aware of all three-hundred-and-sixty degrees around him.

The kitchen is just as he left it. Empty Coke can, cell phone, wallet on the table. He walks through, throws open the back door, scans the yard, the alley. He's unafraid, but not fueled by adrenaline; this is more primal. Territorial. This is an unacceptable violation. He raises his gun, feels like firing a shot at the sky.

'Mother fucker,' he says for anyone to hear. But no one is there.

He goes inside, closes the door. And double-checks the lock.

Back into the front room. He puts his gun on the coffee table and sits down on the couch, the aftermath spread from right to left in front of him. The first blast he heard must have missed the mark, unless it was a warning shot. The blast that hit the window came from far enough away for the shot to spread and take out the whole thing, which means it was fired from the sidewalk, or the street. And the pattern was big enough to penetrate the glass and bring most of it into the room. If he can find all the spent pellets, he can figure out the gun gauge. Better yet, if he can find one of the shell casings outside that kicked out after being fired, he can find out the make.

He stuffs the .38 in his waistband, goes back into the kitchen for a flashlight. He swipes his keys from the kitchen table on the way to the front door, his footsteps hard, deliberate. Inside the shared entryway, he turns to lock his door.

With the key still in the lock his muscles tense, as if sensing the footfall on the sidewalk outside before he hears it.

Then, the familiar twist of metal-on-metal that is the locked doorknob behind him.

In less than a second he's pressed against the wall, gun drawn. A shadow makes its way through the stained glass on the door frame and from his perspective, the shadow is being cast by a very tall person. Not that it matters. If whoever's there has a gun, too, the outcome won't depend on size.

Silence, now, from the other side of the door. He could crawl to the steps and go back to the basement, but hiding in his own home isn't an option. He could sneak upstairs, wait for whoever it is to break in, and surprise! – but the stairs are old and settled and audible under weight. He'd be heard.

Besides, he wants to know who's out there.

The shadow moves, encompassing the left side of the stained-glass window now, the person peering inside.

Weiss knows he has to act fast. He takes a last breath, prepared to hold it until this is all over.

He spins, staying low. He turns the lock with his left hand and pulls the door in toward him at the same time moving left. He shifts his weight back and his ass hits the tiled floor, giving him one clear, surprising shot as the door opens.

'Don't move,' he demands.

Leah giggles. 'What the fuck are you doing?'

CHAPTER TWENTY

'Well, this paints a real telling picture of law enforcement.' Leah stands in the yard watching Weiss search for the shell casings. He's got one ear to the ground, sweeping his flashlight over the grass and the sidewalk.

'What do you want, Leah?'

'What do you think? I want an apology.'

Weiss stands up, aims the flashlight at her face. 'How'd you get here?'

Leah closes one eye, steadies her stance. She's wearing chunky-heeled shoes, but they aren't the trouble. 'I was at Ten Cat.'

'You walked here?' Ten Cat Tavern is nearly a dozen blocks away. She should know better, but it only takes one lemon-drop martini to excuse all common sense from her system. And, Weiss knows, she wants him to be mad.

'What happened to your eye?' she asks.

'Nothing.'

'Silly me; I thought maybe you'd want to talk now.'

Weiss turns his flashlight toward the street, dismissing her. It doesn't take an officer of the law to figure out she's had a few drinks. Weiss finds it kind of pathetic, her being the one to make contact after the other night. But he's done worse. Like the time he crashed her salsa-dancing date with a pitcher of sangria. He drank half of it and dumped the rest on her date's stupid red silk shirt.

'Landlord's going to be pissed,' Leah says, looking at the broken window, always the one to see the glass half-empty after drinking from it.

'If you're just going to stand there, watch for cars.' Weiss gets on his hands and knees in the street, shines the light underneath his car.

'Who do you think did this?' she asks, her steps out to the street less than graceful.

'That's what I'm trying to figure out.' He tries to sound patient, because even if she's drunk and purposely irritating him, she's company. And he has to admit he's not pissed at her so much as he is by the fact that he isn't having any luck. So far all he's discovered out here is that the street sweepers do a pretty damn good job.

He moves up to the Civic in front of his car, checks the angle to the window, aiming the flashlight like a gun. Then he gets down, scans the pavement under the Civic. Again, he's got to hand it to Streets & Sanitation.

'Ray,' Leah says.

He looks over his shoulder. Leah's in the middle of the street.

'Is this what you're looking for?' She bends over. Her tight jeans-skirt stops an inch before he doesn't have to use his imagination, so he doesn't see what she picks up until she walks over and hands it to him.

It's a green plastic striated shell casing. He turns it on its end, shines the light on the brass base, and reads the words stamped around the primer: REMINGTON 12 GAUGE. Same gauge, same color, same fucking brand that's issued by the department.

'Did I crack the case?' she asks.

Weiss turns the casing around in his fingers.

'Should we call the cops?' Her question facetious.

Weiss looks up at her. 'Let's go inside.'

'So you think that your coworkers are trying to kill you because you arrested the wrong person?' Battling the alcohol in her system, Leah's having trouble making sense of what Weiss is telling her. Then again, he's not telling her everything.

'I don't think they're trying to kill me,' he says. 'I think they're trying to send a message.'

'Because you arrested the wrong guy.'

'Because I'm trying to find the right guy.'

'I don't get it.' She sips carefully from a glass of water, though she won't be passing a sobriety test anytime soon. She leans back against the kitchen chair.

'They want me to keep my mouth shut,' he says.

'Maybe they're on to something.' Leah offers a smile he recognizes. She raises her glass for another sip of water and her wide-collared shirt reveals one of her bra straps. Weiss recognizes the color, and he can visualize the rest of the pink, tiger-striped, see-throughish thing, and the matching panties …

He shifts in his seat and tries to push those

thoughts out of his head, but from this position he has a clear shot of her smooth, muscular legs. His erection is instant, and completely beside the point. He puts his hands on the table and reminds himself he's got bigger problems.

'Leah,' he says, 'everything just got so fucked up. I thought I was doing the right thing, and now my own guys are pushing me away.' He can't tell her why, but she can't help him fix this anyway; best he can do is try for some sympathy. 'Every time I put my heart into something ...'

She crosses her legs and presses her lips together, both signs she wants to say something, but isn't.

'What?'

'Ray, people don't push you away. You don't let them in.' She leans forward and a few curls fall over her shoulder. 'You hold everything inside, and you think if you can't fix it, you can't talk about it. Your communication skills suck. It's no wonder someone needs a shotgun to get through to you.'

So much for sympathy.

'Come here,' he says. 'Why don't you get through to me?' He's ready to pull up her skirt and take her right there on the kitchen table, Leah and her know-it-all attitude, compounded by liquid courage, exacerbated by the truth.

He reaches for her, but she holds up a hand like a Stop sign.

'I met someone.'

The words shut him down.

Leah gets up, puts her glass in the sink, balances there momentarily. 'You know what else, Ray? As soon as you get what you want, you don't want it anymore.' She takes her purse from the table, tucks it under her arm, ready to leave.

'Who is he?' he asks.

'His name is Kurt. I've been seeing him for nearly a month.'

'What does he do?'

'He works for the *Sun-Times*.'

'He's a writer?'

'You're changing the subject.'

'I'm just asking. I thought you were over the artist phase.'

'He's a grown-up.'

'I'll call you a cab.'

As Leah disappears into the dark living room and out the front door, Weiss reminds himself again: he's got bigger problems.

CHAPTER TWENTY-ONE

Weiss thought yesterday was bad, but today is shaping up to be equally shitty pretty quickly. He didn't get much sleep after Leah's departure, and this window fiasco isn't a fucking picnic, either. He's been up since six, developing a plan of action.

First things first. It's Saturday, which means there's a pretty good chance that Hal will be showing the upstairs; that means that Weiss had better make the absence of the window look like a planned renovation rather than an executed hit. There's no doubt Hal will back up whatever cheery do-it-yourself tenant story Weiss cooks up, especially since Hal has used Weiss as a selling point before – called him 'on-premises security.' If Weiss can deliver a performance to potential occupants that outshines the high-priced rental agreement, Hal won't care what really happened to the window. Or at least he won't ask.

At eight a.m., Weiss goes outside. He checks around the property, making sure the first gunshot didn't hit the neighbor's house, or someone's cat. Across the street, a new dad pushes a lawn mower around a wooden stork and into his yard. A cloth hangs from the stork's mouth that says WELCOME

GENEVA JANE. Dad waves a neighborly hello; no sign of concern. Weiss waves back, hoping Geneva has kept Dad too sleep-deprived to wonder why Weiss' window is missing.

When he's satisfied no further damage has been done, Weiss goes inside. He sweeps up the glass and the rest of the mess on the floor, no clue how he's going to explain the philodendron to his mother. If he tells her he didn't water it, she'll take him on a guilt trip that spans all the way back to the first day of fifth grade when he made Chuck, the neighborhood wimp, eat grass. On the other hand, if he tells Mom what really happened, she'll come over, pack his things, and move him back home. He guesses he'll have to buy another plant and a duplicate pot, and hope she won't notice.

He measures the window frame and at nine sharp he calls a glass and mirror shop over on Clark Street that does rush jobs. The guy on the phone tries to sell him a tempered, sturdier piece of glass, but Weiss sticks to the same cheap single pane. Guy says two hours in a tone that sounds closer to four and hangs up.

The sun is still on the other side of the house but the heat is everywhere by nine thirty. Weiss sweats in his work gloves as he straddles the window, removing the remaining glass.

He uses a putty knife to dislodge the old, dried putty and the caulk Hal must have put over it like a Band-Aid, further convincing himself that he's not the only one: most of the men he knows are inclined to hide a problem rather than fix it.

His cell rings while he's scraping the top of the wood frame. He jumps down, slips off a glove, and gets the phone from his shorts pocket. Caller ID says it's Pearson. He'd hoped to tackle one problem at a time, but he doesn't want her to know there's more than one. And the last thing she needs is a reason to be suspicious.

'Hey, Sloane.'

'Did you get lucky last night?' She's aiming for playful, but Weiss can hear the anticipation in her voice.

'It's only luck if you don't pay for it,' he says.

'Did you get your money's worth?'

'Wouldn't say I'm satisfied.'

'Guess I owe you.'

He knows she didn't mean it sexually, but it's awkward just the same, because now he's thinking about a forty-dollar blow job from Detective Sloane Pearson. Jed's right about one thing: he needs to get laid.

'Ray,' Pearson says, 'did you get any leads?'

He adjusts his shorts, gives the boys some breathing room. 'Leads,' he says, to get his mind back where it belongs. 'Yeah. About a hundred of them. I asked around, found out there aren't any Lithuanians working the street. A nice young lady suggested I check out the back pages of the *Reader*.'

'Escorts. Of course.' Then, thinking out loud, 'Street whores don't make the kind of cash we found at Ipolitas'. Calling in for exotic, classy girls – that's the traveling businessman's choice. That's where the money is.'

'I made a list, you want to split it?'

'I've got a better idea. You make the calls, and I'll get Ipolitas' phone records. If we work from opposite angles, maybe we'll hit the same point.'

'Okay,' Weiss says, figuring this buys him some time. 'But you still owe me.' He figures this buys him that date somewhere down the line. Assuming she doesn't find out what a liar he is.

'Bye, Ray.'

He flips his phone shut and looks at the time. It's nearly eleven, and he'd planned to pick up the windowpane at noon, so he has plenty of time to lie some more.

He pulls off his other glove and dials Jed.

'Good morning, sunshine,' Jed says, no anger apparent in his greeting.

'Hey,' Weiss says, trying to mask the anger in his.

'You're the one calling me. Sound enthused, would ya?'

'I had a rough night.' Weiss listens for a guilty pause, but right away Jed says—

'Talk about rough, you should have come by Hamilton's last night. My liver hates me. What happened to you? We thought you'd show.'

'Leah.'

'I told you. She's Satan as a woman.'

'Something like that.'

'Wish I'd fucked her.'

'Is that supposed to make me feel better?'

'Sorry, I forgot about your female hormone injections.'

'Jed,' Weiss says, looking out the glassless window,

the joke lost, 'I wanted to apologize. About yesterday. I'm not going to fuck you up.' He rests a hand on the window frame, waits for a hint of remorse, but Jed says—

'Fiore thinks you're a weak link. He says if you keep at it, you're going to bring down the whole district.'

'Why did my name come up?'

'We were tired of talking about our feelings. How do you think? I told him what you said at the Abbey. About the guns.'

Weiss grips the frame. 'And?'

'And he said he was gonna have to find a way to get through to you.'

With a shotgun, Weiss thinks. That's one way.

'What else did he say?'

'I don't know, man. It was just talk. We were pretty loaded.'

Making the idea of taking a shotgun to Weiss' house all the more plausible.

'What time did he leave?'

'Ray, if you want to know about Fiore, talk to him. I'm no good at being the middleman. Unless we're talking about two naked chicks.'

'Okay,' is all Weiss can manage. He notices a red stain on the window frame and only figures out he cut himself when he sees his bloody palm, and a tiny piece of glass embedded there. He'll talk to Fiore all right: on his terms. When he catches the fucker trying to sabotage him. He picks at the piece of glass, wonders what he can say to set a trap.

'I think,' Jed says, 'what we have here,' and his

voice booms like a drill sergeant's, 'is a failyah to communicate.'

'I told you before, I'm afraid we're going to get caught.'

'Nobody's chasing us, man.'

'As far as you know.' And Weiss knows better.

'Ray, I can guarantee you by the end of next week we'll be knee-deep in some other shit. We just have to shut up and stick together.'

Which is why Weiss knows Jed isn't going to want to hear this: 'You're right. I should quit thinking about it. I'm gonna go over to my parents' tonight. My mom invited the whole family, for Billy's promotion.' And for the kicker: 'Maybe I'll talk to my dad about this. Get some perspective.'

'Uh-oh,' Jed says.

'What?' Weiss baiting him.

'My wife is giving me the eye.'

Not what Weiss expected, so he pushes it: 'You think it's okay, though? If I talk to my dad?'

'You do what you gotta do, man,' Jed's words short now, resigned. 'I'll catch you later.'

'We're good, Jed?'

'Yeah. We're good.'

Weiss hangs up, hoping he's said enough to inspire retaliation.

CHAPTER TWENTY-TWO

Weiss is caulking the last edge of the new window when Hal pulls up in his Taurus station wagon. He parks behind the Cavalier and approaches the two-flat, a janitor's-size ring of keys in one hand and his plastic travel mug in the other. He's sporting some alarming white shorts, an orange polo shirt, and a trucker hat that really is a trucker hat – not the trendy kind the pop-culturers in Hollywood wear.

Weiss waves from the window; Hal squints like he doesn't recognize him. Or maybe he's catching a glare from his shirt.

When Hal doesn't buzz the door and Weiss doesn't hear him on the steps up to the second floor, Weiss goes out front to investigate.

Hal's outside on the porch, a screwdriver wedged in the upstairs unit's mailbox. The tool must have come from his back pocket; a pair of needle-nose pliers and a bottle of wood glue are still lodged there, as appropriate as the tight shorts themselves. Weiss has no idea how Hal was able to sit in his car.

'Afternoon, Hal.'

'Hmph.' He jimmies the door open; junk mail flutters from the box.

'I thought you'd be showing the place today.'

'It's rented. Nice couple, getting married in October. She's going to live here next month.' He looks at Weiss. 'Don't get any ideas.'

Hal affixes a new nameplate to the mailbox. 'Zerin-Chavda,' he says. 'An interesting hyphenate. I wonder what their parents talk about.'

'When does she move in?'

'Week from tomorrow. I told 'em I'd have the place painted. You and your buddies interested in a side job?'

'How much?' The idea of having the upstairs key is almost too perfect.

'Three guys, a hundred each.'

'The entire apartment?'

'Can't take more than a day.' Which means it will. 'You ever figure out who had the dog out here?' Which means Weiss better agree to the job.

When Hal steps off the porch and makes a point of surveying the front of the building, looking over at the front window, Weiss says, 'I'll set it up.'

'That's real good.' Hal stuffs the screwdriver in his back pocket, gets his travel mug from the ledge, assumes a good-bye.

'I'll need a key,' Weiss calls after him.

Hal unhooks his key ring from his belt loop, turns over one key after another, none of them marked. He stops, fingers one with potential. Then he cups the ring in his palm, looks up at Weiss. 'I'll bring it by tomorrow afternoon. With the paint.'

'Great.'

Hal closes the mailbox and heads for his wagon,

and Weiss adds the job to the list of things he doesn't want to do.

Shortly after four o'clock Weiss breaks into the upstairs apartment. If Hal notices the lock's been tampered with, Weiss will make up some story about seeing Nick. He's certain Hal will change the lock before he'll have anything to do with the guy.

Once inside, Weiss feels like a thief, even though there's nothing to steal, and he's just here for the view. He decides the floor is going to be a problem: the hardwood is so warped it's like he's on one of those swinging bridges at an amusement park, where one plank moves to compensate for the next. Every step is a creaky giveaway. He doesn't remember hearing Nick up here, but they were on opposite schedules. Weiss would get off work and be ready for some hard rookie sleep when Nick was on his way to sociology class or rugby practice.

Weiss makes his way to the front window, directly above his own. Last year, the city planted a maple tree between the sidewalk and the street. Already it's become a complete obstruction, blocking the street and everything within fifteen feet of the autumn-resistant, leafy branches. Surveillance is an essential part of his plan, and the second floor isn't going to do him a damn bit of good. Looks like he's going to have to take his operation outside.

Weiss can't be certain Fiore was the one who shot out his window, but he decides it has to be one of the guys, and if Weiss thinks like Fiore, he'll have a better chance catching whoever did it. Fiore wouldn't use the shotgun again, though a new window and no mention of the first incident might piss him off enough to shoot it out again – just to make a point. In Weiss' experience, though, Fiore has never taught the same lesson twice. He won't do the window. And he won't drive by.

Fiore wouldn't make a sneaky approach, either; his ego wouldn't let him hide. That's not to say he'll buzz the front door and come in for coffee and civil conversation – whoever did this obviously doesn't want to talk – but he won't risk driving up on Leavitt. He'll be aware of the possibility that someone saw him last night.

The alley is an obvious choice, but it's also a good one. People park there all the time when Leavitt's full or cleared for sweeping or snowplowing. It wouldn't be out of the ordinary for someone to show up at Weiss' back door; Jed always does.

Wherever Fiore comes from, Weiss has to make sure he won't escape. It'd be smart to park in back and strike from the front, or vice versa. The sides of the building have to be secured.

Four thirty. Weiss goes outside, props the metal lid of a garbage can against the gate to the gangway on the south side, by the trash barrels. If the gate's opened, he'll hear it. In the north gangway, the one his Polish neighbors ignore, he spreads the leftover window glass like seed on the pavement. He'll hear that, too.

He walks around the backyard looking for hiding spots. He decides to keep watch from the roof of the garage, which is directly behind his place and level with his back steps. He can see the back of his place plus a good fifteen feet into each gangway; he'll see Fiore before Fiore sees him. Any neighbors decide to barbecue, his backup spot is in under the steps, though he'll be at a disadvantage if Fiore shows up with a flashlight.

At five o'clock he goes inside, showers, wishes he were really going to Mom's.

A half hour before his planned departure, he puts a pepperoni pizza in the oven and calls a few escort services while it cooks. He starts with the numbers in the '(773)/escort' column on his list. The first few are recorded messages for Windy City Divas, a woman named Cheyenne, and Upscale Escorts. The next one is voice mail for someone who calls herself Jennifer X. Weiss doesn't leave a message.

He finally gets a live voice when he's sprinkling packets of crushed red pepper on the pizza to cover the store-bought cardboard flavor.

'Chicago's Most Wicked, this is Amber, I can help you.' Said like she's helped countless others.

'Uh, yeah, hello.' Weiss makes his voice higher and feels like an ass when he hears himself. Back to his real one: 'I have a very specific request: I want a Lithuanian woman.'

'Of course, we have ladies of all ethnicities that would love to meet you. What's your name?'

'Jed' is out of his mouth automatically.

'Well, Jed, if you give me your number, I'll find out who's available tonight and call you back.'

'She has to be Lithuanian.'

'No problem.'

Weiss gives her his number and eats half the pizza while he waits for her to call back. He hopes he didn't just get himself on the escort telemarketers list.

At five minutes to six, Amber calls.

'Hello, Jed. I have the perfect girl available for you tonight.'

'What's her name?'

'Jessica.'

'Is she Lithuanian?'

'What's your definition of Lithuanian?' The sincerity of her question is practiced.

'Was she born in Lithuania?'

'You're not going to ask for her birth certificate, are you?'

'This is important.'

'Jed, we do not take your needs lightly. Jessica is a beautiful, exotic girl—'

'She has to *speak* Lithuanian.'

Nothing from the other end.

'Thanks anyway,' Weiss says, hanging up, and promising himself to be more specific the next time.

At six o'clock he stuffs his phone, a Coke, and his .45 into the various pockets of his cargo shorts. Then he locks up the place, goes out to the Cavalier, and makes sure if anyone's watching they're seeing him leave. He drives up to West Cuyler, a quiet street on the other side of Irving Park, and leaves the car.

He walks around to his place via Damen Avenue and Grace Street because they're busier than the side streets and it's easier to blend in. In the alley, he breaks into a jog, staying close to the garages and, for the most part, out of sight.

He hoists himself up on the garage roof with the help of the neighbor's Buick parked in the alley. On the roof his footsteps sound hollow, and he wonders if Hal still has his 1968 Porsche Cabriolet stored inside. The only time Weiss saw it was the day he moved in: Hal opened the garage door specifically to inform Weiss never to open it. The car had a layer of dust so thick Weiss couldn't tell the color. He could only tell it was a damn shame.

The roof pitches at maybe a 30-degree angle. Weiss sits low and to the right, by the gutter, so someone coming around the corner won't see his shadow.

He removes the gun from his pants pockets and places it on a shingle to his right, by his quick hand. He cracks open the Coke, drinks half of it, and sticks it in the gutter. Then he settles in.

Immediately he hates the wait. Ironic, he thinks, that the other couple of times he's done surveillance, Fiore was his partner. Weiss wishes he smoked, or had some habit that would help pass the time. He cracks his knuckles.

In the academy, he learned that a good trick to staying alert is to name sounds and movements, defining them in the mind's eye. It reminds him of playing stupid name games with Billy when they were kids, stuck in the backseat of the Cutlass on the way to the annual family reunion in Cincinnati. But he doesn't have any better ideas.

Car engine starting a few blocks away. Little kid yelling; delighted, not distressed. Some kind of bird chirping ... His mother is a bird-watcher. Only this could be slightly less interesting. *Airplane, on its way to O'Hare. Diesel truck braking on Irving Park* ... So much noise made by stuff we built. He wishes he could hear the sunset. *Ravenswood train. Cars moving in all directions, from all directions* ... Fiore must be driving one of them. Will he show up here?

An hour and a half later, the shadows in the yard become long and then finally shift to their unchanging nocturnal shapes formed by the streetlights. Weiss quit naming things shortly after he started; he couldn't think of very many creative ways to describe traffic. He's starting to think this plan of his isn't so clever, either.

He tried to think like Fiore; maybe he got it all wrong. What does Weiss really know about the guy, honestly? Fiore's made his feelings known about everything from welfare to the Bears coaching staff to organic fruit, but opinions don't make the man; it's the other way around. Weiss has been working with Fiore for six months and doesn't know anything about how he got the way he is. His family, his past, his life: all of it is a mystery. Being told what to do and what to think all the time made Weiss want to write the guy off as an asshole, know-it-all cop. And now he's sitting here feeling ridiculous while Fiore's probably over at Hamilton's having a beer, wondering why Weiss is such an asshole, know-it-all kid. Maybe Jed's right: they need to communicate.

Weiss' cell vibrates in his pocket and he rolls to his

right to retrieve it and get a look at the caller ID. The display says PEARSON. He punches the ignore button but keeps the phone in his hand, waiting for the voice-mail alert.

And in that moment, as his mind's eye wanders to an image of Sloane, he just misses the face of the man who throws a bottle over the Polish neighbor's fence. It bursts into flames when it hits Weiss' back steps.

All academy training is lost when Weiss jumps off the roof. He realizes in midair that he left his .45 up there, and when he hits the ground hard from the nearly ten-foot drop he knows there's no time to climb back up and get it. His brain chants *Protect yourself* but his body darts across the yard and up the stairs and kicks what's left of the bottle and the fire into the grass, singeing the hair on his leg. The steps didn't catch fire but he doesn't wait to see if the flames sputter out or spread in the yard because he has one objective and that's catching whoever's running. He skips back down the stairs. The neighbor's back porch light comes on, a question mark to the immediate commotion.

Weiss runs through the glass-covered gangway and pushes open the front gate just as another bottle hits and explodes into fire on the front walk, this one thrown on the run, intended target obviously compromised. Seems like it all happened in fast-forward, and Weiss has to stop himself, regroup. Could this be Fiore?

A visual search of the yard comes up empty. No way the guy backtracked, or went through the other gangway, not without Weiss or the neighbors knowing. No way he's quick enough to make it out of sight on this street, either. Unless he has wings he's here, hiding, waiting for Weiss to make a move.

When the second bottle's fire dies out, the pavement a natural extinguisher, Weiss makes out a figure positioned behind a Honda hatchback, his silhouette framed in the driver's window by the street-light. It's too late for Weiss to hide; the guy is watching his every move. And he could be armed.

It doesn't take a risk analyst to figure out Weiss is pretty much fucked. Unless he plans on surrendering, there's only one thing he can do.

He takes a step forward, raises his chin so his voice will carry, and announces to anyone in the neighbor-hood who's listening: 'Fiore, I know you're there.' Finally, his suspicion aired. He hopes someone besides Fiore hears him.

The figure rises, appearing behind the car like a shadow, and for a spilt second Weiss fears death. Then the guy bolts, and Weiss' body takes over again. He breaks into a run, Weiss reaching the near side of the street as the guy hops the other curb. He's wearing black from head to toe so it's hard to make out his height and weight when he gets out of the street's light, but Weiss swears he gets a glimpse of silver hair before he turns back north.

The guy uses the parked cars as obstacles, forcing Weiss to double back around a pickup truck and an SUV to stay on his tail. He's fast, faster than Weiss has ever seen Fiore move, not that Weiss will claim to know the first thing about him any longer.

Weiss is maybe fifteen paces behind the guy when

he reaches the neighbor's freshly mowed yard. The guy cuts right, probably intent on disappearing down another gangway, either as an escape route or a trap. Weiss is gaining on him, but in a dark alley this could get ugly.

'Fiore, stop!'

He doesn't, but the command must be just enough to get him to wonder how much distance is between them, and his curiosity is just enough to turn his head, and he turns his head just enough so that he doesn't see the giant wooden stork before he runs into it. Thank you, Geneva Jane.

Weiss tackles him, ripping the hood from his head, but it isn't Fiore's silver head of hair. It's the eccentrically fashionable, yellow-blond mullet.

The guy tries to crawl away, but now that Weiss has him on the ground, his efforts are pointless, because Weiss has the strength of a man who's done being fucked with. He flips the guy over by his ankles, does a quick once-over for weapons, and finds a Glock-19 in his waistband. Weiss stands up and aims the gun at the guy's chest.

Weiss recognizes him: he was drinking beer next to Shitfer at the Skylark.

The guy wipes blood from his nose and wiggles his jaw like he's resetting it. He looks up at Weiss, and though his expression bares traces of confusion, most likely due to the collision with the stork, he clearly understands the question:

'Who the fuck are you?'

CHAPTER TWENTY-THREE

'Feliks Rainys,' Weiss reads from the guy's driver's license. Feliks looks a little different in the picture: his hair is shorter, he smiles with a mouthful of various teeth. He isn't smiling now.

Weiss has him sitting at the card table in the basement, one wrist handcuffed to a folding chair. A half-ass job, but Feliks hasn't put up much of a fight. The bare lightbulb overhead shines on the top of his blond head, shadows his eyes. Blood has dried brown on his skin from just below his nose and streaked across his cheek.

Weiss stands on the other side of the table, the Glock still trained on Feliks' chest. 'I can tell you from experience,' he says, 'that the nine-one-one response time in this neighborhood is practically record-setting. I can also tell you that I saw the next-door neighbor dialing when I dragged you in here. So I'm guessing you have about two minutes to explain yourself.'

He gets no answer.

Weiss throws the ID on the table next to Feliks' wallet, walks around to Feliks' side. 'Why are you trying to kill me?'

'I would be foolish to kill a cop.'

'But it's not foolish to dump shit in his yard, or blow out his window with a fucking shotgun, or try to set his house on fire?'

'Not if those things had been effective.'

The Glock steady in his right hand, Weiss palms it when he hits Feliks broadside across the face. The Glock's steel magazine release button slices Feliks' skin; blood spurts out of his nose, the previous wound reopening.

'There are two ways we can do this and that's one of them,' Weiss says. 'The other way is for you to talk. I know you, from the Skylark. How the hell do you know me?'

Feliks wipes the blood from his nose with his free left hand, licks some from his lips. 'This is not smart.'

Weiss slams the Glock down on the table so hard the legs wobble. 'You just tried to blow up my house; I don't think you're clear on the definition.' Both hands on the table, he leans over: 'Now answer me: why are you here?'

Upstairs, the anticipated authorities pound at the front door.

'You better start talking,' Weiss says, 'or I'll march you up there and hand you over.'

Feliks looks up at him. 'I am not the one with something to hide.'

'You think I'm hiding something?'

'I worked for Mr Ipolitas; I know you are.'

Weiss rewinds: Sloane told him about Ipolitas' sole employee. Thirty-something Lithuanian on a work visa. Hadn't turned up yet.

Upstairs, the cops knock more forcefully. Weiss picks up the Glock and aims the gun at Feliks' face. 'Third time,' he says, 'they break the door down.'

Feliks closes his eyes. His hard, frustrated face reminds Weiss of Ambrozas. Then one corner of his mouth lifts, exposing a few teeth when he says, 'I will speak to you, but if I am found out, I am as good as dead.'

'Should have thought of that before you fucked with me.' Weiss tucks the Glock in the back of his waistband. 'Sit tight.'

At the door, Weiss takes a second to catch his breath, knowing confidence will be key.

'What took you so long?' he says to the two uniforms when he opens the door.

'Evening,' Officer Chang says. Weiss knows him from the range; he's an excellent shot. Very concerned with accuracy. And, according to Fiore, very much in possession of a number of illegally modified firearms. Weiss makes a mental note.

'I don't think I know your partner.' Weiss looks around Chang at the taller, skinnier, greener cop in his shadow.

'Swigart,' Swigart says, a casual salute.

'He's been around longer than you,' Chang says, setting parameters.

'That's not saying much,' Weiss says, testing them.

'What's the trouble, Weiss?' Chang thumbs the lever of the pen in his hand: click-click, click-click.

'The neighbors called.' Weiss knows denial won't do him any good.

'Said there was a bomb blast,' Chang says, shifting almost imperceptibly to the balls of his feet. 'More than one bomb blast.' His stance is wide, unmovable, in-your-face. Click-click.

'Not a bomb, exactly,' Weiss says, certain to keep his own footing. 'More like an unsuccessful experiment.'

'Testing what?'

'Combustibility.'

'Of what?'

'Didn't you get a look on your way up the walk?' Weiss hadn't cleaned up the second bottle and he doesn't want to get caught in a lie over details.

Chang raises a thin eyebrow. 'Who was here with you?'

'Jed Pagorski.' Everyone knows Jed; Chang will find his part in the story plausible.

'I'd like to speak to him.'

'He left already.'

'A neighbor says you two were fighting. Says you dragged him across the lawn, in through this doorway.'

'We were just messing around,' Weiss says. 'And I didn't drag him anywhere – you kidding me? You think I could drag that fatass up these steps?' Behind Chang, a grin hits Swigart's mouth before he can stop it. He must know Jed, too.

'Where did Pagorski go?' Chang asks.

'Home.'

'When?'

'Ten minutes ago.'

'Was he wearing a wig?' Chang's question out of left field, to throw Weiss.

Weiss keeps his expression as even as he can. He's got to be careful not to find the questions too preposterous, and he can't make his answers argumentative.

Click-click, click-click.

Weiss looks over Chang's other shoulder, across the street, and says, voice reasonable, 'Let me guess: it was the dad who called. The one with the stork. No one like a new parent to blow things out of proportion.'

'It wasn't the guy across the street,' Chang says, 'and we're not talking about proportion here. We're talking about perception. Whoever was here had blond hair. Lots of it.'

Weiss resists the urge to cross his arms over his chest. He feels the Glock against the skin of his back. 'What if I said that Jed's been cross-dressing since he discovered his wife's shoe collection?'

'I'd believe you,' from Swigart.

Chang is the one to cross his arms, pissed because the rookies aren't taking this seriously. 'You made a mess. Why should I cover for you or your nitwit friend?'

'No law against being a nitwit. If I'm not mistaken, though, Chicago does have the most restrictive gun-control law in the country.' Weiss uses his thumb and index finger, mimes a gun, clicks his tongue. Then he says, 'How about if I clean up my mess and we promise to keep each other's little secrets?'

From under Chang's arm: a muffled click-click.

'Chang?' Weiss asks. 'You want to come in, search the place?'

Chang sticks his pen in his shirt pocket. 'We got better things to do.' He jerks his chin at Swigart; Swigart leads the way down the steps.

Downstairs, Weiss throws Feliks a towel from the laundry to clean up his face. His left eye is nearly swollen shut and it's bleeding at the bone where the gun cut him. Blood has pooled on the cement floor directly under his hanging head.

Weiss unfolds another chair, puts the Glock on the card table, and sits across from Feliks. 'Let's hear it. From the beginning, from the moment you got off the boat.'

Feliks uses his free hand to press the towel to his nose, then around his eye. 'I came here to work.'

'For Ipolitas.'

'Yes. I am a gem specialist.'

'I'm sure we have a real need for those around here, what with the shortage of unnecessary employment in the United States workforce.'

'It is my trade.'

'If you worked for Ipolitas, how come you disappeared when he died? Kind of incriminates you.'

'I was afraid I would be arrested for the murder.'

'Would we have a reason?'

Feliks cringes at the fat lip forming below his nose. 'Would you need one?'

'You have a problem with the American justice system, go home.'

'There is no justice. You picked someone to blame and it is too late.'

'It isn't too late if I find out who really killed Ipolitas, which is what I was trying to do, no thanks to you.'

Feliks throws the towel on the table. 'You arrested the wrong man, and the real killer gets away because no one will speak up.'

Weiss sits forward on his chair and speaks slowly: 'We went after Ambrozas because we had a confidential informant who said he had a beef with Ipolitas. When we found Ambrozas, he had unregistered guns in his possession, which made him a murder suspect. Since no one else has come forward with evidence, or a confession, it's up to forensics, and then the court, to decide. If Ambrozas is found innocent, he'll walk.' He's echoing Jed's words now, feeling more confident about them.

Feliks removes the towel from the corner of his mouth. 'The day you arrested Jurgis, I told Fiore that we were meeting at the Skylark.'

Weiss had assumed Shitfer was the snitch, but Fiore never gave a name. 'You're the one who set up Ambrozas? You're Fiore's CI?'

'No.' Feliks crosses his arms, hugs himself protectively. 'Jurgis is my cousin. I am your confidential informant.'

Weiss studies Feliks' face, his likeness to Ambrozas even more apparent. 'You've been harassing me because you want me to help your cousin?' And all this time Weiss thought Fiore was the one pulling his chain. He can't believe he had it backward.

But, Weiss thinks: 'It doesn't make sense. Why would you tell Fiore anything about Ambrozas?'

'I am sure you are aware of his influence.'

Weiss stands up and tucks the Glock in his front waistband. He feels the cold steel of the handle against his abdomen and realizes he's sweating. He turns, walks away, to take a minute to think.

'I have no evidence and I have no confession,' Feliks says behind him. '*You* have evidence. *You* should confess.'

Weiss stares at the concrete wall ahead of him. Feels trapped. Feliks must know about Fiore's arrangement with Ipolitas, and he must have known about the bad blood between Ambrozas and Ipolitas. And he probably knows who killed Ipolitas.

According to Fiore, Ambrozas was trying to play Weiss during the interrogation. Is this another attempt to sabotage him? To get him to go against his own? Weiss isn't going to show his hand. He pulls the Glock, walks around behind Feliks, and puts the muzzle to the back of his head. Feliks' cuffed hand curls into a fist.

Weiss says, 'Imagine the next thing you say will be the last.'

Feliks turns his head so the Glock is at his temple. He looks at Weiss with one eye. 'Your system of checks and balances has its flaws.'

Weiss concentrates on the gun. On staying confident. And in control – no matter what Feliks says, or repeats. 'You sound like a fortune cookie.' His voice is emotionless.

Feliks lets out a slow, even breath. 'I heard an

American saying, that the only way two people can keep a secret is for one of them to be dead.'

Weiss pushes the gun against his skull. 'Which one do you want to be?'

'We all have secrets. But I'm not the one who stole from Mr Ipolitas. I am not the one framing my cousin. And alive or dead, I'm not the one you need to worry about.'

Weiss doesn't need to worry about explaining a dead guy in his basement, either. He reholsters the Glock in the back of his pants. He uncuffs Feliks' wrist and grabs him by a fistful of blond hair. Then he yanks Feliks out of the chair, dragging him by his head toward the basement steps. Feliks moves with him, stumbling, a compliant captive.

At the top of the steps Weiss slams Feliks into the wall and feels his own hot breath as he says, 'I want you to get the fuck out of here and never come back. If I catch you near my house, if I see you in my neighborhood, if I even hear your name … if you enter my world again, Feliks, I will kill you.'

Feliks squints against Weiss' grip on his mullet. Through tight lips he says, 'It seems we both quote Fiore.'

'Get out.' Weiss opens the door and pushes Feliks. He staggers out and down the front steps like a losing lightweight leaving the ring.

'Feliks,' Weiss says, 'I'm keeping the Glock. How's that for evidence?'

Weiss watches Feliks walk up the street and disappear into the night. When he's finally certain Feliks is gone, he wipes the sweat from his face and shakes out his nerves. He dead bolts the lock, shuts out the front lights, and decides to have a beer while he thinks on the latest clusterfuck of information.

CHAPTER TWENTY-FOUR

This morning, Weiss regrets the beer. He had one, then another; midway through the third, the only mental headway made was a jumbled plan to find Ipolitas' killer, which wasn't so epiphanous as it was distressing. Soon after, the combination of alcohol and total fatigue forced him into bed. He didn't dream of Terrence Mann, but a dull headache woke him up, and he felt uneasy just the same.

He reads the entire Sunday *Sun-Times* by nine a.m. Okay, the only thing he actually reads is the sports section; he skims over the rest. Seems like every article from the front page on is rife with finger-pointing politics, newspeak, and spin. The war on terror certainly gave everybody something to bitch about.

He reads a few comic strips, one of which might be funny if he agreed with the cartoonist's slant on welfare. He'll bet the guy drawing the pictures never set foot in a shelter, or took neglected children from their homes when their parents used the government checks for crack. He decides Leah's newspaper boyfriend is a hack if he so much as edits the *Times*' want ads.

Weiss reads his horoscope:

ARIES: Money seems to flow through your hands. Think twice before spending it. Right now you are either too cautious or too impulsive; either way is not right. Nor is procrastination. Strive for proper balance and keep to the middle of the road in any arrangements.

He tosses the paper on the kitchen table. He knows he's procrastinating. He wishes the part about the money were true.

The milk in the fridge expired over a week ago, so he argues with himself over a bowl of dry Corn Flakes and a brown-spotted banana.

It was impulsive to agree to help Sloane; now he's cautiously avoiding her. She's called twice this morning, and in last night's voice mail, she said she had some leads on Ipolitas' phone records. He knows he has to help her, because if she gets ahead of him, she could turn around and point the finger. Just like Feliks.

But if the guys find out he's even talking to her, they'll never forgive him. He could steer clear of Sloane, tell the guys about Feliks. Say Feliks knows about the burglary and the guns. Tell them Sloane, er, Detective Pearson is using this case to get ahead; use her like an excuse. Tell them about the hookers. Ask for help – convince them it's in everyone's best interest to find out who really killed Ipolitas.

That's what he wanted in the first place, isn't it? Before he thought Fiore had turned against him. Before he arrested Ambrozas; before he wrote a false report. As soon as he saw Ipolitas' body, Weiss wanted the truth.

The truth is, Ipolitas is going to stay dead. Ambrozas is going to stay in jail. And the guys? They will still be cops. Because their truth *is* trust. And Weiss knows if he wants to be a cop, he has to find a way to balance the two.

Weiss' cell rings as he's toweling off from a shower: Sloane again. Time to get in the middle of the road, or whatever his horoscope said.

'Didn't you get my message last night?' she asks. The insistence in her voice turns him on.

'Sorry. I was up late.' He won't tell her why.

'Did you have any luck with those phone numbers?'

'Nope.' Leaving out the fact he only called a half-dozen of them.

'Well, get this,' she says. 'I found a lead.'

'That's great.' Not exactly what the expression looking back at Weiss in the bathroom mirror wants to say.

'Name's Ieva Ap ... Apanas ... zev ... sevic – I can't pronounce it. She's seventeen, staying with her uncle Jonas something-or-the-other. His number was in Ipolitas' records. He's a citizen; Ieva's here on a visitor's visa. "Summer fun," Jonas called it. Like he has a clue. I tried to question Ieva but she doesn't speak a lick, so I asked Jonas to translate. I could tell she was playing good girl with him.' Sloane's words come fast, though Weiss tries to think ahead, play out the possible endings.

'So I start talking to Uncle Jonas about prostitution. Drugs. A few gory details. I tell him someone in the community turned up dead. I say "murder." I say I'm sympathetic to vulnerable young ladies in the big city. And his eyes are getting wider, and Ieva's watching him, and her eyes are getting wider, too – she doesn't understand me. She thinks she's in deep. Then he looks over at her, a world's worth of disappointment on his face, and the next thing I know, I've got the name of everybody she's been with since she stepped off the plane.'

'Nice.' Not so nice for Weiss' timeline. He didn't expect Sloane to get ahead of him so fast.

'Any names we know?' he asks.

'Two of the names match the ones on the airline tickets we found at Ipolitas' place. And the kicker? Ieva promises there's nothing illegal going on. She said her friends are "friendly" with the police.'

'You know where to find them?' Weiss hopes not.

'Uncle Jonas told me Ieva's been hanging around this Polish joint – a restaurant called the Red Apple. Doesn't sound like your typical hooker hangout, but I'm going to go over there, see what the draw is.'

'I'll meet you. Can you wait until noon?'

'What, you going to church?' Sarcastic. Her upper hand showing.

'Something like that.' More like confession.

'Say a prayer for whoever killed Ipolitas, because we're gonna catch him.'

Weiss hangs up thinking: *Fuck the middle of the road.* He's got to talk to Fiore.

*

The drive on Addison isn't bad though Weiss will have to take a different route back since all the eastbound traffic is jammed en route to the 1:20 game at Wrigley. A cool breeze off the lake counters the heat, and it'll probably keep long fly balls in the park. *Great day for a game*, Weiss thinks, though tickets are impossible to get this close to the playoffs. He idly wonders how Ambrozas got his.

He won't speculate; so far, all his assumptions have been his mistakes. Best Weiss can do is tell Fiore everything he knows and hope he won't look the other way.

A few blocks past the expressway, Weiss feels like he's driving back in time. The houses are small and dainty and square-framed like they're made of gingerbread. A border of Technicolor-green grass surrounds each one, instead of alleys or other buildings. Every place looks like a home that belongs to a proud owner. There isn't any old money and there isn't any easy money in this part of town. This is what they should mean at the mayor's office when they call Chicago 'the city that works.'

Weiss turns right on Laramie and right again on Roscoe, parks curbside. He doesn't need Fiore's address because he remembers the house: a tan one-and-a-half story A-frame with concrete steps. The way the house was built, it looks like it was constructed around the steps. Either that or the architect was mathematically challenged, because the main floor sits five feet above ground level, the basement is partially visible, and the A-frame top is too slight to be anything but an aesthetic afterthought.

Weiss gets out of the Cavalier, marches across the sidewalk and up the concrete steps. He has no idea what he's going to say, but he's certain his presence here will be enough to start a conversation.

The front door is wood-framed glass, like a big window with handles. A cream-colored shade is drawn three-quarters of the way down, so all that's visible inside on the linoleum is a dirty floor mat and a pair of Fiore's work boots.

As Weiss raises his arm to ring the doorbell, a little white dog with sleep caked in the corners of its eyes appears on the floor mat, yapping in shrill fits like it's being choked. Weiss didn't figure Fiore for a dog person let alone a lapdog person. He finds himself grinning.

Thinking there's a good chance the dog yaps at its own reflection and no one will bother to come to the door, Weiss rings the bell.

He hears 'Just a minute' or something similar from a woman somewhere in the house. The dog stares up at him, no inquisitive tilt of the head, no twitch of the nose; it just stares, as if to say *nobody invited you*.

Weiss steps back from the door, rests a hand on the cast-iron railing along the porch. He doesn't want to appear confrontational, and he doesn't want to get caught looking in the door's window. He watches a daddy longlegs make its way along the siding: on only seven legs it navigates an area where the paint is peeling. On the other side of the porch, a red-orange dog toy is chewed beyond recognition. Maybe it was a hot dog. The shades are pulled closed in the rest of the windows.

Weiss wonders if he imagined the woman's voice. He doesn't want to ring the bell again. He doesn't particularly want to knock, either. Fiore's probably doing this on purpose, to make him sweat.

He raps on the glass. 'Hello?'

This time he definitely hears 'I'm coming.' Same voice.

The dog growls, though its guttural tone sounds more like a whimper. Kind of puts Weiss at ease, just knowing Fiore owns a puny little fluff dog.

That's why he's smiling when the door opens.

'Can I help you?' asks a woman who must be Josephine: Fiore's surprisingly striking, considerably skinny, seemingly hungover wife.

'Mrs Fiore? I'm Ray Weiss.'

Her hazel eyes warm to his name. She keeps one hand on the door frame when she extends the other. 'Ray. We finally meet.'

'I'm looking for Jack.'

Her grip is chilly. 'I expect him back soon. Would you like to come in?' Her smile wanting. 'I have coffee.'

'That'd be great.' Nothing wrong with getting into the wife's good graces.

'Don't mind Captain,' she says, a glance at the dog. 'He's not as fierce as he thinks he is.' She turns, and after a crooked step, leads Weiss inside. Captain stays behind to stand guard.

Josephine uses the hallway walls for balance against her palms, left, then right, then left, like she's making her way toward the cockpit on a bumpy flight. She seems to be favoring her right leg.

'Are you okay?' Weiss asks, because not to would make it awkward that he didn't.

'I'm fine, thanks. Better than yesterday.'

Weiss isn't sure if he's supposed to know what that means so he says, 'Did you hurt yourself?'

'I'm an upright mess,' she says.

As he follows her, Weiss smells a hint of mold that instantly reminds him of his parents' basement. Must be the one-half story, gives the whole place an air like it's stuck in the mud.

They reach the kitchen, a golden-yellow room with dark wood-paneled cabinetry. Fiore obviously doesn't spend his checks on renovations. No wonder he never invites anyone over.

One hand on the brown ceramic sink, Josephine holds herself steady as she retrieves a coffee cup from a countertop mug tree and pours Weiss coffee. 'Have a seat,' she says.

Weiss chooses a cushioned chair that looks like it was meant for the patio, its busy floral pattern faded by the sun.

Josephine moves to the round kitchen table, her cup already there, and places Weiss' coffee in front of him. She rolls a wheeled stool out from under the table that sits her nearly waist-high across from Weiss.

'Sorry, we're out of half-and-half,' she says, no mention of sugar.

Weiss takes his coffee cup. 'Thank you.'

'Jack went to the pharmacy over an hour ago. You know him – he gets sidetracked.'

'Are we talking about the same Jack? The same guy who's so on-point at work he won't even let me play the radio in the squad – the one who runs plates at Stop signs?' Weiss means to keep the conversation light, but Josephine seems too tired to play along.

'I suppose we see different sides of him.' She fingers a strand of her coarse blond hair, her original color fighting gray. Weiss notices her wedding ring, a simple gold band – no engagement ring. She grips her coffee mug with her other hand like it's keeping her from falling off the stool. No rings.

'Did you have a nice anniversary?' he asks.

'That's an odd question. Our anniversary was in May.'

'Oh, I must be mixed up,' Weiss says, unable to look at her. 'Maybe – I think it was Gary Anzalone who mentioned his.'

'I don't even remember what we did to celebrate. Isn't that terrible? Of course, things haven't exactly been normal around here these past months.' Said like Weiss has a clue what she's referring to, which he doesn't. But he does know she isn't wearing the god damn ring he stole for her, and he wonders who is.

'Jack seems like he's been a little stressed lately,' he says, hoping she'll keep talking.

'Right,' she says, sarcasm behind it. 'Because I'm the one who needs help, and he's the one getting it.'

'Help, you mean, professional help?' He forgets he's supposed to know what she's talking about.

'Yeah, "professional."' Looks like the word leaves a taste in her mouth. 'From God knows where, at all hours.'

Weiss uses a long sip of coffee to evaluate her response. Only professionals available God knows where at all hours are emergency medics, bartenders, and prostitutes.

'Will you do me a favor,' she asks, 'and hand me my purse?' She points to the floor behind him, where a stiff black leather handbag sits, its handles upright.

When Weiss picks up the bag he gets a whiff of perfume that instantly registers: the angelic scent from Victoria's Secret. He remembers the blond who was with Ambrozas. She smelled just like this.

'You know,' Josephine says, taking the bag, 'Jack thinks the world of you.'

'He has an interesting way of showing it.'

'He says you're just like he was when he started out.' She opens the bag, rummages through its contents. 'Smart as a whip, problem with authority.'

'I don't think I'm very smart these days.'

'Don't underestimate yourself. Jack doesn't.' Both hands in her purse, she uncaps a pill bottle, taps a few into her palm, recaps the bottle, and takes the pills. No chaser.

'Let me tell you something.' She swivels the stool, puts the purse aside, and swivels back. 'Jack and I were newlyweds when he first got on the job. It was so many years ago. There are times, maybe only moments now, when I see the old fire in his eyes. Like I see in yours. But time ruins us. All of us. However it pleases. And in our own ways, we try to cling to what we remember was good. I remember when my husband and I were in love. That's what I cling to.'

She stands up, as steady on her feet as she has been, and puts her coffee cup in the sink. 'I'm sorry, but I'm feeling very tired. Maybe whatever you wanted to talk to Jack about can wait? He gets sidetracked.' She leans against the sink, her hazel eyes heavy.

'Of course, Mrs Fiore. Thanks for the coffee.'

'You don't mind letting yourself out?'

'As long as Captain doesn't.'

'I'll tell Jack you came by.' She extends her hand again; this time Weiss squeezes it, his smile consolatory.

Outside, Weiss skips down the concrete steps and across the sidewalk and he's starting up the Cavalier in no time flat. He drives off, knowing there's no way he can have a heart-to-heart with Fiore when the guy isn't even telling his wife the truth.

CHAPTER TWENTY-FIVE

Weiss finds a parking spot across from the Red Apple. Sloane is supposed to meet him in a half hour. He untucks his shirt to conceal the .45 in his waistband, puts his cash in his front pocket, and stows his wallet in the glove compartment. He's going to see what he can turn up before Sloane comes in with her badge.

The marquee that hangs over the entrance reads CZERWONE JABLUSZKO, a rudimentary graphic of a red apple below it for clarification. Homemade photo-copied posters are tacked up in the windows and on the entryway walls advertising a Polish Harvest Festival, a folk dance troupe, Wednesday night music at a club called Jedynka.

Inside, the wooden booths are packed with families, the tables piling up with half-eaten plates of beets, sauerkraut, chicken bones, Jell-O. The buffet separates the restaurant from the bar, stretching to the back of the room, the food displayed under orange heat lamps. Women in apple-red aprons excuse themselves around the patrons to refill the troughs of egg salad, pierogis, pork shanks. A waitress flutters from table to table, asking simply, 'Soup?'

Weiss passes through the restaurant and around the

buffet to the bar, where two men prefer to drink lunch. He grabs a stool with a view of the front door, sizes up the room. The bartender is about Weiss' age, sideburns all the way to his thin neck, a Pole's pallor, an absence of enthusiasm. Probably employed through some family connection. The two men facing Weiss on the other side of the square bar are both gray and gray-haired. One watches the bartender fix a drink like he's pouring money; the other stares into his beer like he's drinking the last of his paycheck.

The bartender raises his eyebrows at Weiss as though anyone who skips the buffet has a clear idea about what he wants.

Weiss says, 'An Okocim, please.' Thanks to Jed, he has an appropriate handle on the Polish culture when it comes to beer drinking.

The WGN pregame show is broadcasting on a TV over the bar. None of the men seem interested. The bartender puts a bottle of beer in front of Weiss. He takes a sip then says, to all of them: 'You hear about that guy that got killed up the street? The jeweler?'

'What about him?' The bartender, instantly suspicious.

Weiss raises his beer, announces: 'I'm gonna toast to him. To Ipolitas. *Na Zdrowie*.' Just like Jed says it.

The gray men raise their glasses and say '*Na Zdrowie*' in unison.

'You a friend of his?' from the bartender.

'No,' Weiss says. 'Just heard he was an honest working man, surprised a thief. It's a shame.'

The man drinking his paycheck says, 'I heard he was killed because of a woman.'

The man to his left: 'It was no woman.' His accent thick. 'It was business gone bad. This is what happens when we try to be American. We fight our own—'

'It's not even noon, Tom,' the bartender says, 'spare us the speech.' He turns to Weiss. 'I heard the guy was in deep with the cops.'

'*Pierdolony policiji*,' Tom says.

Thanks to Jed, Weiss has a handle on Polish insults, too. He takes a long drink of beer.

A few minutes later, Weiss sees Sloane show up at the cashier stand and flash her badge. He hasn't exactly made new friends here, but he doesn't want his cover blown either, so he puts a five next to his beer and asks the bartender, 'Bathroom?'

The bartender points to a doorway at the back. 'Through there.'

Weiss slides off his stool and out of Sloane's sight-line.

Through the doorway, he follows a hall that crosses a busy service area. Weiss waits for a waitress to get a set of rolled silverware from a bin. She does a spin-move to avoid another girl who pushes her way out the swinging kitchen door with a platter full of potato pancakes.

'*Przepraszam*, Elzbieta.'

'*Tak*, Lidia.'

Weiss wishes he knew more than the Polish words Jed taught him.

When the kitchen door swings shut and the waitresses are gone, Weiss checks out the cubicle-like area next to the napkin bin. On one side, handwritten notices about various work procedures are posted in English and Polish. On the wall facing Weiss there's a calendar titled *Sierpnia* with dates the same as August. On the other side, next to a telephone, a sheet of yellow paper is thumbtacked to the wall. It lists Elzbieta, Lidia, and ten other names: it's the week's employee schedule. Ta-da.

'Help you?' says a waitress who stops outside the kitchen holding an armful of empty plates to the side of her swollen, pregnant belly.

Weiss points to the bathroom. 'Got it. Thanks.'

As soon as she's in the kitchen Weiss tears the schedule off the wall, folds it up and stuffs it in his shirt pocket. He decides against stopping to take a leak and leaves through the convenient back entrance.

Ten minutes later, Weiss is sitting in his car watching Sloane exit the Red Apple. Her oversized handbag hangs open from her shoulder. Weiss honks and waves, neither of which brings a smile to her face. She comes across the street without yielding to traffic; in fact, she slows an oncoming car to a stop with one hell of a sideways glance.

Weiss rolls down his window. 'You don't like buffets?'

'No.'

'I was in there earlier. I had a feeling we wouldn't have much luck.'

She shifts the briefcase to her other shoulder. 'The hostess said there was no manager. The bartender said there was no hostess. Both of them said they didn't recognize any of the names on our list.'

'They weren't lying.' Weiss flashes the schedule. 'Get in.'

Sloane walks around the front of the car. She's wearing slim black pants and a slate-blue sleeveless V-neck – no jacket. Her shoulders are tight, her arms long. And again, her ass ...

She opens the passenger door, tosses her handbag on the floor and gets in, reaching for Weiss' paper. 'What is it?'

'Employee schedule.'

'You took it?'

'I did. And I checked the names against the passport list. None of them match.'

Sloane looks over the schedule; Weiss looks at her. Her nails are repainted, a pearly pink color, like her lips. Her skin is darker, like she's been in the sun. And she's wearing some kind of lavender-scented lotion. Or perfume. He leans toward her, smelling ... is it her hair?

She stops him with a look. Her eyes match her shirt. She says, 'Ona.'

'Huh?'

'Ona.' She hands Weiss the schedule, sits forward, digs through her handbag.

'Ona?'

'I remember the name.' She takes out a file, scans pages.

Weiss finds the name Ona three-quarters of the way down on the schedule: she works Sundays and Thursdays 10–4, Wednesdays and Fridays 4–10.

'Not from the passports ...' Sloane says. Her black bra strap peeks out from her shirt.

Weiss puts the schedule in his lap and both hands on the steering wheel.

'Not from the names Ieva gave ...' She pulls another file from the bag. Her bra strap is off her shoulder now, hanging on her arm.

Weiss drums his fingers on the wheel.

'Damn it, not from the phone numbers, either.' She closes the second file and her bottom lip fights a pout.

'Hold on.' Weiss resists the urge to reach for her hand. 'Let's rethink this. We have other leads. Maybe we should take a look at the list I made of the escorts' phone numbers.'

Sloane stares forward. She isn't picking up his vibe. She might not even be listening.

'Sloane? I could help you go through Ipolitas' phone records again—'

She holds up her index finger, effectively shutting him up. Then she reaches for a third file in the bag. She finds the page right away.

'Ona Zujaite. She worked at Ipolitas' store for a couple weeks last month. She's the one with the nice handwriting. Remember? The missing Rolex, the diamond earrings, the garnets? She handled those invoices. She might have walked off with the stuff.'

'Think it's the same person?'

Sloane snatches the schedule from his lap and he feels exposed.

She says, 'I think Red Apple Ona gets off work at four o'clock, and we're going to be here to find out.'

Weiss looks at his watch: they have three hours and

change to wait. His appetite is evident, having been jump-started by the coffee and teased by the beer. 'I guess I can't interest you in a buffet, but how about lunch?'

Lunch turns out to be a trip through the drive-thru. No matter that they don't have any idea what Ona looks like, and forget that she is scheduled at the restaurant until four; Sloane doesn't want to risk leaving for a decent meal if the not-so-decent Ona is in the vicinity. Weiss doesn't get the logic, but he doesn't really care about lunch, either. The front seat is as close as he'll get Sloane to the backseat no matter where he takes her to eat today.

He parks the Cavalier just south of the Red Apple so they can monitor the front entrance. He turns on the radio so he doesn't have to make small talk as he plows through a nine-piece order of McNuggets and some fries. He washes the grease down with a Coke, finishing during the last verse of Tom Petty's 'Free Fallin'.'

'There's a parking lot in back,' he says, wiping his hands with a paper napkin. 'One way in and out. You think we should pull in and wait there?'

'According to my information, Ona doesn't drive,' Sloane says. 'Or at least she doesn't have a license. I'm banking on the bus stop up the street.'

Weiss balls up his McBag. 'I'll go back to the lot, get all the plates just in case.'

'Good thinking.' Sloane sips at her small strawberry shake, the only thing she ordered.

Weiss takes his Coke from the drink holder. 'You okay with the windows down?'

Sloane nods. 'Can I drive?' She points to the radio. 'Go ahead.'

Weiss gets out and tosses his trash in a barrel on the sidewalk, wondering if he'll think of Fiore heaving a can through Ipolitas' window every time he throws something away.

There are six cars in the back lot, not counting a minivan crammed with a buffet-stuffed family that's parked by the door waiting for an auntie to finish in the bathroom.

Weiss writes the make, model, and license plate number of each of the cars on the back of the Red Apple schedule, figuring he won't be returning it. He doesn't think taking the plates will do any good, seeing as how Milwaukee Avenue is probably the employees' suggested parking lot, but it was as good an excuse as any to get out of the car. It's not that Sloane makes him uncomfortable. That's not the word for it. Distracted, he thinks; she distracts him.

On his way back to the Cavalier, Weiss decides he'll ask to see Sloane's files. He doesn't know anything about Ipolitas' death: the cause, the official time, the forensic details. Never occurred to him to find out the specifics, maybe because he was busy trying to cover up some of them.

In the car, Sloane chews on a pen while she listens to someone on the other end of her cell phone. Weiss gets in the car, pretends he isn't interested.

'That's great.' Sloane's tone is eager, borderline flirtatious, as it had been earlier over the phone with Weiss. 'I promise I'll return the favor,' she says, looks over at him, connects with a smile. 'Okay. Thanks.' She flips the phone shut like it's an accomplishment.

'The other day you were complaining about the guys at work,' Weiss says, 'but I get the feeling being a good-looking chick has its advantages.'

'I know a guy at Cole Firearms out in Palatine. He's friendly with a lot of the retailers in the area and he's helping me trace the guns we got from Ambrozas.'

'I thought the guns were untraceable.' Trying to sound indifferent.

'Not necessarily. The lab's using acid to try to raise the serial numbers on two or three they think they can salvage. If they get anything, I'm going to meet my guy from Cole for lunch tomorrow.'

Tomorrow is coming too quickly for Weiss. 'What the fuck are we sitting here for if you're going to work that angle?' His profanity is uncalled for; a product of guilt. He cracks his knuckles.

'I'm trying to solve the case, Ray, not make friends.' She looks at him. 'Or enemies.'

'And you say I'm going to fuck you over.' His face feels hot.

'I'm not sure why you're upset.'

'This is a waste of time.' He gets out of the car, slams the door—

'Where are you going?'

'To find Ona.'

On his way back to the Red Apple, he glances over his shoulder, making sure Sloane stays put.

'Back again,' the bartender says to Weiss. The gray men are still there; so is Weiss' half-empty Okocim.

He puts a twenty on the bar and pulls up the stool he sat in earlier. 'Give me another beer. And a shot of whatever it takes, all around.'

'Whatever it takes?' the bartender asks.

'To let me sit here in peace.'

The bartender pours four shots of vodka and ceremoniously distributes the glasses. Weiss slugs his, no waiting for a toast.

How in the hell is he going to get out of this? Jed won't cooperate; Fiore is full of shit. Ambrozas won't talk, but Feliks just might, if he turns up again. The only person who seems interested in the case is a woman Weiss would like to fuck, maybe more than fuck, and he never will because she's about to bring the hammer down on all of them. And Weiss doesn't even know what he's lying about anymore.

WGN comes back from a commercial break and the Cubs are losing 4–1 in the fifth inning. Another thing to piss him off. He takes a drink of beer.

Maybe he should just ask the bartender about Ona, flat out. She's the only one he knows of who can shift the focus back to who killed Ipolitas, instead of who didn't.

The bartender serves Weiss another shot of vodka. 'On the house.' Weiss doesn't say more than 'thanks.' He has to play this right.

He shuts his eyes, relies on his other senses. On TV, Bob Brenly talks about the Cubs' chances against St. Louis in their September series. Across the bar, one of the gray men grumbles something to the other.

Back in the kitchen, the business of dishes. And on the other side of the place, in the restaurant, conversations overlap. A child begs, '*prosze*,' his mother says, '*nie*.' Glasses clink. A waitress asks, 'Soup?'

Of course. Weiss opens his eyes, asks his bar mates: 'How's the buffet?'

'Dumplings are good,' says one.

'Beef stew.' The other.

'Skip the mostacholli,' says the bartender.

'Stuffed cabbage.' The other again.

'Think I'll check it out.' Weiss takes his beer and gets up.

He crosses into the restaurant, sits at an empty wooden booth directly in front of the buffet, and waits for service. It only takes a minute before Lidia, the waitress with the silverware, appears and asks, 'Soup?'

'Did you make it?'

A confused look from Lidia; a communication gap.

'Did you cook the soup yourself?'

'Oh … no.' A smile, embarrassed, but not by her yellow teeth.

'Did Ona make it?'

'Ona? No, no.'

'Then I don't want any. Thanks.'

Weiss sits back and enjoys the rest of his beer. It only takes a minute before Lidia drags Ona around the corner from the kitchen, and points Weiss out to the pregnant waitress.

When Weiss gets back in the Cavalier, Sloane has picked off nearly all her pearly pink nail polish. And apparently, she's also prepared a speech.

'Ray, I'm sorry. I am so grateful for your help, really I am. I didn't mean to send mixed signals – I didn't mean to send any signals. It's just that I'm on the brink here. With my career, with everything. And meeting you hasn't made things any easier.'

'Wait a minute; you asked me for help.'

'I know. I wish I hadn't.'

'You're telling me.' If she had any idea.

'I think we're on the same page here so I'm not going to make an ass out of myself. I'll just ask: can we put this aside? Just until the case plays out.'

'I'd rather put the case aside, see how this plays out,' the alcohol getting a word in.

She smiles at him, a smile that cuts in line to break his heart.

'Okay,' he says.

And that's that conversation.

'Ona is the pregnant one,' Weiss says. 'She'll be out soon.'

On the radio: '*Bobby Skafish here it's a mellow Sunday afternoon a good time for a little* Soma *from the Pumpkins on XRT Chicago.*' The deejay's words skim the airwaves without punctuation.

The Cavalier doesn't have the most impressive sound system so Sloane turns up the volume. The song starts out real soft, a dreamy guitar, then a delicate bass. Sloane's head sways slightly with the light strum of the guitar and when the vocals start the song amplifies and the music seems like it's going straight to her core and coming back out in slow, satisfied breaths.

She doesn't have to say, 'I love this song.'

Weiss loves this song, too, though the memories it rouses work against the current situation. The guitar lulls and builds and he envisions Irene, the Cuban girl who was not a girl and not his first, but she was his first woman. Irene, pronounced in Spanish like his own name, each *E* an *A*: *E-ray-nay*. Her rich black hair, curves all the way around. He understood most of what she said by inflection; the actual words unimportant, like the rest of the world to both of them that night. And this song – loud as a live band on the stereo in her empty summer apartment – Irene, singing the words: 'I'm all by myself … as I've always felt …' no idea what they meant, or what they meant to him. Her feelings, like her stay, admittedly temporary; but she loved him that night.

In the morning, blankets on the floor, cool air in through the window, he slipped away, and thought it impossible that the memory would ever be more sweet than the experience.

'Is that her?' Sloane startles Weiss out of near sleep.

And Ona comes out of the Red Apple.

CHAPTER TWENTY-SIX

'Ona Zujaite?' Sloane asks during her approach, badge held in front of her with a stiff arm. Weiss hangs back, leaning on the hood of his car. He waves, an apology.

Ona assumes a tolerable stance favoring one hip, holding her purse in one hand and her belly with the other. 'What is the trouble?'

'We need to ask you a few questions. Concerning Petras Ipolitas.'

'I have nothing to say.'

'Let us give you a ride home.'

'No thank you.'

'Okay,' Sloane says, 'then we'll meet you there. We'll bring a search warrant to look for the jewelry that's missing from his service inventory.'

Ona looks down at her belly, another thing she lacks the ability to lie about. She takes her time waddling to the Cavalier.

Weiss helps Ona buckle into the backseat. She smells both straight-from-the-oven sweet and kitchen-grime sour and she probably can't wash either out of her uniform, or off her skin. Up close, she is older than Weiss thought. The pregnancy softens her features and endorses her natural beauty, but the time lines around her eyes and lips are deep, like a person who spent a good part of life smoking cigarettes or scowling or both.

Sloane grabs her bag and gets in back with Ona, which Weiss is actually happy about, because it gives him a mirror's-eye view of them both and he won't have to temper his reactions.

When he starts the engine a guitar solo that sounds like Buddy Guy's blasts from the speakers, the volume still cranked. Weiss hits the power switch quick, feeling both sets of eyes on the back of his head.

'Where to?' he asks Ona.

'Rockwell Street. On this side of Peterson.'

Weiss waits for traffic, pulls out heading northwest to Pulaski Road.

'Wait a minute,' Sloane says. Weiss doesn't think she was speaking literally, but there's no one behind him, so he steps on the brakes.

'Ona, your last listed address was on the southside. Twenty-seventh Street – an apartment. I have it in my files—'

'I moved.'

'Do you have any identification that lists your current information?'

A car turns onto Milwaukee behind them so Weiss hits the gas, his eyes shifting between the road and the rearview mirror. It's quiet in the backseat so he figures Ona is going through her purse.

'Is that your passport?' Sloane must have taken it right out of Ona's hands, because she's holding it when Weiss looks. 'This says Ona Lukiene. You changed your name, too?'

'I got married.'

'When?'

'July the twenty-ninth.'

'Four days after your stint at the jewelry store.' Sloane points to the passport. 'And, look here: six days before you had your American passport issued.'

'I wanted it to be current so I can go to Lithuania after the baby is born.'

'Right. A brand-new bouncy U.S. citizen.'

'Don't talk to me that way, I am also a citizen.'

'Hardly.'

'Tell us about your relationship with Mr Ipolitas,' Weiss says over his shoulder, hoping to redirect the heat.

'Any chance he's the father?' Sloane never knowing when to quit.

And Ona preferring not to answer.

'How'd you meet Ipolitas?' Weiss rephrases.

'A man called Feliks Rainys. They worked together.'

Weiss skids the Cavalier to a stop even though the light at Pulaski is barely yellow. He hopes Sloane didn't connect the hard brakes to Ona's statement. He wipes the sweat on his upper lip, decides to shut up and drive.

'How do you know this guy Rainys?' Sloane asks, her focus on Ona.

'We knew each other in Vilnius.'

'So you're friends; you came here, he hooked you up with a job.'

Ona hesitates, catches Weiss' eye in the mirror, nods.

'Do you know where Rainys is now?' Sloane asks.

'I don't speak with him since I am married.'

'Or is it because he knows you stole from the boss?'

'I did not steal. Ipolitas knew I had the jewelry.'

'Oh really.' Not a question.

'I was not going to keep it. I was holding it, for insurance, because he owed my husband money.'

Weiss and Sloane find each other in the rearview mirror. Sloane mouths the word *motive*.

'What's your husband's name?' Sloane asks.

'He had no part in this,' Ona says.

'It was his money.'

'And now he will never have it.'

Weiss adjusts the mirror to watch Ona. She rubs her belly, soothing the baby like it's offended by all this.

'You aren't exactly wowing us with your attitude,' Sloane says.

'I have done nothing wrong.'

'Theft and bribery are legal where you come from?'

'I am changed. I have honest work. And we are having a baby.'

'Babies are born every day in prison.'

Sloane hits a nerve. Ona's breathing gets short, and she clutches her belly. 'I have done nothing wrong,' she says again, near tears, near hyperventilation.

'Maybe you didn't. Maybe it was your husband. What did you say his name is?'

Ona bites her lip, but that doesn't keep the tears in her eyes. Weiss pulls over and stops the car. 'Detective,' he says, 'a minute?'

He gets out; Sloane joins him on the sidewalk. They stand out of earshot, looking back at the car and out over the street like it's some kind of magnificent vista. Pleasant faces, in case Ona's watching; watching, in case Ona's thinking about bolting.

'Why the curbside conference?' Sloane asks.

'You're going to put her into labor.'

'Who cares? She's as good a suspect as any. She's practically confessing for her husband. Can you believe this?'

'Nobody's going to believe it if we have to take her to the hospital because she's been traumatized by a couple off-duty cops.' Weiss remembers his smile. 'We're getting this info off the record and off the clock. Only way it'll help is if it leads to something else.'

'Her husband.'

Weiss turns to Sloane, crosses his arms to appear casual. 'We said we would take her home. Let's make sure she gets there, and she doesn't book the first flight to Vilnius when she does. We'll know where she lives, and then we'll get the grounds to have an official word with him.'

'What if she lies, and we take her to the wrong place?'

'You got the last name from her passport, right? We know the name, we can find him.'

'We're getting so close.' Sloane's fake smile works its way into a grin, enjoying the act.

'All the more reason not to screw it up.'

She sighs. 'Okay. You be the good cop.'

*

Sloane is the quiet one when she gets back in the car next to Ona.

'Ona,' Weiss says, pulling his seat belt across his lap, 'the detective and I apologize for upsetting you. We didn't mean to imply that you or your husband had anything to do with Ipolitas' death. We are just collecting information, and we thought you might be able to help us.'

'His name is Myko,' Ona says.

'What?' Weiss sees the fear in Ona's eyes, and he realizes his curbside talk with Sloane had the wrong effect.

'My husband. His name is Myko.'

'Mee-ko as in Niko?' Sloane asks.

'As in Mykolas. M-y-k-o-l-a-s.' Since she's spelling it out, Weiss figures Sloane is writing it down.

'Please,' she says, 'I will give the jewelry. I did not know what to do when Ipolitas was dead.'

'Do you know who killed him?' asks Sloane.

'No.' Her eyes pleading, terrified.

'It's okay,' Weiss says. 'No reason to get upset. We're taking you home.'

On the phone with dispatch during the drive back to the Red Apple, Sloane is irritated. 'Lukiene.' She spells it out again. Gives the address. 'Okay, run it through LEADS.' Says thanks.

Then says to Weiss, 'They can't find him. No priors, no vehicle registration, no address. I told you she'd lie.'

'We must have missed something. Go over it again.'

Sloane looks at her notes. 'Ona comes to the States. Rainys introduces her to Ipolitas. She works for him for two weeks, steals to get leverage against the money he owes the guy she marries days later, and fails to come forward after Ipolitas is killed.'

'Because of the stolen Rolex, et cetera. Sounds right.'

Sloane chews on her pen, mulling it over. 'Timeline doesn't work. For one thing, you can't just waltz into the States and get married. And, by the looks of her, Ona's been pregnant for at least seven months. Unless her new husband is signing up to care for another man's child, they've been together awhile.'

'She's been living here illegally.'

'And did you hear her comment about "honest" work?'

'Implies what she did before wasn't.'

'Ona says Feliks Rainys introduced her to Ipolitas. Got her a job. She didn't say when. Or what.'

'So maybe she did more than spend a couple weeks polishing gems. Maybe she was polishing—'

'And then she falls in love,' Sloane cuts him off. A terrific grin for his attempt at humor makes it okay.

'Maybe with a "client."'

'Or she gets knocked up and then she falls in love.'

'And she wants out of the "business."'

'Which isn't an option.'

'Unless she gets rid of Ipolitas.'

'Or she gives someone else a reason to do it.'

'Husband,' they say at the same time.

'Still doesn't fly,' Sloane says. 'Why would she go back to work for Ipolitas a few weeks before he was killed? And why would she get in the middle of a dispute between Ipolitas and her husband?'

Sloane rests her forearm on the center console a little too comfortably, a little too close. Weiss shifts his weight away from her, reminding himself he's here for insurance. Same as Ona: to keep in the clear, he's got to make sure whoever did this pays up.

Weiss pulls up outside the Red Apple.

'So, Ray, what should we do now?'

This time, the insistence in Sloane's voice puts up flags instead of possibilities. He needs to be alone, think about this on his own.

'I have plans,' he says.

'Oh.' The disappointed response is too revealing, since she fessed up about her feelings earlier.

'Call me when you hear anything,' Weiss says. 'I want to be there when you talk to Lukiene.'

'Sure.' Sloane doesn't look at him when she gets out of the car.

He'd anticipated offering some smooth parting words, but it's just as well. The way things stand, it's over. Even if they find Mykolas Lukiene tonight, they have to wait until morning for a warrant. And by that time, Ambrozas' case will be in court; Pearson will be in her office, a whole new stack of cases on her desk. And, like Feliks said, no one will speak up, and the real killer will get away, because Weiss will be back at work, his jaw clenched, his mouth firmly shut.

CHAPTER TWENTY-SEVEN

Though admittedly not in his best interest, Weiss finds himself outside Leah's building. It took him all of two minutes to realize he should have stayed with Sloane to rehash the case, maybe work around to that conversation about their feelings again. But without a lock on who killed Ipolitas, he didn't have it in him. He didn't want to have to look her in the eye and lie.

Why he doesn't have the same reservations about seeing Leah is anyone's guess. Weiss wouldn't admit that talk of her new boyfriend bothered him, but he's feeling like he might want her all to himself again. He needs someone familiar, even if she isn't sympathetic. After all, there's more than one meaning to the word *consolation*, and something is better than nothing. He rings her apartment.

'It's Ray.'

The intercom crackles.

'Interesting,' she says.

The door buzzes.

He takes the service elevator. Leah's door is propped open; she's not there to evaluate his approach. He decides it's unfair if she's still mad at him about the other night: he was in the midst of a crisis, and she wasn't exactly helpful. Sometimes she just stays mad for leverage. He hopes this isn't one of those times.

As soon as he pushes open the door he's pretty sure this won't be one of those times. Or remotely like any other time, for that matter. Leah's in her usual spot on the futon, a book in her lap.

But her legs are outstretched, and there's some skinny asshole on the other end giving her a foot massage.

'Ray,' she says, 'this is Kurt.'

Kurt squeezes her foot with one hand and waves at Ray with the other.

'Hi,' they say over one another.

It appears Kurt is unfamiliar with the fact that it's impolite to rub a woman's feet in the presence of another guy, especially one who's previously held the job. It really gets them off to a bad start. Not to mention that the guy has a haircut like a Beatle and an outfit like a beatnik.

'Have a seat, Ray,' Leah says, the seat being the fucking rocking chair. 'Kurt's helping me. I don't get statistics.'

'I'm not much help. I'm better with facts than I am with figures,' Kurt says.

'Okay,' Weiss says to him, a sarcastic thumbs-up.

Leah makes her be-nice face.

'We were getting ready to go over to Giordano's,' Kurt says. 'You want to join us?'

Weiss sits in the fucking rocking chair but he sits forward and plants his feet on the floor so it doesn't rock and he says, to Leah, 'Put your shoes on.'

*

Giordano's is a classic choice, especially because the deep-dish pizza always takes forty-five minutes to get to the table, minimum. Plenty of time for awkward moments. Kurt and Leah sit across from Weiss in a cozy wooden booth, a red-and-white checkered cloth on the table decorated with assorted stains. Kurt seems real interested in the old photos that decorate the walls, and then the menu. Not that he's uncomfortable; it seems like he actually gives a shit. Weiss figures he's writing a mental article about the experience.

'I haven't had Giordano's in forever,' Leah tells them, like anyone cares.

Weiss doesn't offer any small talk, just acts like everything's grand; it's great to be alive. Lets Leah squirm.

The waitress comes by, a college girl stuck in a stupid uniform. 'Hi, guys, stuffed tonight?' Asked first because if the answer's yes, you'll be at her table for a long damn time, and she's got to make an investment.

'May I?' Kurt asks Weiss.

'Go right ahead.' Looks at Leah: who is this guy?

'A large super veggie, garlic instead of broccoli, please.' How cute: Kurt knows Leah's thing.

'And a pitcher of Bud Lite,' Weiss says. He's going to need something to lubricate the situation.

'Can I see your IDs?'

She barely glances at Kurt's; gives Leah's a perfunctory once-over. Weiss gives her the wallet that holds his flat badge; she takes her time, comparing the picture to the real thing, liking what she sees. A smile. 'Thanks, officer.'

He smiles – at Leah, after a glance at the waitress' ass. Life is beautiful.

'So, Ray, Leah tells me you're a cop.'

'She didn't tell me anything about you.' Weiss, loving this.

'That's not true.' Leah, not so much.

'Oh, you're right,' Weiss says, 'you did mention him when you came over the other night.' What? He shouldn't have said that?

'I'm a staff reporter for the *Sun-Times*,' Kurt says.

'Yeah? What do you write?'

'Assignments mostly. Local stuff. City hall. I want to write for sports, but I have to take what I can get for now.'

Weiss resists turning that comment toward Leah.

'So what sports are you into? Football? You seem like a sidelines kind of guy.' Not meant to be a compliment.

'Are you kidding? They'd never let me. I'm a Packers fan.'

Great, Weiss thinks. This changes everything.

After one beer Weiss has only begun to grasp Kurt's extensive scope of Packer facts and lore, not to mention his family's season tickets at Lambeau. If it weren't for the fact that Kurt keeps Leah in the loop, making sure her beer is cold enough and she's warm enough and blah, blah, blah, Weiss would probably forget she was there.

'... it was more than divine intervention,' Kurt says, having been at the Monday night game in Oakland right after Favre's dad died, when Favre threw for a record 399 yards. 'It was like the whole stadium was on some higher plane. Raider fans couldn't even bring themselves to talk trash. It was as close as I've been to God, I'll tell you that much.'

'Wow' is all Weiss can say.

'Yeah' is all Kurt can say.

Leah doesn't say anything.

The waitress stops by, eyes on Weiss: 'Your pizza is on its way out. Another pitcher?'

Weiss looks at Kurt: Should they? Kurt seems down for it.

'No,' Leah answers for them.

'School night,' Kurt explains, though he doesn't need to, and Leah's icy glare even makes Weiss feel sorry for the guy.

Weiss knows when to excuse himself. 'Nature calls.'

He hears Kurt laugh as he makes a quick break for the can. Poor guy.

In the bathroom, Weiss decides his presence isn't doing anybody any good. He and Leah have too much history to blow it all on somebody harmless like Kurt. Though Weiss has to admit he's a little jealous. And not just because of the season tickets.

He plans to duck out politely, let Leah win this one and enjoy her veggie pizza and her boyfriend while she will. But when he exits the bathroom, Leah corners him at the pay phones.

'Can we call a truce, or are you going to torture me all night?'

'Hey, I like the guy.'

'I like him too.'

'One would think.'

'He's nice.'

'He is.'

She steps toward him and fingers the cord of a pay phone, her lips pressed together, her usual prelude to saying something he won't want to hear.

'What?' Weiss asks.

'He's too nice, Ray.' Her eyes catch his. 'I miss you.'

Weiss' hands are in the air, a blameless reaction, which Leah turns into an extremely inappropriate opportunity to wrap her arms around his waist and give him a hot, familiar, candy-flavored kiss. When her tongue slides across his lips, he feels it in his balls. It takes every ounce of moral strength he has to push her away. That, and the thought of those season tickets.

'I'm not doing this now, Leah.'

'It isn't always on your terms, Ray.' She fixes her lip gloss with the back of her hand.

'So you want to go back to the table and tell Kurt you're sorry, you're going home with the asshole? Have some class, Leah.'

'You're the one who came to me.'

'It wasn't my first mistake.' Weiss points to the ladies' room. 'You go in there and do whatever it is you do and don't come out until you can look us both in the eye. I'm going to go out there and have a civil slice of pizza so Kurt doesn't think you just came after me. And then I'm going to leave. And I don't want you to talk to me – in fact, don't even look at me, until I say good-bye.'

Weiss walks away, wiping his mouth. Unbelievable.

'So, Ray,' Kurt says when Weiss sits and slides a fat piece of pie from the elevated tray to his plate. Kurt had been politely waiting to serve himself. 'You think you'd ever want to talk to me, give me the inside scoop on what it's like out there on the street? I have to hand it to you, man, what you do scares the hell out of me. No way I could be a cop.'

Weiss pulls the crust from his slice and takes a bite, washing it down with the end of his beer, getting rid of Leah's candy aftertaste. 'You write something about me and the guys will have my ass. I haven't been on the job long enough to tell you anything but what it's like to be a boot.'

'A boot?'

'New guy.'

'See? That right there is interesting. People don't know stuff like that.'

'Are you going to eat?' Weiss asks, though he knows that Kurt is being polite for Leah. Weiss hates that he's doing the same, in a way, trying to eat and get the fuck out of there. Between bites he says, 'I'll tell you something: the less you care, the better off you'll be.'

Kurt seems to hear truth in the statement, but he doesn't reach for a piece of pizza. Looks like Leah's right: the guy is too nice.

Weiss' cell rings as he's cutting into the mozzarella that melted off his slice onto the plate. It's Sloane.

'What's up?' Weiss asks, realizing he's smiling at the same time he notices Kurt's watching him.

'Well, I have an update. For one thing, I'm an ignorant American.'

'Why's that?'

'We'd been tracing Mykolas Lukiene? That isn't his last name. I came home and Googled him, and one site led to another, and I found out that Lithuanian women change their husband's last name when they take it. It's kind of like how we go from Miss to Mrs; they add a new ending.'

'So did you find the guy?'

'Sure did. Name's Mykolas Lukas.'

'Mykolas Lukas,' Weiss says; doesn't ring a bell. Leah comes back to the table, says something to Kurt that Weiss doesn't process, but her tone is rude, and it distracts him. He shoves his plate out of the way, covers his free ear.

'Turns out Ona wasn't lying,' Sloane says, 'they live right where we dropped her, but it's owned by Lukas' cousin. And the happy couple has only been there a month, so the utilities and everything are still in the previous occupant's name. Anyway, Lukas used to live on the north side, close to his business – he owns a place called Lucky Mike's. It's an electronics store.'

That rings a very loud, very ominous bell. Weiss gets up.

'He has one prior, a misdemeanor for disorderly conduct last year,' Sloane says. 'Arrested, ironically, by none other than your mentor and pal Jack Fiore.'

He swallows back the bile creeping up his throat. 'What's next?'

'I'm in the process of convincing the state's attorney to bug the judge at home tonight. We'll see what happens, but we may have to wait and get him at the store in the morning.'

Weiss can't wait. 'Keep me posted. I'll be there.' He hangs up, takes a twenty from his flat badge wallet, hands it to Leah. He doesn't bother to say good-bye.

CHAPTER TWENTY-EIGHT

Weiss hustles down Sheridan Road to get back to Leah's street, where he left the Cavalier. It's dark outside now, and most of the people in this neighborhood have settled into their apartments or dorms, preparing for Monday morning.

Weiss doesn't have that kind of time. He's got to talk to Lucky Mike before Sloane does.

He thinks about jumping on the Red Line as he approaches Loyola Avenue. Jed lives a few blocks from the stop at Sheffield. The train ride might take a little longer than the drive, but he won't have to look for a parking spot.

Fuck parking, he thinks, and crosses the street. He'll need wheels to get back over to Lucky Mike's place whether Jed believes they're covering for the guy or not.

There isn't much traffic so Weiss takes Sheridan Road all the way down on the late end of a string of yellow lights. He knows the guys in the twenty-third district sit on Lake Shore Drive when they're hot to write traffic tickets. They won't bother with this street, or with Weiss tonight.

Sheridan turns into Sheffield; Weiss turns left at

Dakin and double-parks outside Jed's apartment building. It's a four-story courtyard-style walk-up with about two dozen units. Jed lives on the second floor: looks like every single light in his place is on.

The gate is propped open by someone's unread *Sun-Times*. The press again, Weiss thinks, tampering with security.

He lets himself in and climbs the stairs to Jed's. It's after eight, which means Jed has his ass firmly planted on the couch and he's catching up on whatever he TiVoed last week. He's been known to watch entire seasons of shows over a few days. During his last marathon he watched every single rerun of the 'Ren and Stimpy' cartoon. He spent a week doing imitations that sounded like a constipated Mexican until, after one 'you eediot!' too many, Noise drew his gun and politely asked him to shut the fuck up.

'Hey, Katy,' Weiss says when Jed's wife opens the door. Jed met her during his 'hot girls are stupid' phase, and Katy was perfect – just enough attitude to balance the extra weight on her hips, hips Jed now correctly refers to as 'child-bearing.' She was quick to put Jed in his place, and to take hers: one part wife, one part mother. Jed still thinks hot girls are stupid, but he also TiVoes the Spice Channel when Katy's not around.

'Ray,' Katy says, 'it's been a while.' She kisses him: a peck on the left cheek, then the right. She started that when she got back from a trip to Italy with her sister, after which Jed started thinking he'd better marry her before she picked up any other routines. Like going back to Italy.

'Come on in.' She has what looks like dirt down the front of her shirt, like she's been cleaning house. 'You want to eat with us? I'm making baked ziti.'

'I already ate. Thanks.' He figures the dirt on her shirt is some part of her recipe, since that's how any meal he's ever had here tasted.

'You want a beer? You might as well sit down and stay awhile, Jed's been watching that fucking television since the Cubs game.'

'That's okay.' Weiss never heard anyone call her dainty.

Katy disappears into the kitchen and Weiss takes a seat on the couch opposite Jed's spot, marked by a bottle of Michelob Ultra on the glass coffee table that's surrounded by wet rings, indicating there's been more than one. On TV, Australian-rules football. He wonders when Jed got interested.

'What's up, Vice?' Jed comes into the room with a *Sports Illustrated* in his hand, his bathroom reading. 'I like that one. Vice. Because it can sound tough or it can be fruity. Like if I stress the C – Viissss.'

'It sounds so natural coming from you.'

'Viissssss.' He sticks out one hip, runs his fingers down his torso. 'Swishy.'

'You're the one drinking low-carb beer.'

'Fuck off.'

And then Jed sits down and watches Australian-rules football.

'Shit. Fucking Motlop.'

Weiss doesn't know if that's a player or a team or what. But Jed hasn't asked why he's here and with the TV on, he'll never get around to it.

Weiss waits for a break in game action and then he says, 'The detective. Pearson? She thinks she knows who killed Ipolitas.'

'How do you know?' Eyes still on the TV.

'I was with her.'

That gets Jed's attention. 'With her, like,' he thrusts his hips, 'finally?'

'I was afraid she was going to find out what we did.'

Jed reads the look on Weiss' face. 'Fuck, man, you mean you've been working with her?'

'For us.'

Insert Jed's expression somewhere between disappointment and disbelief.

'Jed. Listen. Pearson thinks it's the guy you told me about: Lucky Mike. You said Fiore and Noise have some kind of deal with him. And you said there was trouble. Did he kill Ipolitas? Is that why we had to cover all this up?'

Cancel disappointment, insert total disbelief. 'We're covering up the murder?'

'I don't know. All I know is what you told me. And if the detective gets to him before we do, we're fucked.'

'You're right we're fucked.' Jed turns off the TV. 'You know the guns I put in Ambrozas' trunk? Noise and I got them from Lucky Mike.' He gets up. 'Katy? Put dinner in the fridge.'

'I swear to you, Ray, I don't know anything about the murder.'

'You said that.'

Weiss drives back up Sheridan, more careful now that Jed's arsenal of extracurricular weapons is in the trunk: custom Ruger MK2, telescopic baton, stun baton, lock-picking set, pistol crossbow. Most of these were purchased shortly after his *Grand Theft Auto: San Andreas* marathon, when he played the video game nonstop, from no shirt on his back to respected gangster and cop-killer with five wanted stars. Weiss also blames the game for Jed's rap collection.

'Noise never told me anything,' Jed says, a variation on his theme.

'I believe you.'

'After the burglary – that was the only time I ever even talked to Lucky Mike. I waited in the car when Noise got the guns.' Jed rips another strip from an old Hanes T-shirt, making impromptu bindings. 'We should call him.'

'Noise? And say what? Jed, they've been keeping us in the dark. You think they're going to want us to be the ones to flip on the switch?'

Jed doesn't say anything. Weiss turns left onto Bryn Mawr, headed for Peterson. They're minutes away.

Weiss uses the silence to review their admittedly hare-brained plan. In a time crunch, there are limited ways to get people to talk. He hopes they won't have to bring Ona and her baby-to-be into the mix.

'Ray?' Jed's voice as colorless as his face.

'Yeah.'

'There's no way any of the guns I planted killed Ipolitas.'

Weiss isn't sure he should tell Jed about the serial numbers. Not yet.

'Ray? Noise wouldn't set me up.'

'We're in this together,' is all Weiss can offer.

Weiss parks outside the building where they dropped off Ona a few hours before. He shuts off the engine and they wait while a thirty-something couple passes by with a stroller and an obedient black Lab.

'Remember when I thought you dumped dog shit in my yard?' Weiss asks.

Jed watches the couple like his life is walking away from him.

'I thought you guys were against me,' Weiss says. 'Turns out, it was this guy Feliks Rainys. He used to work for Ipolitas. And he's Ambrozas' cousin. And, he's an old friend of Lucky Mike's wife. The connections are like something out of Appalachia. And they just keep getting weirder. But if there's one thing I got out of Feliks' screwy mouth, it's that the lines are drawn. It's us against them.'

Jed watches the husband maneuver the stroller around the corner at Thorndale, out of sight.

'Do you remember my wedding day?'

'Sure.'

'You know what I remember most about it? Standing at the head of the church, waiting for Katy to come down the aisle, looking out at all my boys in blue.' Then he rolls the cloth bindings around his fist and says, 'Let's talk to Lucky Mike.'

CHAPTER TWENTY-NINE

Lucky Mike and Ona live in a three-story brick building with a green, street-level door. When Weiss and Sloane dropped off Ona before, Sloane followed her and said Ona let herself into the the first-floor unit on the right.

It's hard to guess whether or not Ona told her husband about her conversation with them this afternoon. Among the variables: Ona told him everything, he's guilty, and they're long gone; or, she didn't tell him anything, he's innocent, and they're in there right now deciding what color to paint the nursery. Calculating the possibilities in between seems infinite, so Weiss and Jed decide the best way to go is without thinking at all – surprise the hell out of them and hope it plays out in their favor. If that doesn't work, they'll split up the couple and hope it divides them.

Jed makes quick work of the green front door's lock and they're inside, Weiss unscrewing the bulb that lights the hallway a nighttime yellow. Then, in the darkness, Weiss pounds a heavy fist on the door. Jed's right behind him, arsenal in tow. They wait, quiet as nobody.

No one answers, so Weiss moves to the left and

draws his .45 as Jed drops to one knee with the lock pins. They won't call out or flash their badges: nothing said here will be admissible in court.

Jed backs away from the door, his sudden movement telling Weiss someone's on the other side. Jed steps to the right of the door, his body flush with the wall, out of the line of fire.

The knob turns; the door opens.

'Hands up,' Weiss says, his voice steel. The way the light falls from the doorway leaves him in the shadows – all except the hand that's aiming the .45.

Lucky Mike raises his hands and his shirt follows, exposing his lanky torso and the bottom of his rib cage. He's at least six foot five and his long arms nearly reach the ceiling. In his right hand, the .357 Magnum looks miniature.

'What the fuck is this?' he whispers.

'Drop the weapon,' Weiss says.

Lucky Mike bends at his stiff, middle-aged knees to put the gun on the floor. As he stands he sees Jed, now facing him, Ruger MK2 drawn.

Lucky Mike puts his bony hands on his bony hips. 'Oh, it's you,' his tone now a pissed whisper. 'What, you having problems with your television?'

'Get the gun,' Weiss tells Jed. 'Get inside,' he tells them both.

'Can we do this somewhere else?' Lucky Mike asks. 'My wife is sleeping.'

A visual consult: Jed shakes his head no.

'Come on, guys. She told me what happened today.'

Jed still shaking his head no.

'Does this building have roof access?' Weiss asks Lucky Mike.

'In the stairwell.' He points to an unmarked door at the back of the hall.

'Jed, stay here and make sure Ona doesn't wake up.'

'You cops and your bullshit compromises.' Lucky Mike is the one shaking his head now.

Weiss coaxes Lucky Mike with the .45. 'Let's go.'

The rooftop isn't worth describing though Lucky Mike seems apprehensive about being there. He shuffles his feet along the tar.

'Keep moving,' Weiss says, the gun pressed to Lucky Mike's right kidney. Weiss feels kind of funny pushing around such a big older guy.

'I do not like heights.'

'But you're tall.'

'I've never had this conversation.'

'Is that sarcasm?'

Lucky Mike turns around, shuffling backward now, Weiss' gun aimed at his gut. 'Can we just stop here, please?'

Weiss has him about ten feet from the northwest corner. The ledge around the perimeter is shallow, two feet high at the most. Weiss points out the ledge. 'You don't want to sit there?'

Lucky Mike sits right where he's standing. 'This is fine.'

Weiss walks around him, the .45 casual in his hand. 'You shouldn't expose your weaknesses. It's easier to get what I want from you that way.'

'It doesn't matter. You cops always get what you want.'

Weiss squats so he's face to face with him. 'Since there's only one of us up here, and one who wants to help you, I think "you cops" is a little offensive. I haven't referred to you as "you murderers," so how about we drop the generalizations?'

'Sure. Whatever.'

Weiss stands up and retrieves a white plastic five-gallon bucket that's tipped on its side near the ledge. He turns it upside down and straddles it in front of Lucky Mike.

'Fact is, you have certain agreements with certain members of law enforcement who have tried to prevent you from taking a murder rap. Unfortunately, they are failing. Which means you have to find another way out of it. One way would be to find an attorney with the conscience of a tick and the expensive legal chops necessary to plead down a murder charge – based, of course, on your intimate knowledge of wayward police activity. You take that route, and you'll certainly be out of jail in time to meet your new baby. Probably at her wedding, but better late than never.'

Lucky Mike finds a pack of cigarettes in his shirt pocket. 'I didn't kill Ipolitas.'

'Save it for the jury. If that's the way you want to go.'

'I assume you will tell me the other way.' He bites the filter of a Marlboro Red with his incisor, takes matches from the cellophane around the pack, and swipes one across the book.

'The other way, or the way I think we'd all like to see this go, would be for you to tell me everything, right now, about Ipolitas, his business, his murder, and the guy who was framed for it. And since we've all apparently worked so well together in the past, I might be able to help you. I'll start by redirecting the detective who's planning to come arrest you in the morning.'

'Where's Fiore on this?'

'You're not the one who gets to ask questions.'

Lucky Mike smokes in heavy pulls. Between them: 'I want to talk to Fiore. I don't make these kinds of arrangements anymore.'

'I know all about your arrangements, Mike. And if this whole thing gets pieced together the way I think it will, you're going to be in jail a lot longer than the rest of us.'

'You are framing me.'

'You are framing Ambrozas.'

'You are twisting the facts.'

'No sir. I'm compromising.' Weiss keeps his eyes on Lucky Mike, letting him know this is as far as it goes.

'I can't compromise. I did not kill Ipolitas.'

'Then you have one chance, right now, to tell me who did.'

'I don't know.'

'Come on, Mike. Your wife gave me more to go on than this.'

'What do you want me to say? I don't know!'

'How about this. I'll name names, you tell me what you do know.'

Lucky Mike stubs out his cigarette like a *no*, but then he blinks an *okay*.

Now they're getting somewhere. Weiss sticks the .45 in his waistband.

'Tell me about your relationship with Ipolitas.'

'We were business associates for a time. He introduced me to my wife.'

'She worked for him.'

'Yes.'

'She wasn't selling jewelry.'

'No.'

'And neither were you.'

'I would help some of the girls he brought over. Help them find work. He would give me part of his profit. But I mostly dealt with his employee, Feliks.'

'I know Feliks.'

'Then you know his agenda.'

'Not in your words.'

Lucky Mike gets another cigarette. Same routine with the biting, the lighting, the smoking. Weiss assumes there must be some mental preparation going on. He shifts his weight, the bucket as comfortable as anything he ever sits on anymore.

'I came here in 1995 after my first wife died of cancer. Our business never recovered after the Soviets left Lithuania. I had nothing, no one but my son. I left him with his grandparents. Came here. It took me eight years to become a citizen, a businessman, and to bring my son here. I enrolled him at White Pines Academy because I wanted him to know his Lithuanian roots. I drove him to Lemont every day. I thought it was important.'

'Why is any of this important?'

'Because that's where I met Feliks Rainys.' He

blows out a ring of smoke. 'I was picking up my son one day and I ran into Feliks. He was on the way to an LIB meeting – Lithuanians In Business. They help each other, promote cooperation between countries, that sort of thing.'

'You went to the meeting?'

'No. But I met with Feliks a few weeks later. Feliks thought the LIB was useless. He felt we were being taken advantage of in American business and who could argue? I've been doing unreturned favors for the police since I opened my store. Feliks was interested in finding ways to make money to send back to Lithuania. He said we could help one another. Then he introduced me to Ipolitas.'

'And you joined Ipolitas' trafficking business.'

'Yes. I remembered what I'd left in Lithuania. Things are no better now. I wanted to help the girls – I helped a number of them find work.' He stomps out the butt of his second smoke, sucks in the night air, says, 'Then I made a mistake. A year ago, my business was suffering after the Best Buy opened on Harlem. I needed help. So I told Feliks about my relationship with the police. He convinced me to introduce Ipolitas to Fiore.'

Weiss has smoked his share of cigarettes. When he was a kid. When he was trying to fit in with the guys at the bar. When he dated a chain-smoker. But this might be the first time he ever feels like he needs one. He reaches over, into Lucky Mike's pocket, and takes the pack.

'It wasn't a setup,' Lucky Mike says. 'Even Ipolitas was reluctant. But I knew Fiore needed someone, you know, the situation with his wife.'

'So you got Fiore a whore?'

'I did no such thing.'

'Then how did Fiore end up fucking one of Ipolitas' women?' Weiss takes out a cigarette.

'I don't know. Ipolitas and I stopped speaking. He owed me money and he wouldn't pay because Ona and I fell in love and left the business.'

'You're lying. Ona worked at his store last month.' Weiss lights a match.

'And I did a job for you cops last week. You think we want to be involved in this? Our family has been split apart. Our values have been completely ignored. We only want to get out, and we are trapped by our past mistakes. We are trapped now because of Feliks.'

Weiss throws the lighted match on the tar. 'Checks and balances.' Totally flawed.

He puts the cigarette back in the pack and tosses it to Lucky Mike. 'Tell me how to find Feliks.'

CHAPTER THIRTY

'He didn't do it.'

Jed follows Weiss out of Lucky Mike's building. 'We're just leaving? Can't we arrest him for something?'

'Yeah. We'll cuff him with your T-shirt and take him to the station for being totally cooperative during an illegal interrogation.'

'What the hell did he say? You were up there forever.'

'He said he's an ex-member of a trafficking and prostitution ring which was headed up by Ipolitas, run by the cryptic Lithuanian who was harassing me, and best of all, patronized by Fiore. And because of that, I think we all got fucked.'

'But this guy didn't kill Ipolitas, so we aren't covering anything up. We're fine, right?'

Weiss pops the Cavalier's trunk so Jed can stow his arsenal. 'Your logic defies all reason.'

'Why?'

'Ipolitas is still dead. Someone still killed him. The wrong guy is still in jail. We are still covering it up, and that means we can still get fucked, especially if Fiore has a "relationship" he isn't telling us about with some hooker.'

Jed slams the trunk shut. 'Ray, I don't think we should risk our jobs over Fiore getting his dick sucked. Who gives a shit who killed the guy? We don't know. We're not responsible. Let it wash out on its own.'

'We're talking about human trafficking. Prostitution. Murder. Sloane isn't going to let any of it slip past her. She thinks the feds are going to trump her as it is.' Weiss walks around to the driver's side door, pops the locks.

'This isn't about Fiore's dick,' Jed says. 'It's about yours.'

'We have to find Feliks Rainys.'

'Hey, man,' Jed says, 'I'm just glad you aren't gay.'

Weiss opens his door, asks, 'You up for a drive to the southside?'

'Does the Pope shit in the woods?'

'God damn, are we going to Indiana?' Jed asks, on the Dan Ryan approaching Thirty-fifth Street. 'Are you sure Lucky Mike told you the truth?'

'It makes sense. This is where we picked up Ambrozas.'

'I can't tell you the last time I was down here. Wait: yes I can. Last year, when Katy made me take her brother to a game versus the Red Sox. Fucking Red Sox.'

'Fucking White Sox.'

Weiss passes the cop shop on Thirty-fifth. 'This is Fiore's old beat.'

'No shit? So that was his base camp. We should call him.'

'And tell him what? That we're looking for his pimp?'

Weiss glances over at the station, lit up with spotlights. Inside, all the ground-floor lights are on, and there's a piece of loose-leaf paper taped up in one of the office windows with the words HELP ME scrawled in Magic Marker. Must be a cop stuck at a desk.

'Man,' Jed says, 'this whole thing just doesn't sit right. I can't picture Fiore with a whore.'

'Have you ever met his wife?'

'Was she at the Christmas party?'

'No. You'd remember if you'd met her.'

'Noise said she was sick or something. I overheard him say she was in the hospital last month.'

'Fiore never talks about her.'

'Yeah, I know. Still, if Fiore's anything, he's loyal.'

'You think his wife would agree?'

'I'm not talking about women, Ray. I'm talking about us. Our loyalty.'

'I think you and I have different interpretations of the word.'

Weiss pulls up and stops at the corner of Lituanica and Thirty-fourth. 'This is it.'

On the first floor of Feliks' supposed residence is an abandoned store. It's surrounded by pavement: a sidewalk, an alley, and a gangway that separates the building from a one-story brick home. The store's exposed foundation is painted white; scabs of water damage make it look like it's crumbling. On the face of the building, the same white paint covers the two first-floor windows, masking the former storefront and whatever's inside. A weathered sign says it's SIN LA R'S GR C RS.

'If this is it,' Jed says, 'I don't want to think about what the guy's hookers look like.'

'Look up there.' The top half of the building had been renovated. The brick is old, but the windows are recent; a faint light comes from one of them.

They get out of the car and walk back to the gangway. A BEWARE OF DOG sign hangs crooked on the chain-link swing gate. Just behind it, there's a windowless gray door with a new wood frame.

Jed sees the door, takes Weiss' car keys. 'I'll get my bag.'

Weiss pulls on his gloves. Then he opens the gate latch, steps into the gangway, and takes out his .45 – in case the dog sign is valid. Weiss pounds on the door with his left hand and then shifts, waiting for a response with his strong side and the gun aimed forward.

He waits. No barking. No nothing. And without any windows on this side of the building, no way to know if someone's coming. He waits an extra few seconds before he beats on the door again.

No response.

Jed appears, his gear bag open, ready to go. He pushes through the gate.

'No one's home,' Weiss tells him.

Jed produces a tiny LED light that he screws onto the end of his telescopic baton. 'I've been wanting to try this thing out.' Its beam is about as powerful as a penlight's.

'What the hell's the purpose of that?'

'It has many uses.'

'Aside from when Grandma borrows it to read the menu?'

Jed switches on the light and shines it in Weiss' face. Then he tucks the baton under his arm, freeing up his hands to pick the lock.

'It's a dead bolt,' Jed says, his tension wrench suspending the lock while he maneuvers the pins. A quick twist of his wrist and the lock turns. 'I am amazing, aren't I?' Jed bags his gear and slings it over his shoulder. Weiss opens the door and moves in first, entering a stairwell. One direction to go: up, to another door.

Weiss hangs back, covers Jed as he rushes up the steps shining the light and aiming his Ruger at the door.

When Jed reaches the top he checks the doorknob: locked. He pounds on the door: no response. He waves Weiss along.

Just as Weiss reaches the top of the steps, Jed kicks, and his boot goes right through the cheap hollow-core door.

'What the fuck did you do that for?' Weiss asks.

Jed reaches through the hole and unlocks the door from the inside. 'Always wanted to.' He pushes the door open and slips in to the left, scanning precise points of the room with the baton light.

Weiss follows, covering, calls out: 'Anyone here?'

The space is open, like a loft, and his voice bounces off the walls. The light they saw from downstairs is coming from the bathroom, the only separate room, at the back. Weiss makes his way to it.

'Hello?' Weiss angles to the far wall, checks behind a bedsheet-covered couch, pokes the nose of his gun behind thin curtains. He knows Jed is just as careful behind him.

He sneaks up on the bathroom, listens. Nothing. Not even a dripping sink. He aims his .45 as he rounds the corner anyway, prepared for anything. Anything is a sink, a toilet, and a stand-up shower with an opaque door.

Weiss backs out, his steps even, moving on instinct. He calls to Jed: 'Are we clear?'

'As a piss before a drug test. But I don't think your friend Feliks could say the same thing. Check this out.'

Next to one of the front windows, in what can loosely be called the bedroom, Jed shines his baton on two suitcases, packed and ready to go. 'I'm guessing those aren't waiting to be unpacked.'

'Holy shit,' Weiss says. 'Feliks is fleeing.'

Jed hoists one of the cases up on the bed.

'Wait, we shouldn't—'

'We already broke into the guy's house, Ray. Let's find out where he's going.'

Jed hands Weiss the baton and he lights the suitcase. Jed unzips the bag, turning it as he does, and when he opens it the top flap falls backward.

'Ooohh, sexy,' he says, presenting a petite woman's blouse to the light. 'This is his color.' It looks tiny in Jed's big-gloved hands.

Weiss roots through the clothes with his free hand. 'This is all women's stuff.'

Jed opens a makeup bag, shows it to Weiss. 'Want

to do makeovers?' He uncaps a bottle of perfume, squirts it in the air.

'There has to be some kind of identification in here ...' Weiss rummages through some sweaters, white cotton scrub pants with pink ribbons, another sky-blue cotton scrub shirt ... and then he smells that god damn angelic perfume.

'Should I open the other bag?' Jed asks.

And that's when Weiss finds, tucked inside the mouth of a white nurse's shoe, a tiny satchel. He puts the baton on the bed, opens the satchel, and dumps all six of the rings he stole from Petras Ipolitas into his hand.

He only hears someone coming up the stairs when Jed pushes him out of the way and aims the Ruger.

Weiss drops to one knee and pulls his gun at the same time, but if he had to draw and fire, he would have been a second behind Fiore, who's already poked his head inside the doorway, fearless.

'Which one of you geniuses busted the door?'

'Christ on a cracker, Fiore.' Jed holsters his gun and moves forward, the bathroom light casting his shadow on Weiss. 'You scared us.'

'Well please, hold your fire.' Fiore steps inside and secures his revolver in his back waistband.

Behind Jed, Weiss stuffs the rings in his pants pocket.

'How'd you find us?' Jed asks.

'I caught Mike on his way out of town.'

Weiss steps up next to Jed. 'How did you know we were at Lucky Mike's?'

'Noise called me.'

Fiore looks at Jed, Jed at Weiss.

'I'm sorry, Ray,' he says. 'I guess we have different interpretations of loyalty.'

Fiore throws a dismissive hand in Jed's direction. 'I'm disappointed, Weiss. I thought you'd ask me to be a part of your secret investigation.'

'You told me to leave it alone.'

'I knew you wouldn't.'

'So what, you're here to shut me down?'

'Not exactly.'

'Is this another one of your backward-ass approaches to teaching me how to be a cop?'

'You're learning, aren't you?'

'Not anything I wanted to know.' Weiss takes the baton from Jed and shines it toward the bed.

'What's that?' Fiore asks.

'See for yourself.' Weiss hands him the baton.

Fiore struts over to the suitcase, shines the light. And by the streetlight coming through the window, Weiss sees Fiore's silhouette change: his shoulders tense and widen, and his head cocks forward, like an animal about to growl.

Then Fiore turns around and unleashes: 'What in the fuck do you boys think you're doing? Your stupid ideas and your stupid toys.' He throws the baton and it hits the floor hard, metal on wood. Jed doesn't move out of the way as it rolls in an arc toward him, stops at his feet. The light shines at the blank wall.

'You break in here, no warrant, no fucking badges, and think you're going to come up with some usable evidence? Or what, you were planning to ambush the guy and Starsky and Hutch him into a confession? Give me a fuckin' break.'

Jed hangs his head; Weiss takes the heat with his chin held high, mouth shut, eyes forward. Fiore doesn't like it one bit. He gets in Weiss' face, spits the words:

'You morons don't have a clue! Even if any of what you've done was legal, do you think whoever was here will come back, now that you've been through the place?'

Weiss feels the rings in his pockets. Keeping them is criminal. Putting them back is out of the question. Why did he take them? And how did this woman end up with them in her suitcase?

'Jed. Pick up your toys,' Fiore says, 'and get the fuck out of here before we all get caught.'

Fiore crosses his arms, watches Jed retrieve the baton, turn off the LED light, and put it in his gear bag.

'Go downstairs and wait,' Fiore tells him. 'Weiss and I will be there in a minute.'

Like a soldier, Jed heads straight for the door without a word.

Fiore walks over to the front window by the bed and leans against the ledge. 'Come over here, Weiss,' he says, a suggestion rather than a command.

Weiss hears Jed's footsteps echo in the stairwell. His own steps are noiseless as he joins Fiore by the window, the second suitcase at their feet.

Fiore looks out the window, waits for Jed to appear. He says, 'This is about a woman, isn't it? The detective?'

This is about a woman, all right, Weiss thinks. He decides the question will be rhetorical.

'Look, I can't blame you. The fall of Troy and all that. Hell, my wife is the only reason I'm still alive. I try to pretend she doesn't hold the cards, but the truth is ...' Fiore pulls his revolver from the back of his pants. 'The truth is, I made a mistake.'

Weiss looks out the window, sees Jed getting into the driver's side of the Cavalier. Wait. What the fuck. Is he leaving?

'That young girl the other night – the little Spanish girl. Melia. Did you see the look on her face when they told her the truth about her man? The man she loves? The father of her kid? I said it before, that poor girl will suffer until she's dead.'

Weiss' breath gets caught in his throat. What's Fiore talking about? And what's he doing with his gun? He isn't aiming it, but—

'We don't deserve the ones who stick with us. We just don't.'

Weiss can't get a word out. He can hardly breathe. Why is Jed starting the car? Is this a setup? What the fuck is happening?

'Weiss. Look at me.'

He does, his eyes burning, watering; his jaw tight.

'Promise me.'

Weiss thinks he nods. His vision blurs with tears.

'I don't like secrets,' Fiore says. 'My FTO used to tell me, "If you want to keep a secret, tell a dead man."' He cocks the revolver.

It takes everything in Weiss' being to keep from crying out. He breathes heavy and fast through his nostrils.

And then Fiore gently thumbs the hammer down, flips open the cylinder, and dumps the bullets in his hand. 'I don't like to talk about this. You want to sit down?'

Weiss wants to collapse. 'Shouldn't we … what if Feliks shows up?'

'Jed's watching.'

Weiss' knees gladly give way for him to sit on the floor next to the second suitcase.

Fiore sits on the bed and begins reloading the revolver, one bullet, another. Then he pauses, says, 'My wife has multiple sclerosis.' And he slips the third bullet into its chamber.

'It's an expensive disease by itself, and this last year, it's been worse. New problems, new medication. She needed help. And the help that I got for her, that was my mistake.'

He looks out the window, staying objective, in control.

'Lucky Mike told me that Ipolitas was bringing girls over, working for cash as caregivers.'

'Caregivers?'

'I know what you thought. Don't insult me.'

Weiss bites his lip.

'I took advantage of the situation,' Fiore says. 'Josephine needed help, this guy needed a sympathetic player on the force.

'In comes this young girl, Paulina, with all her American dreams and all her energy. It was an immediate attitude adjustment for Jo; they really hit it off. She was feeling better. Smiling again. It was like having the place aired out.

'None of it made a shit of difference though. Not as far as the MS anyway. Josephine had what they call a relapse, a few months back. Wound up in the hospital. And Paulina, she had been living with us, so she stayed at the house.'

He loads the fourth bullet, keeping himself in check.

'I'd go to the hospital every day before work, and every day I'd see a little less of Jo. She was losing herself. And every night I'd get home late and I'd see more and more of Paulina. Asking me this or that about Chicago, about work, about my life. She pulled out all the stops.'

Fifth bullet.

'When Jo came home, she and Paulina picked up where they left off. But then, Jo was distant with me. Paulina wasn't. Every night I'd get home late, Jo in bed, and there she'd be, same sweet face, more questions.

'I was exhausted. Overtime for the hospital bills, trying to drum up extra cash however I could. The Job is fucking thankless. It's thankless.'

He pushes the sixth bullet into place and flips the cylinder shut. Then he thumbs back the hammer, turns the revolver, and looks down the barrel from the business end—

'Jack—' Weiss reaches up—

But Fiore holds the revolver there and says, 'It happened once. I got home after a four-to-four and I was buzzed, tired, pissed at the world. And there's that sweet face, and I'm her American dream. I was so fucking stupid.'

Weiss sees Fiore's chest rise, a deep breath, considering. Then he turns the muzzle toward the floor and thumbs the hammer down. He flips open the cylinder again, dumps the bullets out in his hand.

'Paulina must have had it planned, because the next thing I know, I'm being blackmailed by Ambrozas.' He rattles the bullets in his hand like dice. Then, abruptly, he stops and says, 'That is why we covered the murder.'

'You know who killed Ipolitas?'

'I know Feliks Rainys agreed to take care of the blackmail in exchange for my taking care of his problem. And his problem was Ipolitas' dead body. I'm guessing these suitcases are part of his end of the deal.'

'Feliks came to see me. He threatened me. He says you made him tell you where to find Ambrozas. He wants Ambrozas cleared.'

'Paulina must have put him up to it. She must have him on a leash just like she does Ambrozas. She wasn't privy to the fact her fiancé was part of the deal, but fuck her. I wasn't privy to the fact she had a fiancé.'

'Feliks said he and Ambrozas are cousins,' Weiss says, trying not to push.

'It doesn't matter, Weiss. Don't you get it? They tried to fuck with me and I shut them down. Now they're trying to fuck with you.'

'You put us all at risk, Jack. Other people are on to this. Detective Pearson says the feds could take over.'

Fiore reloads the gun as quickly as he unloaded it and aims it at Weiss' face. 'I suggest you work out your thing with the detective, apart from our discussion here. So I don't have to.' He drops his aim to the floor. 'Believe me, you're just a step on her ladder. Don't think she won't kick you while she's climbing.' Then he holsters the gun and walks away.

Weiss lets Jed drive the Cavalier back up north. Jed's been babbling about every damn thing most of the way, overlooking the fact that he completely fucked over Weiss by calling Noise. Weiss adds the indiscretion to the list of reasons he pretty much feels like an asshole. All those nights riding with Fiore, Weiss had no idea what he was going through.

'… that's what we need, man. A new trend. I'm so sick of all this metrosexual pop shit. We're supposed to think these guys with stupid hair and expensive T-shirts are it. What happened to, like, Nirvana?'

'Kurt Cobain killed himself.'

'You know what I mean. What happened to rock?'

'I don't know.' Weiss gazes at the section of skyline visible from the Kennedy. The top floors of the Sears Tower are lost in low clouds.

'Man, I'm fucking starved. You want to get off at North Avenue, go by Kincade's?'

'No.'

'Are you okay, Ray? Did Fiore give you the what-for back there?'

'I don't know what he gave me. I guess he gave me the truth.'

'Truth hurts.'

'Yeah.'

'It won't hurt a little less after a Heineken and a game of Golden Tee?'

'I don't think so.'

'Fine, I guess I'll go home, heat up the ziti, bang the wife.'

And Jed's simple obliviousness is exactly what Weiss envies. 'You're lucky, man.'

'Ray, don't get all snuggly on me. If you really want to get in that detective's pants, you'll find a way.'

Weiss drops off Jed and drives a few blocks over to Lake Shore. The clouds downtown stretch out over the lake into an endless black. To the north, the sky is starless.

Weiss takes the Drive up to Montrose, follows the curled strip of land around the harbor.

The air is cool and heavy, humidity at odds with fall's arrival. Weiss parks and walks out on the longest dock. Across the water, two late-night bikers pedal along the path. On this side, the harbor is calm; the docked boats are barely lulled by the waves. Weiss has never been much of a boat guy. His brother, Billy, sure. When he was about eight, Billy thirteen, the Lieutenant finally decided they were old enough to go along on the annual Coho fishing trip – a day with a boat full of cops and beer and bullshit. Billy caught the biggest salmon. Weiss didn't catch anything, but he got off the boat with his head full of stories and big ideas.

'I want to be a cop,' he told the Lieutenant from the backseat on the drive home.

Billy laughed. And the Lieutenant looked back at him through the rearview mirror with his blue eyes and said, 'You're too smart.'

Weiss takes in a breath of night air and surveys the area, to make sure no one's around. Then he winds up his pitching arm and throws the six stolen rings into the harbor.

CHAPTER THIRTY-ONE

Jed doesn't show for their Monday-morning workout, which is fine with Weiss, because he didn't fall asleep until four something and Terrence Mann kept driving through that fucking intersection until Weiss decided he'd kill the guy himself, if he could just raise his broken arms and shoot. Instead of fitful sleep, he opts for the caffeine in a couple Excedrin and a Coke to get him through the morning.

There's nothing left to eat in the fridge and his stomach is reminding him of it after the caffeine, but he isn't looking forward to leaving the house. It's been raining all morning, the kind of rain that makes for a miserable shift later today.

He finds a box of stale Saltines, some that Leah brought when she made him chili last time it was cold outside. Was it March? Has it been six months since they broke up? He figures the crackers taste like paper anyway, and they'll coat his stomach, so he eats almost an entire sleeve.

He takes a shower and shaves his face clean for the first time since the fight last week. The cuts are healing nicely, thanks to J. Yoon, and the swelling is gone.

After the shower he towel-dries his hair, surprised no one's said anything about the length yet. In the mirror, he thinks he looks young. He thinks he looks too young. After all this, older and wiser he is not.

No word from Sloane this morning. He guesses she had other stuff to attend to since her schedule is more dependent on the court. He figures she didn't get the warrant. Or, she blew off Weiss and went for Lucky Mike on her own. But she didn't find him. Weiss made sure of that.

At eleven thirty Sloane does call. He doesn't answer, though he's only prolonging the inevitable. He doesn't peg her as the sort of woman who will just go away.

He sits on the couch and he's watching *Shootout*, a History Channel show about the Western frontier, when Jed calls. 'Vice, are you working tonight?'

'With Schreiber. That's what Fiore told me.'

'I need your pick for the game. We're all going to watch it at O'Toole's and it's ten to one on the Eagles.'

'Sounds like a safe bet.'

'That's why I'm picking the Lions. It's the first game, man. They got something to prove this year.'

On TV, they're showing a reenactment of the Younger brothers being brought back to town to stand trial after the Northfield bank robbery. Cole Younger had eleven bullets in his body and he still managed to tip his hat to the crowd. Weiss thinks some guys don't know when to quit.

'It's twenty bucks to get in,' Jed says. 'Who do you want?'

Someone buzzes Weiss' front door. He wonders if it's Hal, and instantly remembers the side job, having stepped over the paint cans in the entryway last night when he finally returned home. He gets up off the couch, says, 'Hey, Jed, do you want to get in on a side job this week? I have to paint the upstairs apartment.'

'How much?'

'A hundred each.'

'Forget it.'

'Beer's on me,' Weiss offers, on his way to the front door.

'Maybe.'

'Pizza? I'll get Leona's.'

'I'm hearing you.'

But Weiss isn't hearing Jed, because when he gets to the door he sees that the Lieutenant is the one buzzing.

'I have to call you back.' Weiss doesn't tell Jed the Lieutenant has come calling. During work hours. He wonders if the unexpected visit will be an interrogation.

'Well do you want the Eagles or the—' Jed doesn't get to finish the question before Weiss hangs up and opens the door.

The Lieutenant's hat, flat on top, drips rainwater on his shoulders.

'Your face looks better,' he says when Weiss opens the door.

'I know. I meant to call Mom ...' He doesn't bother with an excuse. 'You want to come in?'

'I'm just passing through.'

'I haven't had lunch yet.'

'I'm on my way to a meeting.'

'Oh.' Weiss feels funny having the Lieutenant standing there on the steps, looking up at him. 'You have time for a Coke?'

'All right.' The Lieutenant sidesteps the paint cans and follows his son inside.

'I haven't been home much,' Weiss explaining the condition of things. He serves the Lieutenant a glass with ice for his Coke; Weiss drinks from a can.

'The ballistics report came back from the murder you worked.'

'Yeah?' Weiss decides maybe he wants a glass with ice, too. Maybe then he won't have to sit down at the kitchen table and look the Lieutenant in the eye. He turns away, pretends to look for a snack or something in the cabinet next to the fridge.

'The guns came up clean,' the Lieutenant says. 'They could only trace partial serial numbers.'

'Can they tell if one was used in the murder?' Weiss tries not to sound too eager.

'There weren't any Glocks in the bunch, Raymond.'

Raymond doesn't know what to say to that. The Glock he took from Feliks is in the back of the silverware drawer. And if it's the murder weapon, the Lieutenant is sitting three feet away from the evidence.

Weiss closes the cabinet, turns around, and watches the Lieutenant pour his Coke slowly, no foam.

'Dad?'

The Lieutenant looks up, his expression unsurprisable.

'I arrested the wrong guy.'

'I know.'

'What's going to happen to him?'

'Judge will give him some time for possession, no doubt. A couple years, most. They'll send him back to Lithuania once he's served. Too bad he'll spend most of his time here in Joliet; he won't have very nice things to tell the folks at home.'

Weiss sits down across from the Lieutenant, his eyes on the table. 'What's going to happen to me?' He stops cracking his knuckles when it suddenly feels incriminating.

The Lieutenant takes a sip of his Coke and puts the glass on the table. 'Did I ever tell you about my Uncle Charlie?'

'The grocer,' Weiss remembers.

'He managed the Jewel on Touhy Avenue. Died before you were born. Charlie was my father's brother. When we were kids we stayed by his place a lot, since Dad worked so much.' His dad: Lieutenant Donald Weiss, the first.

'I remember more than once, staying over, when Charlie'd rush off in the middle of the night, headed for the store.'

'Burglary?'

'Usually. But I'll never forget: one night he let me stay up to play cards. A call came in; he put on his coat. He said the Jewel had been robbed. On his way out the door I asked why he had to go across town at midnight. I said, "Won't the police go?" And he said, "That's what I'm afraid of."'

The Lieutenant cracks a smile before he sips his

Coke, all the while watching Weiss. The smile is contagious to Weiss, like a yawn.

'Do you know how I became a lieutenant?'

'You worked for it,' Weiss says. 'You planned for it. You took the test.'

'And I chose to uphold the law instead of some brother-rules that don't mean a damn thing to anyone but the guys who think the badge makes them a member in some secret club. There's more than one way to get respect, Raymond.'

Again, Raymond doesn't know what to say.

'I'm not here to tell you how to live your life. Never have. Everyone makes mistakes. Hell, you don't learn from them if you don't make them. But when you're a cop, there's one thing that no one ever tells you. And it's so obvious, it seems ridiculous to say it. But I'm going to tell you, Raymond. Just like my father told me: there isn't a single crime that is committed without a mistake. You know why? Because the mistake is the crime itself.'

The Lieutenant pushes his glass away, and then his chair. 'I have to go now.' He gets up, adjusts the buttons on his coat, takes his hat. Weiss follows him through the living room, knowing if he opens his mouth, the words will come out sounding childish.

The Lieutenant opens the interior door, then the exterior, puts on his hat, and steps out into the rain.

'Dad?'

The Lieutenant slows, listening, not enough reason to turn around.

'Did you ever make any mistakes?'

And the Lieutenant turns to Weiss and he says,

'Only one that I regret.' He removes his hat, blinks away the rain on his face, says, 'I never told my son I'm proud of him.'

And again, Raymond doesn't know what to say.

But at least now he knows what he has to do.

CHAPTER THIRTY-TWO

'Feliks Rainys been in here today?' Weiss asks the bartender at the Skylark. 'You know, the guy with the mullet?'

'You're a cop,' the bartender says.

'Makes it all the more likely that you'll tell me the truth.'

The bartender looks around his domain, sizing up the tail end of the lunch crowd, probably wondering if anything he says may be used against him. Weiss sees Shitfer's big head at the other end of the bar, the beer in front of him his only friend.

'I don't want any trouble,' the bartender says, his voice accommodating, his words totally unhelpful.

'You mean trouble like getting arrested for withholding information from a law enforcement officer? Or trouble like having to remodel this joint because someone tosses it from one end to the other looking for a murder suspect?' Weiss raises his voice on that last bit just enough to turn a few heads. 'I just need to talk to the guy. It's in his best interest.' Weiss puts twenty bucks on the bar. 'Yours, too.'

The bartender doesn't touch the twenty. Instead, he picks up a dishrag, wipes down the wood around the money. 'I know the guy you're talking about. He was here last night.'

'By himself?'

'With a woman.' Paulina.

'Where did they sit?'

'Here, at the bar.'

'What did they order?'

'A beer, vodka tonic.'

'Just one round?'

'Two. And dinner. Both had the special. She didn't eat much. It was late.'

'What did they talk about?'

'I have no idea.'

His shrug doesn't fly with Weiss. 'I was a bartender. I know you hear everything, listening or not.'

The bartender tosses the dishrag on the spill mat, picks up a glass, and fills it with beer from the Stroh's tap. 'Something about air travel.'

Explains the suitcases. 'When?'

'Today, this afternoon.'

'Which airport?'

'O'Hare.'

'Airline?'

'Lufthansa.'

'You sure you don't want the twenty bucks?'

'I don't want any trouble.'

Weiss leaves the twenty. 'Buy Shitfer a beer.'

It's just after one o'clock. If Weiss can make it to the airport quick, he might be able to intercept Feliks and Paulina before they disappear through security. He's supposed to be at work in less than three hours. If he can't find them, he'll try to make it back.

The reversibles are headed out on the Kennedy and he's ahead of the rush. When he hits Belmont he calls 411 on his cell.

'I need the number for Lufthansa Airlines.'

They put him through.

He's surprised when a live person says, 'Thank you for calling Lufthansa, this is Nakeisha speaking. How may I help you?'

'Hi, Nakeisha. I'm interested in flights departing from Chicago O'Hare this afternoon, destination Lithuania.'

'Just a moment.' Keypad clicks on her end. 'There are two flights to Vilnius departing today: flight 9130 departs at one fifty-five; flight 431 departs at four forty-five.'

'Shit. Sorry – I'm supposed to be on the one fifty-five and I'm not going to make it. Can you bump me?'

'Let me check availability. One moment.' Keypad clicks. Weiss changes lanes to exit the express in case this doesn't work.

'We do have seats available, sir, however, there will be a transfer charge.'

'No problem.'

'Name, please?'

'Rainys. Feliks Rainys. R-A-I-N-Y-S.'

'One moment.'

'Thanks.'

The digital clock in the Cavalier says 1:36. Then 1:37.

'I'm sorry,' Nakeisha says, 'can you spell your last name again?'

'R-A-I-N-Y-S.'

1:38.

'Hello, Mr Rainys? There must be some mistake, you're already booked on the four forty-five.'

Weiss floors it.

Floors it, that is, until he hits dead-stopped traffic at the 90/94 split. The rain. It has to be the rain. Weiss turns on AM780 and waits until 1:48 for the traffic report. They say it's a half hour from downtown to the airport. They lie.

His cell rings while he's weaving in and out of lanes, getting nowhere fast. It's Sloane again. Her voice mail earlier confirmed what the Lieutenant said about the ballistics report. She also said the state's attorney made her look like an ass over the Ambrozas thing, so the judge wouldn't give her a warrant for Lucky Mike. She was at a dead end.

The fact that she's calling back now suggests she found a way around it.

'Sloane,' Weiss says when he answers. 'Good news this time?'

'Not exactly. Our disgruntled john theory is out the window. One of Ipolitas' clients just came forward. Her name's Kathy May.'

'A woman?'

'Yeah: a single mom who works nights and needs affordable child care. Ipolitas wasn't running a prosti- tution ring; he was bringing over Lithuanian babysitters. May was afraid to speak up for fear she'd get in trouble for hiring an illegal, but then her eight-year-old tells her a police officer came to visit the nanny last week while mom was at work – the kid was supposed to be asleep, so he was afraid to say anything – go figure. Anyway it turns out it's an undocumented stop, since no one called the cops and there's no report, and especially since the nanny apparently slapped the guy.'

'Shit.' Weiss wonders if it was Fiore. 'When was this?'

'She thinks it was last Monday. She's bringing the kid in when he gets out of school.'

'Who's the nanny?'

'Her name's Paulina Zujaite. You know what that means? She's Ona's sister.'

Weiss comes up on the sign for the I-190 West exit to O'Hare. 'I'll call you back.'

Weiss gets to terminal one, United and Lufthansa, at two twenty. The gold and royal blue LUFTHANSA sign marks his destination. He takes his flat badge and conceals his .45 in his boot and leaves his car in the white crosswalk, a no-no, but he flashes his star and his smile at the female officer yelling at lingering drivers.

She bats her big brown eyes at him and says, 'Don't go flyin' nowhere.'

Just inside the door marked ONE, Weiss finds a sign for the security checkpoint, which lies behind the United ticketing on his left. The women's bathroom is directly in front of him; he takes a seat on a bench next to the door in view of the whole area.

He watches people enter the checkpoint, wondering how people can be so clueless, holding each other up in line because they put their passports away or they didn't take the change out of their pockets.

The display on his phone reads 2:27. International flights recommend a two-hour lead time, so either he missed them, or there's no way he'll miss them. Unless he talks himself out of this and gets in the car at three, so he won't be late for work.

What will he say, anyway? *Excuse me, Feliks, are you fleeing the country because you killed your boss?* If he didn't, he damn well knows who did, and there's no way he's getting out of the country without telling Weiss the truth.

Weiss has checked the display on his phone nearly every minute and he's seen hundreds of faces pass through the terminal. At 2:51 he promises himself he'll leave at 3:15. At 2:58 he makes it 3:30.

At exactly three o'clock he sees Feliks and the girl with the golden curl come toward him, Feliks managing three bags, Paulina the tickets. They get in line to show their identification and they don't see Weiss step into line right behind them.

They speak to one another in hushed Lithuanian. Paulina is more beautiful than Weiss remembers. Her hair is brushed up in a last-minute bun, and her clothes are unfashionable, but her skin is flawless and vibrant; her beauty one of a kind. Even knowing what he does, Weiss has to admit he can understand Fiore's attraction.

And, knowing what he does, he has to restrain himself from hurting Feliks. He taps him on the shoulder. 'Excuse me, Feliks,' Weiss says, 'where do you think you're going?'

Feliks and Paulina turn to him, and at seeing Weiss there, the horror in Paulina's face seems extreme. But there's an explanation:

'Fancy meeting you here.' Fiore comes from behind Weiss, puts his arm around Paulina's waist, and discreetly reveals his gun. 'Why don't we all step outside?'

'I am not going anywhere with you,' Paulina says to him, trying to get free.

'What are you going to do?' Feliks asks. 'Take us out right here?'

'I can't let you get on that plane,' Fiore says. 'Fight me, Feliks. Give me a reason.'

'We are leaving, Jack,' Paulina says. 'We are doing what you told us to do.'

Fiore looks at Weiss: *Don't believe her*.

'How'd you know?' Weiss asks him.

'Shitfer called me. I thought you could use a hand.' His letdown look makes a pang of guilt rattle Weiss' nerves.

The couple in front of them moves their bags forward, creating a gap in the line that instantly annoys the people behind them.

'Let's step out of the way,' Weiss says.

'Listen to the officer,' Fiore says. He slips his gun in his coat pocket and pulls Paulina under the dividing rope.

One of Feliks' bags gets caught as he ducks under the rope and Weiss detaches it, staying close. Travelers cross paths in front of Weiss and Feliks, separating them from the other two. Weiss spots Paulina's blond head across the walkway. They're stopped outside the women's room next to a public-access defibrillator, a heart decal covered by a lightning bolt marking its cabinet. Weiss grabs the strap of one of Feliks' bags and drags him over.

'This is going to end badly,' Feliks says to Weiss.

'Please, Jack,' Paulina says as they approach.

'There's no other way to handle this. I don't think Officer Weiss will let a murderer walk.' His face is red, his hairline sweaty.

'You can't,' she pleads.

'I gave you a chance,' Fiore says. 'I'd hoped you'd make it out in time.'

The statement provides an equal sign for everything Weiss had been trying to add up. 'It was you?' Weiss asks Paulina. 'You killed Ipolitas?'

Paulina looks at Weiss, then at Fiore, whose face is like a suspect's, indignant and telling.

'You were covering for her?' Weiss asks him. 'You did all this to get her off the hook?' Weiss thinks of Ambrozas, of Ona, of Feliks. 'Everyone's been covering for you,' he says to Paulina. But her eyes are still on Fiore, his face indignant, and telling something far worse.

'He wasn't covering for her,' Feliks says.

Fiore takes a step back, distancing himself. His face turns pale, in a feverish sweat. Details swarm around Weiss' periphery, but his attention is drawn to Fiore's face: his anger, his insistence, his attitude – it's all gone, and he's left with nothing but defeat in his voice when he says, 'I told you I made a mistake.'

Weiss doesn't know how long he stands there, rewinding, playing it all back. It's long enough for Feliks and Paulina to show their boarding passes and remove their shoes and place their belongings in plastic bins and slip through the metal detectors. It's long enough for Fiore to walk away, to get lost in the mix of international travelers, a silent departure. But it isn't long enough for Weiss to understand. Weiss rewinds, rethinking things through a different lens. Still, he can't understand. He can say it, but he can't understand: Fiore killed Ipolitas. Fiore was covering for himself.

Then, from somewhere deep in his bones, Weiss is called to action. His vision clears; everything around him appears in crisp detail. The rush and the noise of the airport floods his ears. And he is agile with adrenaline as he sprints back toward the door marked ONE to catch Fiore.

CHAPTER THIRTY-THREE

Weiss ducks out the automatic door that leads to the street where he left his car and he barely has both feet outside when he hears a woman scream. She's seen the cop who let Weiss park in the white zone, who has her gun trained on Fiore. He's crossing five lanes of traffic on foot, his revolver in plain sight.

Weiss dodges a fat man pushing a family's worth of luggage on a cart, knocking a handbag from the top, its contents spilling to the floor.

'Police!' the man shouts.

'Police,' Weiss shouts back, producing his star and moving on.

Weiss jumps over a group of suitcases waiting to be checked at the nearest vestibule. 'Fiore! Stop!' He skips past a crowd of tourists, flashing his star – 'Stay back! Get everyone back!' – he yells at the skycap.

Weiss stops at the yellow curb to get a read on the scene. In the street, cars honk and weave to avoid Fiore. He's crossed three lanes of traffic and reached a set of concrete median barriers, only noticing them once they're in his way. He backtracks, walking against traffic, to get around them.

In the two lanes of traffic on the other side, cars zip

by. Fiore moves with no indication he'll run, as though he has the right of way, and the right to get away.

'Get these cars stopped!' Weiss yells at the woman cop who's behind him now, on her radio. She holsters her gun and runs out into the street to the left, where a band of Chicago and American flags welcome travelers. Weiss moves straight ahead, toward Fiore. Approaching traffic slows quickly at the woman cop's command, screams to a stop at the sight of Fiore's gun.

A group of passengers stop on the walkway above Fiore that stretches from the terminal across the street to the tram platform and the rusting gray parking structure. Weiss waves them away, but they stay to watch the scene below.

'Fiore!' Weiss reaches the point where he's directly across from Fiore, now on the other side of the concrete medians in the traffic thru-lanes. He walks toward a sign that says EXIT TO CITY like a lost man. Weiss stays ten paces away. 'Fiore, please,' Weiss begs. He draws his gun carefully and says, 'Don't make this worse.'

Fiore stops and turns to Weiss, the revolver at his side. 'It can't get any worse,' he says. A pack of cars that snuck around the woman cop move past them. Fiore's looking at Weiss as though he's waiting for the cars to pass, but his eyes are beyond the moment. He turns and resumes walking, diagonally now, across the outer lanes.

Traffic has stopped, though the lower level rumbles below them with taxis, buses, and limos, and the roar of air traffic echoes overhead. Weiss jumps a median and says, 'Fiore,' taking cautious steps toward him. When he catches up, side by side so he can see Fiore's face, he says, 'Tell me what happened.'

Fiore continues on, in no particular hurry, carrying his gun by the barrel now. Weiss walks with him, five paces away.

'I made sure the scene was clean,' Fiore says. 'I brought you there – not to get you into trouble. To get help. I had to write the report. I had to make sure there were no mistakes.'

Weiss recognizes the look on Fiore's face – the same look he had when they 'found' Ipolitas. Before, Weiss imagined it expressed a special alliance they shared. Now, Weiss knows it's nothing but plain desperation.

'The mistake,' Weiss says, 'was the crime itself.' He feels strength from his father's words.

Fiore stops and turns to Weiss. He raises his revolver and offers it to Weiss by its handle.

'Do me a favor, Weiss. Shoot me. I can't bear to see my wife again. Not after this.'

'I'm not going to kill you. You owe me the truth. And you owe it to Josephine, too.'

'What's she going to do if I tell her? She's trapped, Weiss. By her disease, and now by me.'

'You trapped all of us, Jack: you killed a man. You killed a man and you blamed someone else.'

'He ruined me. He found my weakness and he sent Paulina to ruin me.'

'It was more than one night with her, wasn't it, Jack? Fall of Troy, and all that? Is that why she had the rings?'

'It was blackmail. There was no end to it unless I ended it.'

'So all your talk about trust, and loyalty, that was a bunch of shit? A way to cover up the truth? You lied to me. You made me a part of your lie.'

'I had to lie to you. You're too good a man to keep my secrets.'

Fiore turns his revolver around, aims it at Weiss. Weiss doesn't back off; instead, he keeps inching forward, his gun aimed just the same.

'What now, are you going to kill me?' Weiss asks. 'Ambrozas is in jail, Feliks and Paulina are gone, and I'm the only loose end? You told me, Jack, just like your FTO told you: only a dead man can keep a secret. Is that your solution?'

Fiore lowers his revolver. Weiss is close enough to him to see the tears brimming in his eyes.

'This isn't a secret I expect you to keep,' he says. 'I just can't be there when my wife gets the news.' Fiore puts the revolver in his mouth.

Weiss lunges forward. 'Jack, wait—'

But the bullet keeps the rest of his secrets.

CHAPTER THIRTY-FOUR

The store's alarm doesn't startle anyone. Two blocks away, at the corner of Foster and Ashland, Johnny Giantolli hears it while writing a citation for a red light violation. He could have let the driver off with a warning, but the driver gave him lip, and he's not in the mood. He can't believe he got stuck working today, of all days.

A block away, at Ravenswood and Farragut, a real estate agent assures his prospective buyers that the alarm is no indication of trouble in this neighborhood. He wipes the dust from his patent leather shoes, having given the couple a walk-through of the loft before the renovations are complete. The youngish wife beams at her husband: they're moving to the city. What an adventure.

In the store's parking lot, a new mother straps her colicky baby and her sister's boy into the backseat of her mid-1990's SUV. Thinking the alarm comes from the expensive BMW a half dozen spaces away, she curses whoever owns it, the fucking yuppie with his head up his ass. The boy hears her curse – she can tell by the look in his ever-questioning eyes. She'll admit she's got a short fuse, but she didn't expect life to turn out this way. She thought she might drive a nice car, and have someone else to babysit. To pick up the dry cleaning. She had no clue about stretch marks.

The store's manager is on his knees behind the counter, his head down, praying for his life. He didn't get a very good look at the man who has him at gunpoint, nor did he see the other man who's emptying the cash register. The manager is sorry he didn't take the week's deposit to the bank during lunch. He is also sorry he tripped the alarm, because the man with the gun keeps threatening to kill him over it. The manager wonders if his ex-wife will see him on the news tonight, and if she'll regret being so mean.

Nearly two miles from the store, at Guild Hall, Gina Petrakoulas, Channel Five, is distracted while she rearranges calla lilies to create an appealing shot for the camera. She's got thirty seconds of airtime. Thirty seconds to tell viewers about the cop who killed himself for undisclosed reasons – all the department will say is that he was 'troubled.' What's troubling is that she's stuck waiting at the site of the funeral reception, hoping for a newsworthy interview, while the other field reporter has been sent to cover breaking news on the southside where corrupt cops are suspected of racial profiling. Gina can guess who's next in line to make anchor.

Across the street from Guild Hall, at the Queen of Angels Catholic Church, a guy from the ninth is saying a few words about Fiore that are nothing to write about. But it's not his fault; nobody really knows what to say. Fiore's wife, Josephine, is seated in the front row, having made her way there with the help of a cane. She's just steps away from the closed casket, though she cannot smell the flowers that adorn it. Instead, she smells heavy aftershave, which more than one officer has used to mask the whiskey he drank at Hamilton's this morning.

Josephine sheds no tears. She had a feeling. She knew he was gone when Ray Weiss came to see her the second time. She knew Jack finally found a way to afford their problems – her problems. She knows now just how much her husband loved her.

A representative from the National Police Suicide Foundation is in attendance: his organization has already stepped in to provide financial assistance. The Department has been good to Josephine, too; better than it had been to her husband. They're making charitable contributions. They've paid for the casket.

And they've shown up in numbers: the pews are filled with officers, because this service is a part of duty. Lieutenant Don Weiss is one of them, his hands clasped, praying for his son.

The priest calls for the congregation to join him in reciting the Beatitudes. Jed has no idea what those are. Katy nudges him when he resumes scraping the paint from under his fingernails. His back is killing him from helping with Ray's side job, but the last thing he'll do is complain, because he's one of the guys carrying the coffin out of here. *Be in control*, he thinks. *It's all under control.*

Noise sits on the other side of Jed. He is the only one at the service who hears the alarm, two miles away. He believes Fiore's suicide is a crime. He wishes crime was stoppable, just once.

Detective Pearson has trouble paying attention to the priest; maybe because Ray Weiss and the girl with the pretty dark curls whose hand he's holding are sitting three rows ahead of her. Weiss only spoke to Pearson once after Fiore's death. He said that even though the Ambrozas case washed out, he was sure she was on her way to becoming a respected member of the boys' club. He also told her that the truth would always be her most powerful weapon. He didn't say anything about seeing her again.

He didn't say anything about returning to Montrose Harbor, either. After Fiore died, he went back there to throw the Glock into Lake Michigan. Because the truth isn't going to kill him, too. Not yet.

No, the store's alarm doesn't startle anyone, and Weiss has known all along that it's human nature: we keep moving along, oblivious, until something stops us. The hard part, afterward, is to find a way to keep going.

ACKNOWLEDGEMENTS

Thank you to all those who offered insight and assistance this time around, including Sergeant Dave Anderson, Detective Sergeant Dave Putnam, Officer Dave Casarez, and Sergeant Mike Black; Doug Lyle, Terri Nolan, Anna Kennedy, Linda Cessna, Kurt Kitasaki, and Kathryn Campbell; and, of course, Katie Kennicott.

Thanks also to Scott Phillips, Kevin Adkins, and Ken Harvill for each one's often-solicited perspective. As always, thanks to David Hale Smith and Kelley Ragland – the voices of reason; and to Keith and Matt – the voices. Finally and forever, thank you to Kevin, and to my family – especially my parents: my first readers, biggest fans, and best friends.

Keep reading for an excerpt from

PERSON OF INTEREST

by Theresa Schwegel

CHAPTER 1

Springtime hasn't always depressed Leslie McHugh. When she was a girl, she looked forward to the days when the sun would try to stay in the sky just a little longer, signaling everything below to get up and get going: to sprout and bud and bloom. She could even feel herself open up, a blossom, roused by the season's potential. A flower.

And then she started working at Sauganash Flowers and Gifts for ten bucks an hour.

Today she sits at the front counter, flipping through an American Floral Distributors product catalogue, waiting on six o'clock. Behind her, a giant poster of a fresh rose–covered wedding cake fades with each passing year, and there's not much to look forward to. Business has been dead since Easter, so Raylene took the afternoon off, let Leslie close up shop. She sits, her enthusiasm as stagnant as the humid air. She hopes the phone doesn't ring, because if it isn't a customer it's Raylene, calling to make sure she didn't cut out early. Either way, she's stuck.

At twenty to six she ditches the catalogue and gets up to treat the leftover flowers. One by one, she takes the buckets from the cooler: the six varieties of roses, the daffodils and the hyacinths, the tulips. She transfers each bunch into its own new bucket filled with fresh Chrysal solution and, once immersed, draws a sharp knife across the stems of those that look a little peaked.

Afterward, she returns the buckets to the cooler, so that the happy daffodils and the showy purple hyacinths may sit like trumpets and bells, on display at eye level to announce to the customers another glorious day. That's what their positioning is supposed to do, anyway. Leslie, being the one in charge of keeping them alive, finds the whole scene contrived, and very sad. Each flower holds on for dear life here, being treated and temperature-controlled like a corpse until it's bundled or bouqueted and sold to someone who thinks a spray of pastels will brighten up their little corner of the world.

When she's through with the cold-stored flowers, she uses a mister to keep the warm-climate plants hydrated: the zinnias, the completely out-of-season sunflowers. Raylene buys those in the lightest yellow, so customers think of summer instead of fall.

Leslie takes the dirty buckets to the back and cleans them out with bleach and water, the familiar solution no less abrasive to her poor corroded nostrils, her roughened skin. The bleach still stings her thorn-pricked fingers, and she's never away from this place long enough to get the chemical smell from her hands.

At five to six, the front bell rings. Great, she thinks: just in the nick of time, some husband forgot his anniversary, or some woman wants to browse.

When she trudges up front, she wishes she'd have

closed up early, because it's not just someone. It's Niko Stavrakos, her daughter's newest boyfriend.

Leslie feels like she should check her hair. 'Niko, is that you?'

'Mrs McHugh,' he says on his approach, arms out. 'Yassas.' He addresses her formally, but his kisses to both cheeks are as familiar as those from any one of her cousins. He's twenty, too old for Ivy, she thinks; too polite, in any case.

Leslie hasn't seen him in a few weeks and he seems taller; plus, he's grown his sideburns, shaved them to clean rectangles that cut his jaw. He'd introduced himself to Ivy at the Heartland Café three months ago, and Ivy said he was 'nice'. He's more than nice.

'What are you doing here?' Leslie asked him.

'I need to buy some flowers.'

'Don't tell me you and Ivy are fighting. I was going to ask her why you haven't been around—'

'It's nothing like that. I'm a busy guy.'

'If the flowers are for Ivy, I can tell you she will not be impressed.'

Niko scratches at one of his sideburns, tolerant, but like he's already had this conversation. 'They're for my mother. She hasn't been feeling well; you know the Greek-mother thing, right? She has too much to do to be sick.'

Leslie isn't exactly thrilled to be lumped into the Greek-mother category: visions of her own mother, busy and frumpy, ruin any possibility of feeling attractive.

Maybe Niko senses her annoyance because he says, 'Ivy suggested I come see you.'

'That's a surprise. She doesn't exactly respect her mother the way you seem to respect yours.'

'Ivy's young,' he says, picking up one of the cheap plush chicks left over from Easter off the front display, turning it around in his hands. 'Anyway, my mother is pretending she's not sick, and I thought I would bring her a little something to keep her going.' He tosses the chick back on the display and smiles at her like his mother has nothing to do with it.

How thoughtful, Leslie thinks, careful not to let his smile lead. He watches her mouth as she says, 'Let me show you what we have available,' and she wonders what he's watching when he follows behind, over to the cooler.

She slides open the door, says, 'These Casteras are nice, I just clipped them,' and takes a bunch of the slender, beautiful brick-red-tipped roses from their bucket.

'They're nice. But what about these?' He points to the bucket of Madame DelBards, the bright, velvety bestsellers.

Leslie puts all but one of the Casteras back in the bucket, keeping it to convince him otherwise; isn't it just like a man to believe the bigger and brighter, the better.

'The Casteras are very fragile,' she says, 'but they're worth the price.'

'You mean they're expensive, and they'll die?'

'Sometimes the beauty of the thing lies in the moment.'

'I don't know, these big ones look nice.' He turns the bucket of Madame DelBards around on the shelf, checking them out.

'They do last longer, but you could buy them at the grocery store. The Casteras are unique.' She twirls the single rose between her fingers.

'But they die.'

'Everything dies, Niko.'

'Geez,' he says, his hands up, surrendering. 'What was I thinking? I'm going to buy my mother roses so they'll die? She'll take it as a bad omen. She'll freak out.'

'She shouldn't. I can't imagine anyone getting too worked up over a flower.'

He considers the Casteras, and reconsiders. 'I better get the ones that last the longest. So they'll be alive until she feels better.'

'Fair enough.' Leslie selects a dozen of the freshest roses and takes them to the counter, all the while feeling Niko's eyes fastened on her. He doesn't make conversation and she doesn't know what to say; there's something between them, but she doesn't know what.

'You talked to Ivy today?' she asks, the best she can come up with.

'No, not today.'

Leslie hasn't, either. She pretends wrapping up the roses takes all her attention.

As she's tying the bow around the box, Niko says, 'I'll bet you never get flowers, with this job and all.'

'This job, yes, that's one reason.' She doesn't say that another would be because these days, Craig is about as romantic as a carp. He blames his job, though he's been a cop for more than twenty years and never this much of a jerk. She hands Niko the box, says, 'Ivy's father works a lot.'

'Well, it would be silly for him to waste money on flowers when they aren't as pretty as you.'

She can't look at him but she says, 'Niko,' her tone dismissive, embarrassed.

'I'm sorry,' he says. 'You know us Greek men. We can never resist beauty.'

'You know us Greek women,' she shoots back. 'We can always resist your charm.'

She still doesn't look at him. Silly boy.

After Niko leaves, Leslie closes up shop, and she doesn't make much of his visit until she goes out to her car. There, stuck between the windshield and the wiper, is a single Madame DelBard rose.

CHAPTER 2

It's been said that the Chinese take gambling so seriously that a man would bet his life's earnings on the number of seeds in an unpeeled navel orange. Craig McHugh can't remember where he heard that, but after playing Pai Gow with Mr Moy and company for a month and a half, he's pretty sure it's true.

Moy shuffles the cards, fifty-two plus a joker. This is nothing like a friendly game with the boys, where the cards give you something to think about between sips of Heineken. Where winning an argument over the Cubs' outfielders or beating a guy to the punch-line of a joke you already read in Playboy is equally satisfying. Craig stretches his neck to relieve his tension headache, and also to get a subtle look around the room.

Only three men are pressing their luck tonight: Craig, Fish Eye, and Dandelion. Craig hoped for some bigger players, some guys with better connections, but Dandelion said Moy wiped out a whole table that morning with a string of flushes. The fact that Dandelion turned up again, resilient against his own loss, is an obvious indication as to where he acquired the nickname, his round yellow face notwithstanding.

Fish Eye traps a Viceroy between stained incisors and lights up, the only other thing to do here aside from setting cards. He takes a long drag; his right eye swims around in its socket. Craig's never sure where the guy is really looking. Maybe nowhere particular. Maybe everywhere at once.

The den sits at the back of Chu's China Delight, behind the kitchen. From the outside, it's dressed up like a walk-in meat locker; a heavy steel door guards the small, smoky room and its rickety card tables, its precious dice. Plenty of meat in this place, Craig thinks. Fresh, stupid meat.

The locker's cooling system serves to circulate air since there are no windows in the room. No decoration, either; only cards, players and endless minutes between hands. Minutes when someone might get tired of losing. Or of the house rules. Or of being quiet. Craig's spent enough time and money here to know there are plenty of bones to pick with Moy; it can't be much longer before the seams of this carefully set scene spread and fray and he gets a glimpse backstage – back to where Chinatown does its real business with the Fuxi gang. That is the reason Craig is here, waiting on Moy to deal another hand.

Moy pauses like he's listening to the cards. Apparently they tell him to reshuffle.

Outside the Pai Gow den, boxes of wooden chopsticks, soy sauce packets and almond cookies sit stacked against the unpainted wall adjacent to the service door, waiting to be sorted and shelved after the three p.m. delivery. The service door leads to the alley that runs parallel to Argyle Street. The only white men who use this door besides Craig wear uniforms with logos like Halsted Packing House or Chicago Meat and Produce Market, Inc. Craig doesn't wear a uniform, but he'd say he does business just the same.

Moy is still shuffling.

Craig hears the business of the kitchen in the next room: the chopping of bok choy, the sizzle of egg foo yung dropped in hot peanut oil. Craig would never get takeout from this place. He's seen the cooks at work: their eyes on the televised horse races; cigarettes hanging from their drying lips, ashes fluttering into the wok as they stir-fry pork for kung pao. If it is really pork, soaking in plastic buckets of purple-red marinade beneath fluorescent lights softened by the kitchen's general layer of grime.

The customers don't seem concerned with quality as they come in, hurried, to order by number from inaccurately glamorized photographs of combination plates. The front of the place is a well-designed stage. 'Number sixteen, no MSG,' they may say, and they'll receive an obedient bow, though the latter request won't make it back to the kitchen. The customers won't know any better; they'll love the sticky white rice packed into wire-handled cartons stamped with the Chinese character that represents wealth, fortune, and luck, though it could just as easily signify rat piss. They'll rave about the chow mein noodles, unaware they came prepackaged, as ethnic as a Ritz cracker. And they'll actually believe the cooks are Chinese.

Knowing all this doesn't make Craig feel any better. He's just glad the only thing on his plate at this place is the game and, if he's lucky, another name, another link in the Fuxi chain.

In the den's thick air, Fish Eye's cigarette smoke mingles with the oily smell that sticks to Craig's clothes, his hair, his skin – like he's been glazed with it. It stays with him long after he's lost his allowance for the night, another unappetizing reminder of the job. He'll probably never eat another egg roll.

Finally, Moy deals the cards, seven hands for only four players, four cards to the dungeon, as are the rules. Moy places every card on the table like it's deciding a fate. Then he rattles three dice in a cup and tips them out onto the table to determine the order of play.

Craig thinks the whole ritual is time suckage, as if the motions affect who gets what cards, but win or lose, he can't complain. Not to these men. The odds have to tip in his favor eventually, don't they?

Craig's dealt his cards last: a pair of aces, the joker, a jack; the rest slop. He could set three of a kind with the aces, or split them. It's a toss-up; worst case, he'll wind up with a push, which means he doesn't win or lose, save for the house's ten percent. He takes an impatient breath.

Mr Moy's thin lips stretch horizontally across his face, his smile all lines like a stick figure. 'It('s a) good thing (there's) no bluff(ing) in Pai Gow,' he says, Craig mentally fixing Moy's broken English as he speaks. 'You('re a) terrible bluff(er), Mickey.'

'Yeah,' Craig says, unnecessarily rearranging his hand, playing the role of the malleable whiteface, the unlucky Irishman known as Mickey. That his badge and his gun are in the glove compartment of the unmarked, GIS-monitored car down the street is concealed quite well, he thinks. And that he's here, running his own game on the Kuang Tian tong, Moy's upfront 'community' organization that will be his link to the Fuxi Spiders gang, is the real bluff. When he nails the Fuxis for handling the bad China White – the heroin cut with fentanyl – that's been killing junkies from here to 187th Street, Moy won't be so certain about his bets.

Craig splits his aces.

Mr Moy shows his cards: low hand is an ace-jack; the high hand, three deuces. The house wins. Again.

And now Craig has to wait some more while Moy goes counterclockwise around the table, comparing his hand to Dandelion's, then to Fish Eye's, and finally to Craig's, all as precisely as he calculates how much more each man owes. Gives Craig plenty of time to figure out he's down a little over two grand.

Moy snatches Craig's cards and begins the whole ritual again, his face listless, despite the fact that he just raked in another couple hundred bucks.

Craig pushes back from the table, his irritation an inevitable tell. He can't help it; he feels like he forked over some sensibility with that last twenty dollars. 'Mr Moy,' he says, 'I want to know something: how come the house always gets lucky?'

Moy's expression doesn't change. Like he isn't even listening.

Craig catches the back of the chair as he stands up to keep it from tipping back and clattering to the floor. 'I'm just saying, maybe it's fate. But tonight? The cards are playing like your command of English. Convenient.'

Moy looks up at him, through him. A dare.

Craig didn't plan to be the one to pick a fight; he promised he'd keep cool, let the others' losses get the best of them. But damn this game: there's no strategy. No skill. It isn't fate, and it isn't fair.

And it doesn't matter. It's work.

Craig sits. Moy has no idea what they've both got to lose.

Moy resumes shuffling, and eventually deals. When he gets to Craig he pauses, a card pressed between his fingers like he's second-guessing Mickey's seat at the table. Craig thinks this is the start of something, and he's right, but it's not because of Craig; the next thing he knows, three men dressed in black from hair to heel bust in on the den like a SWAT team.

Maybe he should've, but Craig didn't order the SWAT team.

'Mr Moy,' Craig says, 'what's happening?'

Moy says nothing; he meets the intrusion like a man sentenced to death, his face long ago through with emotion.

Craig doesn't know Mandarin or Cantonese or whatever the hell language one of them is yelling at Moy, but the gun the man wields speaks to Craig pretty clearly: he could die here if he doesn't do something.

More men in black, who knows how many, crowd into the room like insects teeming toward the dark. The leader repeats his demand, to Craig it sounds something like: 'Ayy doww, Su naaan . . .'

Craig pushes his chair aside and crouches: he's got his backup Walther .380 tucked into his boot and fuck this undercover simple-guy act; if he's going down, he's doing it shooting as Detective Craig McHugh, twenty-three years serving, Chicago PD.

Or maybe not. Because before he can get to the gun, one of the men grabs Craig by his thin hair and yanks him to the floor. Another's knife, a threat at Craig's throat, is a reason to cooperate. When he looks up, he meets a pair of eyes so empty he knows there'll be no negotiation. He shies away from the serrated blade, shielding his face with his hands, and someone else steps on his fingers; his eyes begin to tear and he loses sight of the blade as he tries to jerk his hand away.

He hears Dandelion cry out; he isn't sure he makes any noise himself when someone kicks him in the stomach, stealing his breath. There are black-shod feet all around, and it is futile to think he can go for his gun but he tries anyway, reaches until he is stopped by the blow of a heavy boot to his back, and then he is kicked again, and again, and again.

I'm going to die in this shitty place, he thinks. Die nameless and disappear, without knowing why, accepting this fate on behalf of some crooked Chinamen.

Confusion dilutes the pain and as he slips from clear consciousness, he tries to hold on for his mind's auto-replay of his life. The frames slow to lingering photographs, and finally stop on an image of his wife. It's when she was a girl, about their daughter's age – the way he'll always remember her: long black hair tangled by the lake water; olive skin kissed a shade darker, cheeks flushed by the summer heat, and her eyes, smiling at him like they used to, when things were so good.

And that awful yellow bikini, the one that tied in white strings at the sides, covering just a little of everything he always wanted to protect.

Fate, Craig decides, is a bitch.